C000061077

CHRISTOPHER BUSH

THE CASE OF THE APRIL FOOLS

With an introduction
by Curtis Evans

DEAN STREET PRESS

INTRODUCTION

THAT ONCE vast and mighty legion of bright young (and youngish) British crime writers who began publishing their ingenious tales of mystery and imagination during what is known as the Golden Age of detective fiction (traditionally dated from 1920 to 1939) had greatly diminished by the iconoclastic decade of the Sixties, many of these writers having become casualties of time. Of the 38 authors who during the Golden Age had belonged to the Detection Club, a London-based group which included within its ranks many of the finest writers of detective fiction then plying the craft in the United Kingdom, just over a third remained among the living by the second half of the 1960s, while merely seven—Agatha Christie, Anthony Gilbert, Gladys Mitchell, Margery Allingham, John Dickson Carr, Nicholas Blake and Christopher Bush—were still penning crime fiction.

In 1966--a year that saw the sad demise, at the too young age of 62, of Margery Allingham--an executive with the English book publishing firm Macdonald reflected on the continued popularity of the author who today is the least well known among this tiny but accomplished crime writing cohort: Christopher Bush (1885-1973), whose first of his three score and three series detective novels, *The Plumley Inheritance*, had appeared fully four decades earlier, in 1926. "He has a considerable public, a 'steady Bush public,' a public that has endured through many years," the executive boasted of Bush. "He never presents any problem to his publisher, who knows exactly how many copies of a title may be safely printed for the loyal Bush fans; the number is a healthy one too." Yet in 1968, just a couple of years after the Macdonald editor's affirmation of Bush's notable popular duration as a crime writer, the author, now in his 83rd year, bade farewell to mystery fiction with a final detective novel, *The Case of the Prodigal Daughter*, in which, like in Agatha Christie's *Third Girl* (1966), copious references are made, none too favorably, to youthful sex, drugs and rock and roll. Afterwards, outside of the reprinting in the UK in the early 1970s of a scattering of classic Bush titles from the Golden Age, Bush's books, in contrast with those of Christie, Carr, Allingham and Blake, disappeared from mass circulation in both the UK and the US, becoming fervently sought (and ever more unobtainable) treasures by collectors and connoisseurs of classic crime fiction. Now, in one of the signal developments in vintage mystery publishing, Dean Street Press is reprinting all 63 of the Christopher Bush detective novels. These will be published over a period of months, beginning with the release of books 1 to 10 in the series.

Few Golden Age British mystery writers had backgrounds as humble yet simultaneously mysterious, dotted with omissions and evasions, as Christopher Bush, who was born Charlie Christmas Bush on the day of the Nativity in 1885 in the Norfolk village of Great Hockham, to Charles Walter Bush and his second wife, Eva Margaret Long. While the father of Christopher Bush's Detection Club colleague and near exact contemporary Henry Wade (the pseudonym of Henry Lancelot Aubrey-Fletcher) was a baronet who lived in an elegant Georgian mansion and claimed extensive ownership of fertile English fields, Christopher's father resided in a cramped cottage and toiled in fields as a farm laborer, a term that in the late Victorian and Edwardian era, his son lamented many years afterward, "had in it something of contempt....There was something almost of serfdom about it."

Charles Walter Bush was a canny though mercurial individual, his only learning, his son recalled, having been "acquired at the Sunday school." A man of parts, Charles was a tenant farmer of three acres, a thatcher, bricklayer and carpenter (fittingly for the father of a detective novelist, coffins were his specialty), a village radical and a most adept poacher. After a flight from Great Hockham, possibly on account of his poaching activities, Charles, a widower with a baby son whom he had left in the care of his mother, resided in London, where he worked for a firm of spice importers. At a dance in the city, Charles met Christopher's mother, Eva Long, a lovely and sweet-natured young milliner and bonnet maker, sweeping her off her feet with a combination of "good looks and a certain plausibility." After their marriage the couple left London to live in a tiny rented cottage in Great Hockham, where Eva over the next eighteen years gave birth to three sons and five daughters and perforce learned the challenging ways of rural domestic economy.

Decades later an octogenarian Christopher Bush, in his memoir *Winter Harvest: A Norfolk Boyhood* (1967), characterized Great Hockham as a rustic rural redoubt where many of the words that fell from the tongues of the native inhabitants "were those of Shakespeare, Milton and the Authorised Version....Still in general use were words that were standard in Chaucer's time, but had since lost a certain respectability." Christopher amusingly recalled as a young boy telling his mother that a respectable neighbor woman had used profanity, explaining that in his hearing she had told her husband, "George, wipe you that shit off that pig's arse, do you'll datty your trousers," to which his mother had responded that although that particular usage of a four-letter word had not really been *swearing*, he was not to give vent to such language himself.

Great Hockham, which in Christopher Bush's youth had a population of about four hundred souls, was composed of a score or so of cottages, three public houses, a post-office, five shops, a couple of forges and a pair of churches, All Saint's and the Primitive Methodist Chapel, where the Bush family rather vocally worshipped. "The village lived by farming, and most of its men were labourers," Christopher recollected. "Most of the children left school as soon as the law permitted: boys to be absorbed somehow into the land and the girls to go into domestic service." There were three large farms and four smaller ones, and, in something of an anomaly, not one but two squires--the original squire, dubbed "Finch" by Christopher, having let the shooting rights at Little Hockham Hall to one "Green," a wealthy international banker, making the latter man a squire by courtesy. Finch owned most of the local houses and farms, in traditional form receiving rents for them personally on Michaelmas; and when Christopher's father fell out with Green, "a red-faced, pompous, blustering man," over a political election, he lost all of the banker's business, much to his mother's distress. Yet against all odds and adversities, Christopher's life greatly diverged from settled norms in Great Hockham, incidentally producing one of the most distinguished detective novelists from the Golden Age of detective fiction.

Although Christopher Bush was born in Great Hockham, he spent his earliest years in London living with his mother's much older sister, Elizabeth, and her husband, a fur dealer by the name of James Streeter, the couple having no children of their own. Almost certainly of illegitimate birth, Eva had been raised by the Long family from her infancy. She once told her youngest daughter how she recalled the Longs being visited, when she was a child, by a "fine lady in a carriage," whom she believed was her birth mother. Or is it possible that the "fine lady in a carriage" was simply an imaginary figment, like the aristocratic fantasies of Philippa Palfrey in P.D. James's *Innocent Blood* (1980), and that Eva's "sister" Elizabeth was in fact her mother?

The Streeters were a comfortably circumstanced couple at the time they took custody of Christopher. Their household included two maids and a governess for the young boy, whose doting but dutiful "Aunt Lizzie" devoted much of her time to the performance of "good works among the East End poor." When Christopher was seven years old, however, drastically straightened financial circumstances compelled the Streeters to leave London for Norfolk, by the way returning the boy to his birth parents in Great Hockham.

Fortunately the cause of the education of Christopher, who was not only a capable village cricketer but a precocious reader and scholar, was taken up both by his determined and devoted mother and an idealistic local elementary school headmaster. In his teens Christopher secured a scholarship to Norfolk's Thetford Grammar School, one of England's oldest educational institutions, where Thomas Paine had studied a century-and-a-half earlier. He left Thetford in 1904 to take a position as a junior schoolmaster, missing a chance to go to Cambridge University on yet another scholarship. (Later he proclaimed himself thankful for this turn of events, sardonically speculating that had he received a Cambridge degree he "might have become an exceedingly minor don or something as staid and static and respectable as a publisher.") Christopher would teach in English schools for the next twenty-seven years, retiring at the age of 46 in 1931, after he had established a successful career as a detective novelist.

Christopher's romantic relationships proved far rockier than his career path, not to mention every bit as murky as his mother's familial antecedents. In 1911, when Christopher was teaching in Wood Green School, a co-educational institution in Oxfordshire, he wed county council schoolteacher Ella Maria Pinner, a daughter of a baker neighbor of the Bushes in Great Hockham. The two appear never actually to have lived together, however, and in 1914, when Christopher at the age of 29 headed to war in the 16th (Public Schools) Battalion of the Middlesex Regiment, he falsely claimed in his attestation papers, under penalty of two years' imprisonment with hard labor, to be unmarried.

After four years of service in the Great War, including a year-long stint in Egypt, Christopher returned in 1919 to his position at Wood Green School, where he became involved in another romantic relationship, from which he soon desired to extricate himself. (A photo of the future author, taken at this time in Egypt, shows a rather dashing, thin-mustached man in uniform and is signed "Chris," suggesting that he had dispensed with "Charlie" and taken in its place a diminutive drawn from his middle name.) The next year Winifred Chart, a mathematics teacher at Wood Green, gave birth to a son, whom she named Geoffrey Bush. Christopher was the father of Geoffrey, who later in life became a noted English composer, though for reasons best known to himself Christopher never acknowledged his son. (A letter Geoffrey once sent him was returned unopened.) Winifred claimed that she and Christopher had married but separated, but she refused to speak of her purported spouse forever after and she destroyed all of his letters and other mementos, with the exception of a book of poetry that he had written for her during what she termed their engagement.

Christopher's true mate in life, though with her he had no children, was Florence Marjorie Barclay, the daughter of a draper from Ballymena, Northern Ireland, and, like Ella Pinner and Winifred Chart, a schoolteacher. Christopher and Marjorie likely had become romantically involved by 1929, when Christopher dedicated to her his second detective novel, *The Perfect Murder Case*; and they lived together as man and wife from the 1930s until her death in 1968 (after which, probably not coincidentally, Christopher stopped publishing novels). Christopher returned with Marjorie to the vicinity of Great Hockham when his writing career took flight, purchasing two adjoining cottages and commissioning his father and a stepbrother to build an extension consisting of a kitchen, two bedrooms and a new staircase. (The now sprawling structure, which Christopher called "Home Cottage," is now a bed and breakfast grandiloquently dubbed "Home Hall.") After a falling-out with his father, presumably over the conduct of Christopher's personal life, he and Marjorie in 1932 moved to Beckley, Sussex, where they purchased Horsepen, a lovely Tudor plaster and timber-framed house. In 1953 the couple settled at their final home, The Great House, a centuries-old structure (now a boutique hotel) in Lavenham, Suffolk.

From these three houses Christopher maintained a lucrative and critically esteemed career as a novelist, publishing both detective novels as Christopher Bush and, commencing in 1933 with the acclaimed book *Return* (in the UK, *God and the Rabbit*, 1934), regional novels purposefully drawing on his own life experience, under the pen name Michael Home. (During the 1940s he also published espionage novels under the Michael Home pseudonym.) Although his first detective novel, *The Plumley Inheritance*, made a limited impact, with his second, *The Perfect Murder Case*, Christopher struck gold. The latter novel, a big seller in both the UK and the US, was published in the former country by the prestigious Heinemann, soon to become the publisher of the detective novels of Margery Allingham and Carter Dickson (John Dickson Carr), and in the latter country by the Crime Club imprint of Doubleday, Doran, one of the most important publishers of mystery fiction in the United States.

Over the decade of the 1930s Christopher Bush published, in both the UK and the US as well as other countries around the world, some of the finest detective fiction of the Golden Age, prompting the brilliant Thirties crime fiction reviewer, author and Oxford University Press editor Charles Williams to avow: "Mr. Bush writes of as thoroughly enjoyable murders as any I know." (More recently, mystery genre authority B.A. Pike dubbed these novels by Bush, whom he praised as "one of the most reliable and resourceful of true detective writers"; "Golden Age baroque, rendered remarkable by some extraordinary flights of fancy.") In 1937 Christopher Bush became, along with Nicholas Blake, E.C.R. Lorac and Newton Gayle (the writing team of Muna Lee and Maurice West Guinness), one of the final authors initiated into the Detection Club before the outbreak of the Second World War and with it the demise of the Golden Age. Afterward he continued publishing a detective novel or more a year, with his final book in 1968 reaching a total of 63, all of them detailing the investigative adventures of lanky and bespectacled gentleman amateur detective Ludovic Travers. Concurring as I do with the encomia of Charles Williams and B.A. Pike, I will end this introduction by thanking Avril MacArthur for providing invaluable biographical information on her great uncle, and simply wishing fans of classic crime fiction good times as they discover (or rediscover), with this latest splendid series of Dean Street Press classic crime fiction reissues, Christopher Bush's Ludovic Travers detective novels. May a new "Bush public" yet arise!

Curtis Evans

The Case of the April Fools (1933)

> The whole business was extraordinarily puzzling, and
> in the words of his old nurse, there was some jiggery-
> pokery somewhere.

THE APRIL FOOLS' DAY setting of *The Case of the April Fools*
(1933), Christopher Bush's ninth Ludovic Travers detective novel and second "holiday" mystery (after the 1931 Christmas tale
Dancing Death), is possibly unique within the Golden Age of detective fiction. The novel is notable as well in another, ultimately
more significant, way. It marks the ascendance, in all the rest of
the Bush mysteries, of Ludovic Travers to the top of the sleuth
heap, so to speak. No longer would Travers's Durangos associ-
ate John Franklin appear in the books, though Superintendent
George "the General" Wharton would continue for nearly the
next quarter-century to play a major role in the series--although
he does not appear in either *The Case of the Unfortunate Village* (1932) or *The Case of the April Fools*. In the latter his place
is taken by his former "right-hand man," Chief Inspector Norris,
who proves in the case to be quite as capable as his formidable
mentor. Unlike many other mystery writers during the Golden
Age of detective fiction, Christopher Bush did not feel the need
to aggrandize his amateur gentleman sleuth by depicting police
detectives as dunderheads.

Travers comes into this case quickly, by way of stage producer Courtney Allard and his colleague Charles Crewe, the two of
whom are negotiating with Durangos, the mammoth consulting
and publicity firm of which Travers is a director, for the lease of
a theater. In a novel uncommonly sensitive to fine class distinc-
tions, even by the standards of the Golden Age, Travers adjudg-
es Allard and Crew rather an odd couple indeed.

> Whatever else Crewe was, there was one thing he certain-
> ly was not—a man of the class and breeding of Allard.
> Allard...for all his affectations...looked like a gentleman

and spoke like one. Crewe was trying hard to look like one, and making none too good a hand of it. Little tricks of accent and gesture would keep butting in, and Travers was finding it difficult to place him.

Travers learns at his meeting with the pair that Crewe has been subjected to a series of death threats in the mail. Crewe dismisses these threats as a "rather nasty joke" and Allard later invites Travers down to his country house, "The Covers," to carry on the business negotiations at greater length. Having previously overheard Allard and Crewe in an odd discussion about him at Fragoli's, a favorite restaurant of his that appears more than once in the series, Travers concludes that he is intended to be the butt of some sort of joke at The Covers, where his stay would coincide with April Fools' Day. Yet being insatiably curious--"the fact that there are two sides to every question was for him merely an excellent reason for hunting for a third"--Travers decides to accept the proffered invitation; and on Aprils Fools' Day he finds himself confronting a situation that is no joke at all: a double murder at The Covers, committed under the most bizarre and seemingly impossible of circumstances. "Put [X] in his room under the conditions that existed the morning he was killed, and the whole of Maskelyne and Devant's and the Royal and Ancient Society of African Wizards couldn't have killed him," avows an astonished Travers, referencing the famous English magicians David Devant and Nevil Maskelyne.

Soon the dilettante author and amateur sleuth is unsubtly sidling up to the local superintendent investigating the murders --"My uncle happens to be the Chief Commissioner. I mean... well, I sort of know people."--and he is most gratified when the "same old gang" from Scotland Yard—Chief Inspector Norris, Sergeant Lewis (Did Colin Dexter read Christopher Bush?) and medical examiner Menzies--appears at The Covers to take over the investigation. "Ghastly thing to say," he declares, sounding something like Dorothy L. Sayers's Lord Peter Wimsey, "but it makes one feel quite at home."

The case Travers and the Scotland Yard gang investigate— the case of the April Fools--develops into a classic country house mystery with a raft of suspicious characters, including Susan Allard, Courtney Allard's sister, who obviously has something to hide; Preston, an abruptly absent chauffeur; and the other weekend guests at The Covers, who are brusquely dismissed as people of no account by Mason, the ossified Allard butler ("began here as a pantry boy"). These individuals are Margaret Hastings ("slangy and, as Travers guessed, somewhat of a vulgarian with a spiritual home well in the middle of the front row of the chorus"); Spence ("the crime reporter of the *Evening Record*, looking very natty in plus fours and polka dot brown tie"); and the Americans Henry Drew ("lean and sunburnt, with wrinkled-up eyes that twinkled pleasantly, and looking generally as if he had stepped straight out of a Wild West novel") and Taylor Samuels ("with a husky, intimate voice and a manner so genuinely friendly, and a plumpness of person that would have placed him in the front rank of really successful confidence men"). Lurking nebulously in the wings is a mysterious Chinaman named Wen Ti, but do not let that dissuade you from reading, for this ingenious detective novel never ventures anywhere close to thriller territory.

One especially intriguing aspect of *The Case of the April Fools* is that as the plot unfolds it becomes clear that Bush has based the character of Taylor Samuels on the American actor Roscoe "Fatty" Arbuckle, one of the most popular comedians of the then recently passed silent film era. (Bush was obviously a fan of silent film comedy, for in a couple of books from the period he also compares Superintendent Wharton's physical appearance to that of another silent film comedian, Chester Conklin.) A dozen years earlier Fatty Arbuckle had become embroiled in what is regarded as the first great Hollywood sex scandal. The imbroglio began when actress Virginia Rappe fell ill at a party Arbuckle had given at the St. Francis hotel in San Francisco. After her death four days later, Arbuckle was accused of raping and thereby mortally injuring Rappe (due to his excessive weight); he went through three trials before finally being acquitted. In retrospect the case against Arbuckle appears to have been a farrago of nonsense, cynically perpetuated by a politically ambitious prosecutor. Nevertheless a legion of self-righteous American moralists did its best to keep the comedian from working in film again. The year before the publication of *The Case of the April Fools*, Arbuckle managed to launch what turned out to be a brief comeback, making six two-reel comedy films, which were quite successful in the US, although in the UK the officious British Board of Film Censors refused to allow the showing of the films, citing the more than decade-old scandal. Only three months after the publication of Bush's novel, Arbuckle passed away from a heart attack, at the age of 46.

Christopher Bush, certainly no moralist in his own life, makes clear that Travers believes Taylor Samuels was most ill-used in the United States, at the thundering behest of, as he witheringly puts it, "American womanhood." But just what precisely were Samuels and his colorful cohorts up to during that deadly country house weekend that culminated in a dastardly double murder on April Fools' Day? It is up to Travers and Chief Inspector Norris to find the solution to the bizarre crime—and to readers to beat them to it, if they can.

CHAPTER I
TWO MYSTERIES

THE UNEXPLAINED is always intriguing, provided one can be reasonably sure of ultimately arriving at some sort of explanation, whether it be by one's own efforts or at the good pleasure of the perpetrator of the mystery. Ludovic Travers loved nosing things out; it was said of him indeed that the fact that there are two sides to every question was for him merely an excellent reason for hunting for a third. That afternoon—a Monday, and the twenty-ninth of March—he was to be intrigued by two things that were apparently in no sort of relationship to each other, and both of them rather ridiculous.

First was that new poster on the huge sign. It was about forty feet long and fifteen high, and as its main colouring was an intense yellow, there was not much chance of its being missed. Somewhat low down in the centre of the yellow ground was a name in black block lettering, occupying perhaps a third of the length:

ZONA FOX

and what that precisely meant was more than Travers at the moment could fathom. There had been posters like it and he frowned as he recalled those other names in their black lettering on the same yellow ground—PEG LORNE, had been one, and SAM LEPPARD, and FRANCIS PEROLLES. And each of the posters had had the biggest mystery of all—the same that now hit him clean in the eye as he stood there on the pavement looking across the road. From each top corner of the yellow poster came an arm, as though a man of gigantic stature were hidden behind and was reaching round to embrace the sign in full. But nothing of the actual arms could be seen; they were concealed in the draping sleeves of a vivid green, oriental garment. And there were no fingers protruding from the sleeves. In their place was more black lettering that fell down slightly to the position that the fingers would have occupied; from one sleeve half the name and the rest from the other, and the full name:

WEN TI

Travers frowned again as he tried to make sense of it. Was the green-sleeved WEN TI a mandarin, and was ZONA FOX meant to be in his clutches? Was all this publicity that had been lavished on billboards and buses and electric signs merely the heralding of a melodramatic serial in one of the popular periodicals? Were PEG LORNE and SAM LEPPARD and FRANCIS PEROLLES also in the mandarin's clutches? Was Peg the heroine? Francis would surely be the hero, and perhaps Sam was the villain, though the fuller Samuel would have sounded much more sinister than its shortened form.

Quite a good guess, that serial business, thought Travers, and he was still nodding to himself as he entered the main hall of Durangos' vast building that reared itself superciliously alongside Charing Cross Station. He nodded abstractedly as the doorman gave him a director's salute, and then turned abruptly and made his way to the Publicity Department that housed itself in the east wing of the ground floor.

"Tell me," he said to Roberts, who had charge of the London area, "that Wen Ti poster business. They've got a new one just outside our own door. What's the idea of it all? A new book, or serial, or what?"

Roberts nodded most portentously. "I've been ferreting round Abermanns—they're doing it, you know—and I can't get hold of a thing. Never knew them so close. Someone's spending the devil of a lot of money for some reason or other. I'd have said it was a musical comedy—only we don't know a single name that's been published. This Peg Lorne and Sam Leppard and so on."

Travers nodded. "Exactly. Most intriguing affair. Let me know personally if you get hold of anything definite, will you?" and he moved off.

Once in his own room he dismissed the Wen Ti business from his mind and ran over again the papers in connection with the Mermaid Theatre, of which Durangos were negotiating the lease. Courtney Allard was toying with the idea of purchasing and was due at any moment. What he was like, Travers, except from rumour, had no notion. He had known old William Allard—of Calcutta and Shanghai—and had known that he had left the best part of a million pounds to his nephew. He knew also that the nephew had a very pretty taste in cars and had already burnt his fingers pretty badly over at least one musical show in town. Still one can go on making a fool of one's self for quite a time on a million.

Allard came on time, and with him was another man, whom he introduced as Charles Crewe. Allard resembled his reputation. His face was piscine, with eyes that bulged and chin that receded and nose that dominated the whole. He was very tall, and Travers' six feet three was slightly topped. His hair was fair and mousy, his gait a kind of shuffle, and his manner a general boredness that manifested itself in a drawl and an affectation of sleepiness from which he awoke at intervals to utter some remark that was meant to be shrewd, and often—frankly enough—was humorous in an unexpectedly cynical way. He wore green socks and fawn coloured flannel trousers, and on the whole was clad with the same unexpectedness that occasionally gleamed from his conversation.

Crewe, his friend, fascinated Travers. His hair was jet black and his eyes dark and curiously magnetic. A much older man than Allard—about thirty-five, in fact—he looked like a great tragedian in the making. He was not tall; five feet eight or nine it might be, but he looked wiry and calculating and volcanic and a whole lot of other romantic things. And whatever else he was, there was one thing he certainly was not—a man of the class and breeding of Allard. Allard looked a fool and, Travers guessed, was nothing of the sort. But for all his affectations he looked like a gentleman and spoke like one. Crewe was trying to look like one, and making none too good a hand of it. Little tricks of accent and gesture would keep butting in, and Travers was finding it difficult to place him.

The room where they were sitting was what Travers had made it. On the walls were a William and Mary mirror and a few coloured prints. It was, in fact, so like the private room of a sane and wealthy poet that the portable typewriter on the knee-hole writing-desk gave one quite a shock. As for the business palaver, Travers did none of that. An expert came in, and all Travers had to do was to contemplate the company through his horn-rims like a very modern Buddha and chime benevolently into the conversation when requested. Then Allard expressed himself as perfectly satisfied and the expert departed. Allard made as if to rise, then settled down again.

"I suppose," he said shrewdly, "you haven't such a thing as a set of statistics about the Marlowe Theatre? I mean, it's rather off the track, like the Mermaid—same area, in fact. It might give one some idea about things. There are such things as unpopular sites, you know."

"We've got the very thing for you," said Travers. "I can't have it brought in because it's as big as that wall. Complete map of the whole theatre area, showing everything absolutely up to date, including the figures for—in some cases—last week. Like to see it?"

Allard rose at once. "You coming, Charles?"

Crewe kept his seat. "I don't think I will, if you don't mind. I suppose you won't be long?"

"Five minutes," smiled Travers. "You know where the cigarettes are."

When they got back again he was sitting just as they had left him, legs crossed in the easy chair and holding the gold-topped cane in his glove hand.

"May I get you tea before you go?" asked Travers.

Allard consulted the platinum wrist-watch. "Frightfully early. Good of you and all that. You coming, Charles?" As Crewe rose he made an explanation. "Charles isn't in very good form these days. I really ought to have told you why he came along. You see, somebody's threatening to do him in."

"Do him in?" Travers raised his eyebrows politely.

"Yes. Threatening letters and all that. We asked about it at Scotland Yard, but they referred us to the local police. Not their show, you know."

Travers was rather at a loss. "Do I understand that someone's threatening to murder you, Mr. Crewe?"

Crewe smiled feebly. "I suppose that's what it amounts to. We don't know who the fellow is, and we think it's somebody playing a rather nasty joke. Court has a policeman parading the grounds at Marbury every night just for luck, and that's all there is to it."

"The papers have got hold of it now," said Allard. "Haslington gaped a bit in the *Record* this morning. Perhaps you saw it?"

"I didn't," said Travers, "but I certainly will do."

Indeed, no sooner did he get back to the room after seeing them into the lift, than he sent for that morning's *Record*. The gossip columns—presided over by The Masquerader, *alias* Lord George Haslington—had a paragraph.

Outside the Benvenuto I ran into Courtney Allard, who was looking remarkably fit after his visit to Nice. He tells me the track there is in capital fettle this year. With him was Mr. Charles Crewe who is likely, so they tell me, to make things pretty lively in the theatrical world very shortly. Mr. Crewe, by the way, is either the most unfortunate person in England at the moment or the victim of a foolish joke. *Somebody is threatening to murder him!* The prospective victim is, however, bearing up remarkably well, though the police, I may divulge very confidentially, are treating the affair with every seriousness and have already taken certain precautions. The curious thing about the whole matter is that Mr. Crewe owns up to a knowledge of at least four people who might really like to murder him, though all four are citizens of the United States and were, when he last heard about them, still in that fortunately far-off country.

The paragraph left Travers little wiser than before.

Half an hour later Travers, having finished with the office for that afternoon, made his way in the biting wind along the Strand and across Trafalgar Square to the Haymarket for a peep into the window of a firm of antique dealers where that morning, he had seen what looked like a Ralph Wood figure. The figure was still there, and Ralph Wood or not, he didn't like the look of it. It seemed for a moment to be genuine enough—and then there would be a little shiver in his dawning enthusiasm that warned him all was not well. A final look and he renounced it for good, and with Fragoli's only two doors away, decided on tea instead.

Travers liked Fragoli's. He liked the tiny cubby-holes set all round, each large enough for a table for four. The orchestra was playing decorously as he took a seat in one of the remoter cubby-holes, and in a couple of minutes he was lying back in the comfortable chair awaiting the arrival of tea-cake and honey and a pot of China tea.

It was then that the second curious thing happened. He was not even aware that the farther table was occupied, since he had reached his own by sidling along the edge of the floor. He might in time have become aware of voices, but as his head went back and leaned cosily against the wall, the sound came through clearly—and almost the first word he caught was his own name!

The voices he recognized at once. There was no mistaking that unique noise made by Courtney Allard—a sound that seemed to be produced painfully in the stomach, oozed through some tube or other to the back of the palate and then pushed out with the smallest possible movement of lips and jaws. And there was no mistaking the main pattern of the voice of Charles Crewe, with its variations of Cockney and nasalism. As for the morals of the matter Travers saw no harm in listening, and after the first sentence or two wild horses wouldn't have pried loose his head from the wall.

A.Ludovic, I think the name is.

C.Hm! Ludovic Travers. I think I've heard it somewhere. Doesn't he write books?

A.Yes (*dubiously*), I believe he does. He's frightfully wealthy so they say. His father left him a lot, and those financial fellows are always in the know. Looked a bit of a fool, don't you think?

C.(*An indistinct mumble, then*) That's just what I've been thinking about. He's the very chap you ought to ask down. (*The voice became positively eager.*) You know, the sort of society incompetent who's the soul of honour and all that. Wouldn't tell a lie for worlds; no

end of a reputation and a jury'd believe every word he
said. Ask him down, Court! See if he'll bite.
A.Wouldn't be a bad idea. *(A pause.)* He looks rather
bat-eyed.
C.Why not let him know everything? A sort of chap
like that wouldn't give anything away. Besides, he'd be
pretty useful as a witness. He and Spence between them
ought to pitch a yarn anybody'd swallow.
A.*(A grunt.)* I think that's a damn good idea. What's the
best way to manage it?

And at that moment Travers' waiter arrived. He cleared his
throat gently and spoke to the waiter with a husky voice that was
amazingly unlike his own. "I'd rather like to go a little farther
that way, I think. See if there's a table, will you?"

The waiter reported one, two cubby-holes along, and Travers
unobtrusively transferred his headquarters. As he munched
his tea-cake, spread cloyingly with honey, he watched dancers
circling round, tapped to the rhythm or nodded his head, and
every now and again gave a queer little smile of utter enjoyment.
It had all—or certainly most of it—been so devastatingly true.
He *did* look a bit of a fool. He *was* most decidedly bat-eyed, and,
as far as society went, he *was* the world's worst incompetent.

And just what was it that he was supposed to tell to a jury?
Travers smiled to himself again. Perfectly delightful it must be
to talk to a jury; to get them into one's confidence, as it were,
and have a real heart-to-heart chat. And what was it he was to
bite? Anything to do with that lease business of the afternoon?
Surely not. That sort of thing could be made fool-proof. There
couldn't be any swindle in that. And who was the Spence whom
Crewe had mentioned as the second of two witnesses in the
mouths of whom something mysterious was to be confirmed?
Nobody that Travers knew himself, in all probability, though
he knew plenty of Spences; Montagu, for instance, the leader
writer of *The Times*, and Herbert, the bibliophile—though it
couldn't be he unless he'd got rid of his gout; and Sir Percy of

Spence and Harmer the stockbrokers, not to mention Spence the special crime reporter of the *Evening Record*.

And there was another thing that was intriguing Travers. Crewe had suggested that he might be told everything. Just what everything? And why the confidence? What was it that he wouldn't give away? Travers hooked off his glasses and polished them—the surest sign in the world that he was puzzling his wits—then hooked them on again rapidly as he caught sight of Courtney Allard dancing with the elder of the Wendley girls. A moment later he had caught the waiter's eye, and in five minutes he was on the pavement outside the Fragoli wondering just how to fill in the time before dinner, and finding himself going over from the beginning that slice of conversation that had come apparently out of nowhere and was likely to end heaven alone knew where.

He thought about it all again a good few times before the next morning, and yet the letter, when he opened it and realized whom it was from, gave him quite a shock. Allard must have got the private address from the telephone directory. It looked, too, as if he employed a secretary—the missive was so beautifully typed on the most beautiful paper and signed with the most convincing flourish. It read convincingly too.

DEAR TRAVERS,

I have been giving the matter of the Mermaid lease a good deal of thought and have decided that I would like things to get along a little more quickly. It seems almost certain, in fact, that the matter will go through; the only thing is another issue has arisen which makes the purchase unlikely unless it can be carried through within the next few days.

What I would like you to do is to let me have an abstract of the whole of the proposition as your people outlined it to me yesterday afternoon, and I should like you to bring it yourself if that could possibly be managed.

Now I come to think of it, this is what I would suggest. Come along at any time on the Wednesday and stay the night. You know The Covers at Marbury, just along the Guildford Road and well back. There will be some really interesting and unusual people there, and we will give you a good time. Business can be included at your own convenience.

Do come. We would love to see a lion of your magnitude.

Yours sincerely,

COURTNEY ALLARD.

Quite plausible that, in parts, and most unusual in others. Normally Travers would have smiled rather frigidly at such an overture, and the whole thing, the more he examined it, struck him as the effort evolved by a lady secretary who had been given a free hand and a certain amount of material. The sort of people, too, whom Courtney Allard was likely to have at The Covers, seemed hardly worth the hour's journey and the brief encounter and the discomfort of a strange bed.

And yet, in spite of all that, Travers did what he felt to be the most absurd thing he had ever done—he wrote and accepted gracefully. And nothing having been said to the contrary, he proposed to take his man Palmer down with him. The whole affair was so peculiar, and the preliminaries had been so unusual, that Travers felt somewhere in his bones the desire to have during that short visit a witness and an ally somewhere close at hand—if one might speak so of the servants' quarters. But just what it was that Travers was anticipating he had no definite idea. There was nothing, for instance, about the cutting of throats or holding to ransom; it was just that he had a hunch of sorts, and that he didn't like the gentleman with the magnetically shifty eyes, and he didn't trust Courtney Allard with his pursed lips and cod-fish face, and he didn't like the sound of The Covers which stood back from the road. And there was that little matter of the bloodthirsty fellow who was said to be threatening to murder Crewe. Not that he himself bore any resemblance to Crewe—but the best of murderers are liable in their excitement to make mistakes, and what use Palmer would be under those circumstances Travers didn't know—unless somebody was urgently wanted to identify the corpse.

CHAPTER II
MEET THE FOLKS

ON THE Wednesday morning the first thing that caught Travers' eye in the middle of the general news page of the *Record* was a half column referring to that interesting person, Charles Crewe.

ANONYMOUS LETTERS THREATEN
MURDER
DEATH WITHIN TWENTY-FOUR HOURS
POLICE SUSPECT HOAX

The story added very little to what Travers already knew. Mr. Charles Crewe was staying at The Covers, Marbury, with the famous sportsman, Courtney Allard, after spending some years in the States. A fortnight previously he had received a letter saying simply that his time had come—a bald enough statement in all conscience and capable of only the one interpretation. No clue could be gathered from it. The postmark was London and the letter was typed on fair-class paper. The curious thing was that as far as he was aware, nobody in America knew that he was in London, and was certainly not aware of his precise whereabouts. A week later another letter had arrived, typed, but on paper of a different kind. This announced that the sender had been unavoidably delayed, but that Crewe had no more than a week's further respite. It added, moreover, that Crewe himself was perfectly well aware of the sender's identity. The whole matter, the story said, had been reported to the local police and to Scotland Yard. Mr. Crewe himself was not disposed to treat the matter too seriously, and the police, while taking certain precautions, were of the opinion that the affair was in the nature of a practical joke. Mr. Courtney Allard, for all that, was offering a reward of a hundred pounds for discovery of the author of the anonymous letters. This had been on the arrival the previous evening of yet another letter, narrowing the time of the supposed murder to twenty-four hours.

Now Ludovic Travers was of a suspicious turn of mind, and all sorts of curious questions began chasing through his brain. For the life of him he couldn't see that in this peculiar instance two and two made four. Had such letters been addressed to himself he would certainly have taken reasonable precautions, and there was Charles Crewe walking openly about London in the company of a person—Courtney Allard—who was so conspicuous that he might as well have announced his movements with a drum and fife band. Then there was the question of the newspapers, all of which he sent for as soon as he reached his office. Those accustomed to deal in stories of human interest of the frankly sensational type had their accounts of the Charles Crewe affair; the staider papers had never a word of it, and that was decidedly fishy. And the most suspicious thing about the whole business was that the next day was April the first—when practical jokers flourish most. True the murder seemed to be promised for that very night, but Travers was already hazarding a guess that whatever there was in the shape of murders would be conveniently postponed to coincide with the Feast of All-Fools.

Travers timed his arrival for half-past six, sufficient daylight to see his whereabouts and sufficiently late to be near to dinner. Palmer went with him in the Bentley, and in the case were the papers relating to the Mermaid lease, with an agreement all ready to be signed on the dotted line. It was about an hour's drive, and as he drew in at the imposing gates of The Covers he was agreeably surprised. The house did stand back from the road—a quarter of a mile back—in grounds that were extraordinarily well laid out, with wide stretches of lawn and hundreds of ornamental trees. In front of the house was a vista that led away over spacious park-land, and a lake lay in the hollow between the woods that ran almost to the walls at the east side.

The great hall looked cosy with its log fire, and from somewhere was the sound of cheerful voices. They grew louder as

Travers followed in the butler's wake to a door on the far side, and developed into a hubbub as he was announced.

The room, which appeared to be the lounge, seemed for the moment full of people; some standing by the fire, some sitting round casually, but all consuming cocktails which an energetic gentleman was shaking vigorously at a table in the immediate background. There was quite a hush as Travers came in. Courtney Allard shuffled across the carpet, shoulders hunched as usual and head well forward.

"Hallo! See you found your way. Come and meet the folks, as they say in the best circles."

It was all very informal. Sue Allard, Courtney's sister, was slim and dark, with a face that was moulded like her brother's and yet seemed to have all the good points that his had missed, and a pair of brown eyes and a pleasant smile that made her quite a charming person to know. Margaret Hastings would be about thirty and was made-up to kill. She was petite, and vivacious with only too obvious an effort; slangy and, as Travers guessed, somewhat of a vulgarian with a spiritual home well in the middle of the front row of the chorus.

Of the men Travers recognized one at once—Spence, the crime reporter of the *Evening Record*, looking very natty in plus fours and polka dot brown tie. Henry Drew, the lad who was officiating at the cocktail table, was lean and sunburnt, with wrinkled-up eyes that twinkled pleasantly, and looking generally as if he had stepped straight out of a Wild West novel. Taylor Samuels was also an American, of the quiet, homely, almost middle-aged type, complete with horn-rims that were larger than Travers' own, and with a husky, intimate voice and a manner so genuinely friendly, and a plumpness of person that would have placed him in the front rank of really successful confidence men. Charles Crewe was funereal as ever, with a temporary heartiness that reminded one of an undertaker on his annual holiday.

"Still alive, I see," smiled Travers.

"Yes," said Crewe, and his face suddenly clouded. "All the same I'd rather hear you ask the question to-morrow night."

"Perhaps I will," Travers told him cheerfully, and blinked round at the company. "I must say you've got an extraordinarily good escort."

"You ought to see the cops!" giggled Margaret Hastings. "How many are there, Court?"

"Only a couple." He explained to Travers. "Local men, you know. They came on duty at dusk."

Travers made a face. "Sounds pretty serious?"

Allard nodded knowingly. "Best to be safe. If some silly ass is playing a joke, the laugh won't be all on his side. You'll have a cocktail? Henry, mix Mr. Travers what he wants. Fatty, you put the phonograph on, and for God's sake let's be cheerful."

Samuels waddled amiably over to the phonograph and fiddled with the pile of records. He chose the *Wedding March* from *Lohengrin*.

"Oh, my God!" wailed Margaret Hastings. "You're not going to play that damn thing again!"

"Sure I am," beamed Samuels. "It's a great little tune. What's wrong with it, anyway?"

Before that could be discussed the voice of the majestic butler was heard at the door.

"Mr. Franks, sir."

The gentleman who entered was tall, dark and handsome in an artificial sort of way. There was something of the floor-walker about him, and he seemed none too much at ease as he walked the few yards across the room to meet Courtney Allard. His clothes, too, were just a bit too new, and even to Travers' eye had something of the foreign in their cut. When he smiled, the clear-cut face lost all its fineness and cheapened in a flash. When he spoke it was only too obvious that he didn't exactly belong, and that what he lacked in acclimatization he was likely to make up in assurance.

It was curious how the room had hushed as soon as the new-comer's name had been announced. Samuels had switched off the *Wedding March*, Henry Drew had let the cocktail shaker down to the table, and Courtney Allard's face had brightened as he turned to the door. Stranger still was the attitude of Margaret Hastings as soon as the newcomer made his appearance. Travers was standing alongside her, waiting gracefully for his drink, and he saw the whole thing—how her lips parted as she gave a little gasp; then the flush of hectic red that ran over her powdered face. As Allard brought Franks up she still seemed to be mesmerized, and when Franks set eyes on her, his eyes narrowed and a flush ran over his face too.

"Don't say you two know each other?" said Allard, who couldn't help but notice something remarkable about the gushing Margaret.

Franks smiled sheepishly. "I think I have met—er—the lady somewhere before. Miss—er—"

"Hastings—Margaret Hastings."

"Oh, yes!" Another smile, that might have been cynical. "How do you do, Miss Hastings? Very pleased to meet you."

Margaret Hastings suddenly got up. "I think I'll go and dress for dinner. I've got such a lot to do."

"Then you'll have to wear something different from what you had the last time I saw you," drawled Henry, and resumed the shaking.

"I'm going too." Sue Allard overtook her at the door and the men were left to themselves.

Travers received his drink and nodded round with a, "Here's how!" Henry began on another. Samuels abandoned the phonograph and came across to the fire.

"What time is dinner?" Travers asked.

"Half-past seven."

Travers finished his drink at a gulp. "Then if you don't mind I think I'd better go up." As he caught Spence's eye the gong sounded.

"I'll come with you," said Allard. "I'm afraid you're going to be rather annoyed when you see where we've put you."

There was a general stirring in the room as they passed out. Allard waved the footman back and Travers asked for his man to be sent up.

At the head of the stairs they turned left to a corridor and there was the bedroom at once.

"Perfectly charming room!" said Travers, as he ran his eye round it.

Allard smiled. "You haven't seen the snag. There are two rooms here. My aunt always used one as a dressing-room and one as a bedroom." He moved across and opened the far door. "Here we are, as you see. Another bedroom and bathroom and all that. The problem is, which will you have? If we come up together, it doesn't really matter. If you take the inner room you won't be disturbed."

"But doesn't that door lead anywhere?"

"It's fastened up," said Allard. "It used to be her maid's room. Crewe's using it now. You see," he explained, "it isn't often we have such a big party as we have at the moment—all in single harness, so to speak. Also people don't like those damn big bedrooms like barns. They'd rather have something small, like these."

"Which one are you using at present?" asked Travers.

"Well, at the moment, this one."

"Good enough!" said Travers. "Then I'll have the outside one. We won't quarrel over turns in the bathroom."

Palmer was waiting in the outer room when they re-entered.

"This your man?" asked Allard. "Because he might bring tea for both of us in the morning. What time'd you like it? Breakfast's on at nine."

"Eight o'clock too early?"

"Not a bit. Give us time for a yarn before feeding time. You'll take the bathroom now?"

"Thanks, I will," said Travers.

Allard nodded cheerily and went through to the other room.

As soon as the door closed Travers motioned to Palmer. "Find out which room Mr. Spence is in. Ask him to wait till I come, and let me know."

He hustled through his dressing and in ten minutes was in Spence's room, which turned out to be on the other side of the house. Spence had hustled too, and he drew a chair up to the electric heater for Travers.

"Well, what special pleading brought you here?" smiled Travers.

Spence seemed not the least perturbed at the question.

"I know. Damn funny, isn't it? I came down early this morning to see about all this murder threat business, and damned if Allard didn't ask me to come along, so naturally I went back to town, packed a suit-case and came back before the blood was shed."

"What a life!" sighed Travers. "Why wasn't I a special crime reporter? Still, between ourselves, you're none too sure about the blood?"

Spence grinned at him. "I know whatever happens I'm sitting pretty. I'm sure of a story either way."

Travers leaned forward confidentially. "What would you say if I told you I knew you were coming here? Knew it last Monday!"

Spence's eyes opened. "But how the devil could you know that? I didn't know it myself."

"Let me tell you a little conversation I heard," said Travers, and did so. "Don't let that get any further, by the way, unless the necessity arises."

"Talking about me, were they?" He shook his head. "I wondered why the Old Man wasn't surprised when I told him I was coming here for the night. I've a good mind to call up and find out."

"Take my advice and leave things alone," Travers told him. "What's it matter if Allard did fix it up? You're here and that's the main thing. Know any of these people at all?"

"Not a one," said Spence, "and I generally flatter myself I know the names at least, of most people Courtney Allard would be friendly with. Very mixed lot, what?"

Travers smiled enigmatically. "Hearts of gold, no doubt. The wee-est bit rough-diamondish on the outside." He laughed. "That's a bit mixed too. What about coming to see the whereabouts of my room, then we ought to be getting down?"

That was probably the most amazing meal Travers had ever sat through, and it was amazing in so many ways. The dining-room was a superb room, beautifully furnished and impeccable in taste. The service—butler and a couple of footmen—was perfect. The food was superb.

Sue Allard talked away, to Spence and Travers mostly, and the others seemed to confine themselves to a methodical and accurate progress through the meal. And if ever people were uncomfortable, they were. There was a feeling of restraint that made everything difficult. Travers felt so sorry for everybody that he put a tactful feeler.

"Well, what's making everybody so gloomy? Not the murder business?"

"Exactly when is zero hour?" added Spence.

Allard's face remained severe. "Six o'clock. That's when Charles ought to have been dead, according to the latest letter." He looked round the table. "What I suggest is we don't mention the matter any more. Anybody referring to it puts a quid of the pool."

"Gosh! I wouldn't like you to be sheriff in my home county," said Henry.

"Five bucks a word is some fine!" said Samuels, and smiled round as if he was going to add something really humorous.

Allard cut in with, "Talking of America, how would you explain all this gold business? Effects on trade and all that sort of thing."

"Oh, do tell us about it!" exclaimed Sue Allard. "I never seem to understand what the papers say."

Travers protested laughingly, but had to give his lecture. So the meal progressed. Crewe put in a careful question or two; from Samuels and Drew came an occasional, "Is that so!" or, "You don't say!" Franks was fatuous. Margaret Hastings was so quiet that Crewe became solicitous about a headache, and it was plain that he and the lady had at least an understanding, if they were not definitely engaged. And none of them seemed in the least at home. There was trouble with knives and forks and spoons; trouble about just what to say to the servants; trouble about just what to say to themselves, and altogether it was not at all a lively affair. None of them seemed to be drinking much either; it was as if some embargo had been placed on what might loosen tongues, and it was not till the end of the meal when Allard really pressed Franks to try the kümmel that the inhibition was released.

Then almost before the kümmel had had time to settle, Allard was suggesting a general adjournment to the billiard-room. Sue Allard went off with Margaret Hastings and said they'd be in there later. Travers said he never played, but he'd come along in a minute or so. What he had been hoping was that Spence would rise to it and stay too, but Spence hailed the billiards like an enthusiast. Surprisingly enough it was Samuels who said he'd stay and keep Travers company in the lounge.

"No, you won't," said Allard curtly. "You'll come along and play billiards. It'll do you good."

"Gosh! Court," and in spite of the humorous way he contemplated himself, Travers felt there was something of rebellion in the reply.

"You don't expect a man like me to go hoppin' around that billiard table." He shook his head. "I guess Mr. Travers and me'll look better fillin' a couple of chairs."

Travers waded in. He liked the look of Samuels. "I quite agree. You run along and we'll join you later."

In the lounge Samuels sank heavily into an easy chair, produced a large handkerchief and mopped his forehead.

"That was a great little meal!"

Travers gave him a shrewd look. "All the same, you'd sooner have sat opposite a porterhouse steak and a mug of Pilsener."

His eyes opened. "How'd you guess that?"

Travers laughed as he held the light for the other's cigar. "Pure instinct. You'll have some whisky? I'm pouring myself one."

Samuels looked round as if he feared to be overlooked. Then he gave a sigh of what was either relief or exasperation. "Just what you're having is good enough for me."

He watched while Travers squirted the soda, and gave a nod of satisfaction as he took his first swig.

"And how long have you been over here, Mr. Samuels?"

"Three days." No sooner were the words out when he looked startled. "Hell! I shouldn't have said that. You live in one of these old houses, Mr. Travers?"

"Good Lord, no!" said Travers quickly. "I mean—well, perhaps I shouldn't have said it like that. What do you think of The Covers?"

"I've struck places like it in Hollywood—" began Samuels, then stopped again. "Forget it! You do the talking, Mr. Travers, then I'll be safe. That was a great line of thought you wrestled with at dinner—all about the gold standard and—tell me some more."

Travers laughed. "We'll find much more interesting things to talk about than that."

So they talked about English weather and the war and whether Paris was all it was supposed to be and newspapers and murders, and it was then, when the glasses had been filled again and half emptied, that Samuels looked round nervously as he put his question. He lowered his voice.

"Talking of murders, there's one you folks had over here that I've heard an awful lot about, but somehow I never seem to get the inside dope. I wonder if you know it. The Mercer Case."

"The Mercer Case?" Travers frowned. "Yes. I remember it well. About twenty years ago it'd be."

"About that." He looked towards the door again. "I thought maybe we hadn't got hold of the real inside information over there."

Travers frowned again. "There wasn't anything to conceal as far as I know. Mercer was a Harley Street doctor—that implies he was a pretty wealthy and fashionable physician, if you follow me. He was very well connected socially, and his wife was a prominent society woman before she married him. All that happened was that Mercer went mad and nobody knew it till it was too late. He told one man he—the man, that is—was suffering from cancer, and this man blew his brains out, and they discovered afterwards that there wasn't a word of truth in the diagnosis. That made people sit up and think. Before they could take action Mercer had poisoned his wife with an injection of prussic acid. He was really mad then, but all the excitement came when his patients had to be re-examined and re-diagnosed, as it were, to see exactly what harm he'd done. I should have said that when it was found out about the unfortunate cancer man, there was an outcry about murder. That was just on the eve of the other affair. I'm afraid I've got it very muddled, but it caused a tremendous sensation at the time."

"And this fellow Mercer? He gave himself a shot of the same dope that killed his wife?"

"Oh, no! They got him away perfectly quietly. Broadmoor he was sent to. That's a prison for the insane. As far as I know he's still there. At least I never remember hearing of his death."

Samuels folded his arms across his waistcoat and nodded heavily.

"Still bughouse. That's a rotten end for a man with a brain like that."

Courtney Allard must have opened the door very quietly, because he was almost on them when he spoke.

"A brain like what?"

Samuels gave a start. "Gee! Court, you scared me stiff. Whose brains, you said? You'll make Mr. Travers blush. I was just complimenting him on his oration on that gold problem."

"Well, come along and be friendly," said Allard with a manner that was meant to be hearty.

Samuels heaved himself out of the chair and Travers followed suit. As they entered the billiard-room Allard took his arm and drew him back for a moment.

"Old Samuels been boring you with his yarns about the States?"

"The States?" asked Travers, and assumed a positive bewilderment. "Good Lord, no! We've been discussing the weather principally. Besides, isn't he a Canadian?"

Allard shook his head. "He's American all right. Get yourself a drink as you go through."

A quarter of an hour later they went upstairs together, all rather talkative and cheerful after the drinks and the game. Allard forgot his ban on the murder business, and they saw Crewe into his room and heard the key turn from inside after his final good night.

"Any other door?" asked Travers.

"Only the one into my room," said Allard. "And I bet he locks the one window."

Just before Travers actually turned in he popped his head inside Allard's room to say good night. Allard made a gesture for quiet and tapped the wall. From Crewe's side came an answering tap. Allard put his mouth to the wall and grinned as he hollered.

"Let us know when you're dead!"

From the other side came an indistinguishable noise which Allard, ear to the wall, evidently identified as the voice of Crewe. Travers nodded with feigned joyousness, then escaped to his bed. Two minutes after his head hit the pillow he was asleep.

CHAPTER III
TAKE AWAY TWO

VERY EARLY in the morning Travers stirred and was suddenly wide awake. For a moment he thought it was the birds that woke him—they were just beginning to twitter outside his window—and then he became aware of a sound in the outside corridor. In a moment he was out of bed and had gently turned the handle of the door.

The corridor, as he could see it in the half light, was empty, and there was now no sound. Then, as he was about to close the door again, the figure of a man came in sight, turning the right angle at the end of the corridor. Travers closed the door till there was only a slit—and waited. The man, whoever he was, went straight past without a glance to either side, though he seemed to be treading warily. In that fraction of a second while he passed, Travers could see that he was wearing a raincoat, buttoned to the neck, and his face had nothing furtive about it. It was rather the face of the kind of man that might have dined at Courtney Allard's table; the face of an outdoor man; a soldier, perhaps, or a hunting man.

For a moment Travers was tempted to tiptoe on his tracks, then he thought better of it and got back into bed, though for some time he lay there listening. This was the day when things were to happen. There was to be something which he, as an obvious fool, was to see and not see; something to which he would be prepared to swear to a jury; something that Spence was to corroborate; something for which he and Spence had been especially inveigled down.

When he woke again it was with a start, and he realized he had been dreaming about Samuels—that he had signed the Mermaid lease, and had said he was going to turn the place into a talkie. In that moment of waking, too, Travers knew something else—that somewhere or other he had seen Samuels before.

Before the questioning had begun, there was a tap on the door and Palmer entered with the tea and good morning. Outside in the corridor could be heard the sound of voices—the servants with the main tray of tea things—and Travers sat up in bed.

"See if Mr. Allard is awake first, Palmer, will you?"

He yawned and stretched while Palmer went through to the other room. Allard was heard to speak; then he gave a holler.

"Travers! why not have it together in your room?"

"Splendid! Why not?"

Palmer reappeared and set out the cups. Then Courtney Allard's face came round the door.

"Come along a second and see if Crewe's survived the night."

Travers got into the dressing-gown and went in. Allard was listening, ear to the wall. He whispered.

"He's all right. He's just opening the door for the man."

His face expanded to a grin, then he let out such a holler that Travers was startled.

"Hallo, Charles! Still alive?"

There was an answering tap from the other side. Allard, with his ear again to the wall, reported the sounds as, "Of course I'm alive!"

"Well, that's that!" said Allard cheerily. "Now what about a spot of tea?"

Palmer laid out clothes while the tea was being drunk, and then went through to do the same service for Allard, whose man was being loaned to others of the men. When the cigarettes were alight, Travers ventured to mention business.

"When do you think it will be convenient for you to go into the matter of the lease?"

"Immediately after breakfast, I think, don't you?" said Allard. "I suppose you're in no particular hurry?"

"Must get back before lunch, as I told you. Not that I want to rush you into anything, of course."

"My dear fellow," said Allard, "I'd never suggest that you were rushing me. It was extraordinarily good of you to come at all." He felt in his dressing-gown pocket and gave a start. "Excuse me just one moment!" and he moved off—with, for him, a singular haste—towards his own room.

Palmer reappeared again almost at once. "Your bath in a quarter of an hour, sir?"

Travers glanced at the wrist-watch. "Do capitally."

As Palmer passed out to the corridor, Allard re-entered the room. Before he could reach the table there was a sound from his own room, or beyond, as if something were falling against the wall. There was the noise of falling crockery—a cry!

Allard's eyes goggled as he clutched Travers' arm. "My God! What was that?"

Travers held his breath and listened. There was no further sound.

"Crewe's room, wasn't it?"

"Crewe's room?" He stared, then made for the door. "We'd better go and see."

Travers overtook him in the corridor, though it was Allard's hand that reached the door-knob first. As he opened the door he began the question.

"You all right—"

His voice broke off suddenly, and Travers, peering round his shoulder, saw why. Lying by the window, as if it had slithered down by the wall, was the body of Crewe. The window itself was wide open, but there was a little shadow beneath it where the body lay between the bed and dressing-table. The jacket of the dead man's sleeping-suit seemed to have been torn back. The handle of a knife protruded from his ribs, and round it was an island of red which fell away to where the material of the jacket held it up. The face of the dead man was deadly pale, and his eyes were black blots on white paper.

Allard began to make queer little noises, and as he backed into the doorway Travers took his place. He moved across the room to the window and looked out. Nothing could be seen except a wall that fell sheer away, the creeper thing that grew on it and the shrubbery at the foot. Then he saw something on the stems of the leafless creeper, something that looked like blood. The stems, too, seemed to be newly marked as if by feet, and one or two smaller twigs were hanging broken.

He turned away and caught the goggling eyes of Allard staring frightenedly. It seemed as if something had happened for which he was totally unprepared; something outside the schedule.

"Is he . . . dead?"

Travers nodded. The mouth of the body was set in a gape that could mean nothing else. Then, as he backed again, he saw that the knife was some sort of dagger, and the handle looked like wood, though from where he stood it was none too plain. But he saw that his feet were leaving impressions in the thick, black rug. Something might be trodden on or obscured, and he moved more warily to the door again. Allard's hand was shaking.

"I say, this is dreadful! . . . You know, we only meant it as a joke."

Travers rounded on him in a flash. "Meant what as a joke?"

"Well, this murder business." He caught Travers' eye and looked away, moistening his lips nervously.

Travers nodded. "I see. . . . Well, it isn't a joke now. Those policemen still about?"

Allard shook his head. "They went off at daylight—or should have done. You think . . . you think we ought to tell the police?"

Travers snorted. *"Ought* to? We've damn well *got* to. And the doctor. 'Phone's in the lounge, isn't it?"

He pushed Allard gently out and closed the door.

"You go to your own room and I'll be up again in a second or two. If anybody should happen to come, don't let them go in."

He darted off along the corridor and down the stairs. The hall was deserted, but he found a bell and pushed it.

It was fortunate that the butler came almost at once, for Travers was getting very confused with the directory.

"What's the doctor's number, Mason? Or would it be quicker to send for him direct?"

Mason gave a start. "The doctor, sir?"

"Yes," said Travers curtly. "And hurry."

"I beg your pardon, sir. May I?" The butler took off the receiver and asked for a number. He squinted round while waiting.

"Anybody hurt, may I ask, sir?"

"Mr. Crewe."

"I see, sir." He nodded imperturbably, and turned as his call came through. As soon as he had hung up, Travers put his hand on the receiver.

"What number's the police station?"

As he looked away beyond the butler's head he saw that the time by the grandfather clock was eight-twenty, or just short of it. It was at that moment that there was a sound like a shot. It seemed to be coming from outside, and above where they stood. Travers stopped breathing.

"My God! What's that?"

Mason was perfectly unalarmed. "Probably a car backfiring, sir. They're always doing it."

Travers remembered the racing cars and nodded in agreement. Mason gave the number and he got through almost at once. A sergeant said he'd be round in a couple of jiffs, and he'd certainly let the superintendent know as the gentleman requested.

There was a strange, hesitating look on Mason's face when Travers turned round again.

"I've been thinking, sir," he said quite nervously, "that there couldn't be any cars out this morning. The head chauffeur left yesterday, sir—I mean this morning, sir."

Travers looked hard at him. "What *do* you mean, Mason? You mean it *was* a shot we heard?"

He turned at once and made for the door, Mason at his heels. At the landing where the corridors branched he collided with Spence, in dressing-gown, and the lather still on part of his unshaved face. Spence clutched his arm.

"What's the matter? Did you hear anything?"

"Don't know," said Travers. "Did you?"

Spence frowned. "I did hear something that sounded like a shot, and then I thought it wasn't, and then I thought I'd come along and explore seeing as how"—and he caught sight of Mason standing a stair or two down, and ended with—"well, seeing as how."

"Come on then," said Travers, and the three moved on. Outside the door of Crewe's room he stopped.

"Crewe's lying dead in there. I've just sent for the police and doctor."

"Dead! You mean . . ."

"That's right. He's murdered. Not a word to a soul downstairs, Mason. You understand? And you'd better go back and have the doctor or whoever gets here first, sent up. And tell my man to come here at once."

He watched the butler disappear, then turned to Spence.

"We'll have a peep in here as a precautionary measure, though we shan't find much. Unless . . ."

The word tapered off as his eyes swept the room for the second time that morning. The body of Crewe still lay beneath the window, though it had fallen forward and now sprawled with grotesque arms like a Moslem prostrated in prayer. Nearer to the door, on his back, lay Allard, eyes staring at the ceiling and lips gaping with that cod-like expression he had worn so often in life. There was no need to ask what had killed him, as Travers and Spence, kneeling by the body, at once knew. A bullet had caught him at the angle of the jaw and had ploughed upwards to the skull. The blood was still seeping down the neck where the orange-yellow of the sleeping-jacket was heavily stained.

Travers licked his lips as he backed again to the door. His eyes roamed round the room and saw the changes that had taken place since he saw it last. There had been a desperate struggle. The broken crockery had been kicked here and there. The small bedside table had been overturned and the rug was askew.

"What's happened to the pistol?" came Spence's voice.

Travers shook his head. It was not the absence of the pistol that was troubling him at the moment, but the fact that the room was all wrong. Everything was wrong. Up to a point it had all fitted, and then things had gone so startlingly astray that there was no sense in it.

"What's worrying you?"

Travers looked round half startled, and realized that Spence was there.

"Sorry! Afraid I was wool-gathering." He shook his head. "This room's all gone wrong. Allard shouldn't have been here at all."

Spence looked at him. "What do you mean?"

"Just what I say. Everything was what we suspected it to be, though you wouldn't commit yourself. This shouldn't have been a murder at all! It was all a fake. Allard owned up as much when he and I found Crewe dead in here a few minutes ago. I heard that shot downstairs while I was 'phoning and mistook it for the backfire of a car. Then the butler told me it couldn't be a car, and I knew what it was—or thought I did."

"What'd you think it was?"

"Ask yourself the question. What ought it to have been? Here's Allard who'd made a pretty fool of himself by rigging up all that murder stuff and found as a result that he'd been responsible for a man's death. What I guessed was that he'd shot himself—and in his own room."

"But he couldn't have shot himself! I mean, well, look at the line of the shot. He wouldn't shoot himself under the chin."

"I know. That's part of what's wrong. And there's no revolver, as you said. And there's been a third person in here, or else I'm very far wrong."

"How do you know it?"

Travers smiled wryly. "Who took the revolver? And who fought with Allard and did all that? They even kicked the other man's body over. And he shot Allard and made his getaway." He broke off. "I say, I shouldn't go there if I were you. We'd better leave things as they are. And there won't be anything to see."

Spence leaned out of the window for all that before he came back to the door.

"What's troubling me," he said, "is not how the chap got out, but how he got in. And, if you like, how he got out and in."

"What's wrong with the door?"

"But that implies someone living in the house; someone quite close. Someone, for instance, who knew you had gone downstairs and Allard was in here alone with the dead man."

Travers gave another wry smile. "But he wasn't in here at all! I left him going to his room."

"All the better," said Spence calmly. "The murderer came back after killing Crewe because he knew that the coast was clear. Allard surprised him here, and that's that."

"Rather a nerve, don't you think, to come back again after killing Crewe? Must have been something desperately important to bring him back again, especially after having made his escape down the creeper stuff with blood on his hands!"

It was Spence's turn to make the wry face. "So you noticed that, did you?" His eyes suddenly popped open. "Perhaps he never left the room after all! No, that's wrong. There must have been two of them. One may have left and the other didn't have time to go before you and Allard got here."

In a flash he had gone across to the huge wardrobe that stood by the windowless wall opposite the bed. With his handkerchief for a glove he turned the handle. Travers, close behind him, saw that he had been right. On the bottom of the wardrobe, in the empty space that should have been used for hanging suits, were the marks of the muddy feet of the man who had stood there. Travers scowled.

"It still isn't right. If there was mud on his boots, he must have entered from outside. And what's that curious thing?"

In the far corner of what would otherwise have been an empty space a dressing-gown was hanging; the one that Crewe would doubtless have worn if he hadn't been surprised and killed. It reached to within a foot of the bottom, and Travers had seen beneath it when he stooped to look at the mud. Now he drew back the dressing-gown for Spence to see. Spence stared, then looked puzzled.

"I know what it is. It's a dutch hoe!"

"So it is," said Travers, and looked bewildered. "But how extraordinary! I mean, it's like finding a cauliflower in your bed, or something perfectly ridiculous like that."

There was a tap at the door. He nodded to Spence to back out of sight, and opened it himself.

"Oh, it's you, Palmer. Come inside." He explained to Spence. "It's all right. Palmer's perfectly discreet."

Palmer gently cleared his throat with the most respectful of coughs in the presence of the dead.

"Something's been happening, sir."

Spence wondered afterwards why he hadn't smiled.

Travers nodded. "Looks like it, doesn't it. By the way, just after you left the room—my room, that is—you passed by here. Did you hear anything happen?"

Palmer nodded gravely. "I did, sir. I heard the falling of a cup and saucer—at least I thought that was what it was, sir, and then there was a noise which I thought was the gentleman swearing, sir—at the accident, as it were. I stopped for a second, sir, and then I went on again. You see, it was no business of mine, sir."

"Quite right of you." He thought for a moment. "Get off back now and find out for me—you'd better make a diagram—where all the guests were sleeping; everybody except the staff. Be discreet about it, and don't thrust yourself under the noses of the police when they get here."

Palmer departed. Travers and Spence looked at each other.

"Well, what now?" asked Spence.

"Outside first, I think," said Travers, and led the way. He locked the door and stood there for a moment holding the key.

"Perhaps I'd better stay here till someone comes. I take it you're itching to get through to your paper?"

Spence smiled self-consciously. "Isn't that what I'm here for?"

Travers smiled too. "Perhaps it is." He held out an arm as the reporter went to move off. "You'll take a piece of advice from one old enough to be your . . . your uncle? Don't theorize. Give the facts and wrap them up nicely. And see that my name's not mentioned."

CHAPTER IV
WORD OF HONOUR

SPENCE WAS fortunate in just managing to reach the telephone as the forces of law and order arrived. The doctor, a middle-aged, colourless sort of man, came with them, and Travers received the whole procession—butler at their heels—at the head of the stairs. It was soon evident that neither the superintendent nor the sergeant had much use for him. It was even more evident that they were wholly unprepared for what was inside the room. Travers, having introduced himself and received in return, "Oh, yes. Perhaps you'll be so good as not to leave the house, sir, like the others," nodded an acknowledgment and went along to his room. Before he had been in the bath a minute, with Palmer fluttering round anxiously at the coolness of the water, a policeman tapped, and put his head unceremoniously round the door.

"Would you be so good as to come along at once, sir? The superintendent'd like to see you."

Travers nodded graciously. "At the very earliest moment," and went on with the tepid bath. Then he shaved hastily, got on the beginnings of a costume and finished with the dressing-gown. A slap at the hair with the brushes and a polish of the horn-rims and he was ready to forgive and forget.

The doctor had already gone; so had the butler. Outside the room a constable was sitting, and inside it were two gentlemen in a state bordering on panic.

"My God, sir! this is terrible," began the senior, who looked as if Monday's malefactors before the local bench were the lowest depths of his recent criminal experience. "You know anything about it?"

"Quite a lot," Travers told him, and began the details.

"Wait a minute, sir," interrupted the sergeant. "Let's get this all down."

Travers continued methodically. He left only one thing out—that Allard had owned up that all the Crewe murder threats had been bunkum. And he mentioned nothing about clues or deductions, and that not from obstinacy or secretiveness, but just that it would have been butting in on other people's jobs, and what was visible in the room itself was sufficient matter for anyone's thought. Where he himself stood close by the door, his foot almost touched the back of Allard's head, and whichever way he looked he always came back to its staring and perplexed-looking eyes.

The superintendent looked at him with considerable interest when the lucid recital was over.

"You're not a lawyer by any chance, sir?"

"Lord, no!" said Travers, rather too quickly. He hesitated for a bit. "The fact is—I know you won't think I'm blowing about it at all—I happen to have been mixed up in quite a few murder cases in my time and . . . well, if I can be of any use, perhaps you'll let me do anything I can."

The other looked uncommonly gratified. "You haven't anything particular in your mind you were thinking of, I suppose, sir?"

"I hadn't," said Travers. "You've notified the Chief Constable?"

"Five minutes ago, sir! As soon as we stepped inside this room we knew we were up against something."

"I know," said Travers. "What with the publicity and everything it's going to be the very devil. You've looked out of that window?"

"You mean the blood and the way he got out?"

Travers prevaricated with a nod. "Quite. You've doubtless followed that up."

The other two looked at each other. "We've got a couple of men down there in those bushes trying to trace steps, if that's what you mean, sir."

Travers nodded again. "The very thing. And if I might suggest it, I'd get a statement at once from the footman who brought his morning tea—as the last person actually to see him"—he moistened his lips as he pointed to the body of Crewe—"definitely alive. And might I have another look?"

"Why not, sir?" He turned to the sergeant. "You bring that footman here now."

Half-way across the room Travers suddenly paused. He looked at the disordered bedclothes, and the eiderdown that was trailing on the floor, then he leaned over and gently lifted the pillow. Underneath was a clear impression of an object that was no longer there. He turned his head quickly, and with a remark on his lips saw the superintendent looking out of the door, through which the sergeant had just gone. Travers replaced the pillow as gently as he had lifted it and moved on to the window.

The room, and another that lay alongside it on its right hand side, were in an inset between the two wings of the back of the house. All that could be seen from it was the wall falling sheer to the shrubbery beneath, on the edge of which a constable stood on duty. Except from the corresponding window of the neighbouring room, the room of the tragedy was therefore not overlooked. Beyond the shrubbery were the woods that skirted the lake and then ran back to the park-land. Travers became aware that the superintendent was at his elbow.

"Who is occupying that room next to us?"

"Nobody," said the superintendent. "The bed isn't made up or anything as far as I could see."

"Odd, don't you think?" remarked Travers. "Mightn't it be as well to find out why a room like that—conveniently at the head of the stairs—wasn't made use of? Especially as the house was rather full."

"Who'd know about it, sir? The butler?"

"Or the housekeeper. Or perhaps Miss Allard. Very smart of you, if I may say so, having a man to watch the back."

The other was pleased at that, as Travers had anticipated. He struck further while the iron was hot.

"I'd like to see your Chief Constable when he arrives. If he should decide to call in Scotland Yard, there's a suggestion I'd like to make to him." He took off his glasses and began a tentative polish, the surest sign that he was thinking somewhat hard. "My uncle happens to be the Chief Commissioner. I mean . . . well, I sort of know people."

"Indeed, sir?" The superintendent seemed very impressed. "Colonel Grant is Chief Constable, sir, as you probably know. I'll tell him what you say as soon as he gets here."

"And what now?" asked Travers. "Going to lock up?"

"I thought so, sir." His eyes suddenly fell on the door and he came across, picking his way between the sprawling legs of the staring Allard. "What about this door? Any connection with the room the other side?"

Travers had been itching to look at that door for himself, and now he and the superintendent examined it together. But not much examination was necessary. The door was bolted from their own side top and bottom, and neither bolt had been moved for months. Then when the room had been closed and the constable outside given his orders, the two went into Allard's bedroom. From that side two new bolts had been placed on the door and they, too, had not been moved for some time. Travers, leaving the other to tackle the footman who was waiting on the landing, completed his toilet and made his way downstairs.

Mason was waiting in the hall and Travers all at once realized that it was well over the hour for breakfast.

"Where *is* breakfast?" he asked the butler.

"In the breakfast-room, sir. This side of the lounge."

"Good. And the news has got out, Mason? Everybody knows it?"

The butler lost his suavity, as he shook his head gloomily. "The staff are very upset, sir. Luckily they know it's nothing to do with them. By a curious coincidence, sir, everybody is accounted for. It happened to be the staff breakfast at the time, sir."

Travers nodded. Any other answer might have been difficult. "And Miss Allard? Who broke the news to her?"

"Mrs. Hall, sir—the housekeeper. She took it very well, sir, if you know what I mean. She's a lady, sir, is Miss Allard."

Before Travers could go into the question of whether or not the implication was that the others were not ladies, there was the sound of voices arguing at the front door. Mason looked inquiringly at Travers and the two went over together. On the porch the constable on duty was confronting Taylor Samuels, who was looking slightly flustered.

"Morning, Samuels," said Travers. "What's all the bother?"

Samuels explained. "The officer here says I'd no right to be out. I told him I'd been for my regular constitutional, and he doesn't seem to think I've got any right to a constitutional. I told him if he'd a digestive system like mine he'd understand."

Travers smiled. "What is it, officer? You've had orders not to allow anybody out?"

"That's right, sir—not without the superintendent's permission."

"But nothing about stopping them from coming in."

The constable looked a bit glum. "Well, I suppose not, sir, if you look at it that way." He turned on Samuels. "And what time did you go out, sir?"

"Time? I guess it was a half-hour ago. I've tramped right round this ranch and I'm a steady goer, so I guess you can work it out."

"Went right round the park, did you, sir?"

"Haven't I just told you so?" said Samuels plaintively.

Travers laughed. "That's all right, officer. Come along in, Samuels, and have some breakfast."

With the outer door closed again he took the fat man's arm and pulled him round. Though the look was not too serious a one, Samuels seemed uncomfortable.

"Do you know what happened upstairs before you went out?"

"Happened?"

"Yes. In Crewe's room."

Samuels shook his head. "No, sir! And what did happen?"

"Crewe's been murdered—and Allard too."

Samuels' fat, unshaven cheeks began to wobble, and his eyes bulged. Travers steered him over in the direction of the breakfast-room. As he opened the door Mason's hand shot forward first. Then, before Travers could follow in Samuels' wake, the butler spoke quietly.

"May I speak to you a moment, sir?"

Travers closed the door again and stepped back. Mason moved across the hall and stopped in the corridor that led to the servants' kitchen.

"That man Samuels, sir." The disrespect was only too apparent. Travers guessed, and guessed rightly, that the butler was working off the feelings of the last few days. "He was wrong, sir, about going out. You know when I came downstairs, sir? That was when he went out, sir, and he slipped round that corner just before they got here."

"You mean he didn't pass in front of the window."

"He went out what I might call sneakingly, sir. I looked through the window myself, sir."

"I see. And that'd be how long ago? Quarter of an hour?"

"Not more, sir." He took Travers into his confidence. "What could the master have meant, sir, having people like them in the house?"

Travers shook his head. "Don't know, Mason. What are they, do you think?"

Mason snorted. "You're a gentleman, sir, and you know the sort they are. Some theatrical troupe is the opinion of the servants' hall."

Travers nodded. "Down to breakfast, are they?"

"Only the one who came last night, sir—that Mr. Franks. Mr. Drew was sound asleep when last seen, and Miss Hastings is suffering from what she calls shock." He suddenly put his hand on Travers' arm with a gesture that was almost touching in its timidity. "What is all this terrible business, sir? Do they know anything?"

"Not yet, Mason," Travers told him. "You're an old servant of the family?"

"All my life, sir. I began here as pantry boy." He pulled himself together. "But I'm keeping you from your breakfast, sir."

Before he could answer, Travers saw him stare, and followed his gaze. Sue Allard was going quickly across the hall, and her manner was that of a woman who wants to be unobserved. She was wearing a tweed costume and beret, and was carrying a small brief-case. The door in the corner closed on her before they could have spoken.

"What door's that?" asked Travers quickly.

"The library, sir." Mason looked at him nervously.

"Is there an outer door?"

"There is, sir, but it's kept locked. She has a key. She and the master have keys, sir—and I have one."

"She lives here?"

"Oh, no, sir! She lives in town. She came down specially on Monday."

"I see." He frowned for a moment, then turned. "Just go about your business normally, Mason. Don't say a word about this. Or about Mr. Samuels."

He went quietly across the hall and gently turned the handle of the library door. Sue Allard was bent over a desk with her back to him, but he could see that she held the lid down with one hand and was rummaging in the drawers with the other. Then she held the lid up with her body and rummaged impatiently with both hands, turning over papers and cramming them back. Travers waited till the search had ended—and fruitlessly—then gave a little cough. Up went the lid of the desk in a flash as she turned. When she saw who it was she gave a little smile. Her face was pale, and he knew she had been crying.

"Good morning. . . . You gave me a start. . . . I thought . . . I mean . . ."

"Sorry," smiled Travers. "Silly of me butting in like that." He gave a little nervous cough. "May I say how dreadfully sorry I am about . . . what's happened." He cleared his throat.

"You won't mind my asking it, but you're not thinking of going away? I mean, we've all got to stop here. It's absolutely vital."

She was biting her lower lip as she gave him a look. It was an appraising look, and Travers thought what a fine, clean-looking woman she was; a thoroughbred to the finger-tips, and a man's woman every time. He wondered, too, what she had thought of those amazing people her brother had collected in his house. It was she who spoke first.

"I know what you think. You think it's rotten of me." She shook her head passionately. "I know it's rotten."

Travers nodded gently. "But you've got to go."

"Yes. I've got to go." She gave another little, tentative smile. "I'm glad you said that. . . . And you won't give me away?"

"Not if you tell me where you're going."

She bit her lip in sudden apprehension, then seemed to see where the danger could be avoided.

"To town. That's all. I'll be back again before lunch. I've just got to go. You know I've got to go."

"And you wouldn't like to tell me exactly where?"

She shook her head. "One day . . . perhaps." She watched him as she picked up the case. "I'll be back before lunch—word of honour."

"And you'd have nothing to tell the police if they questioned you?" Her lips suddenly quivered and he turned away. Then he gave her a smile. "Look here, I hadn't better see you go. If you'll give me a moment to get out, then I shan't have to tell all sorts of tales." He turned at the door. "If you give me another moment or two, I may be able to talk to the policeman at the door—if that would help."

The constable was seated on the porch. He hopped up as Travers appeared.

"Did I understand you to say one could go out if the superintendent's permission was obtained?"

"That's right, sir," the constable assured him. "Was you wanting to go out then, sir?"

Travers thought. "I don't quite know, yet. . . . You've had breakfast?"

"And forgotten it, sir."

Travers grunted. "Yes. I suppose you have. Which reminds me that I'm most frightfully hungry myself."

He gave a cheery nod of farewell and went in again. The superintendent and the sergeant came in sight at the head of the stairs and he waited for them.

"You were quite right about that footman, sir," the super told him. "He was in the room when Crewe shouted to Mr. Allard. He left the tea on the table by the bed and Crewe in bed."

"Good," said Travers. "By the way, I'm just going to have a spot of breakfast if you should want me. You wouldn't care for some coffee?"

The super shook his head. "Not for me, sir. My sergeant's taking over for a bit while I see how those men are coming along outside." He caught the questioning look. "Those two following up the footprints under that window."

"Oh, yes," said Travers. "Of course. I forgot the footprints." He stood there lamely for a moment, then nodded and moved on towards the breakfast-room door. He was thinking of Sue Allard and wondering whether she had got clear and what she had hunted for so frantically in the desk and why it was so urgent that she should go to *town*.

As he entered the room he saw Franks sitting at the breakfast table, head morosely leaning on his cupped hands, while Taylor Samuels, eyes on plate, was shaking his head lugubriously. But it was what he was saying that pulled Travers up short.

"Yes, sir!" Samuels was saying. "I guess that lets out Wen Ti."

CHAPTER V
MORE ABOUT WEN TI

THERE WAS NO knowing what Travers might have heard if Samuels had not happened to glance up at that very moment. He gave what seemed like a warning cough and hoisted himself to his feet.

"Guess you're mighty hungry, Mr. Travers. Take this seat and warm yourself."

"No, too near the fire for me," said Travers, and pushed him down again. He smiled over at Franks. "Good morning. Sleep well?"

"Slept like a log," said Franks, who smelled of hair-oil. He was looking more of a musical comedy hero than ever; each hair in place and a general air of nattiness about him. "Perhaps it might have been a bit better if I hadn't."

"You mean . . . this awful business?" and Travers stopped in the act of helping himself to porridge. But there were no revelations.

"Well, yes and no," said Franks. "What I was getting at is if some of us had been awake we might have been in time to do something. You know all about it, don't you?"

"Precious little," said Travers. He took a seat on the other side of the table to have a good look at him. "You know this place pretty well?" was his first feeler.

"Never been here in my life," Franks told him, and gave a quick look at Samuels. Then he wiped his mouth with the napkin and made the further remark as quite an afterthought. "The fact of the matter is, I've been down the south of France."

Travers saw some daylight. "That's where you ran up against Allard?"

Another quick look at Samuels, and he changed the conversation. "Well, I did meet him there. . . . You any ideas on this business?"

"Very few," temporized Travers. "What I'm really anxious to find out is if either of you knew much about Crewe." He turned sharply at the buffet as he put the question. "You knew him, Samuels, didn't you?"

"Sure," said Samuels promptly. "I knew him in the States. Henry knew him too. He asked us both over here. Sort of business deal we had on."

Travers sat down again. "I see. And what was his particular line?"

"Well. . . ." He hesitated. "Theatrical, I reckon you'd call it. He was interested in theatres." He shook his head portentously. "He was a great guy. One of the best ever, but he sure got a bum break for a man who comes home after ten years." He rose heavily from the table and found a chair by the fire.

"By the way, didn't someone tell me Crewe was going to marry Miss Hastings? I mean it's pretty rotten for her."

Samuels nodded, even more gloomily. "Sure. That's another tough break."

"Where did Crewe run across her? Do you know?"

"Nope," said Samuels, and spat his cigar end deftly into the fire. "When Henry and I got here it had all kinda happened?"

"Yes," persisted Franks, "but he must have said something?"

"Forget it!" the other told him. "There ain't no marryin' or givin' in marriage where he's gone."

Spence came in briskly. "Good morning, everybody. Mr. Travers, that superintendent wants to see you outside as soon as you're ready."

"Ready now," said Travers, and gulped down the rest of his coffee. "Where've you been all this time, by the way?"

"Tell you later," said Spence, making for the buffet.

"Wish I was in as well with those cops as you are, Mr. Travers," said Samuels mournfully. "And what about that Scotland Yard of yours? When are they due to arrive?"

"Mr. Spence'll tell you all about that," smiled Travers, as he moved off to the door. In the hall the superintendent was waiting, and a strange constable with him.

"We've found out something—the car the murderer should have got away in! Hidden in the wood about half a mile away. Looks as though you disturbed him or else he got the wind up."

What had happened, apparently, was that the two men whom the super had detailed to follow up footprints from beneath the bedroom window had found nothing at all, since the leaf-mould left no traces; but they had hunted about in the woods round the lake and beyond, and had ultimately come out at a back road which led from the far side of the park to a field gate in a side road. There in the wood had been an empty car, hidden by the tall laurels and rhododendrons with which all the woods were sprinkled.

"I understand you're an authority on cars," said the super. "We'd like you to have a look at it."

Travers smiled. "I don't know who told you that, but I'd certainly like to see it. Why not take my car? We'd be there in a couple of minutes."

"Good idea, sir!" He stopped as Mason came into the hall. "Just a minute, Mr. Travers. Oh, Mason; you don't happen to know if everybody's in the house as I ordered? My men say they saw a car going out of the front drive from the garage as they were coming back here."

"Everybody's in as far as I know," said Mason. "The car you saw would be the head mechanic. He acts as Mr. Allard's private chauffeur too. He was leaving last night but stayed on till this morning. There's the other mechanic at the garage. He'll tell you anything you want to know."

"Right," said the super, and moved off again. "Come along, Mr. Travers. We'll see what they say at the garage."

The garage was an immense place, surrounded by an acre or two of concrete. Only one open car seemed to be there, but there was a Rolls limousine and a Daimler on which the dungareed mechanic was, at the moment, at work. He went over to Travers' car at once.

"Anybody taken a car from here this morning?" asked the super.

"Stolen it you mean, sir?"

The super looked at him. "Why? Is there one stolen?"

The man smiled. "Not that I know of, sir. If you mean what cars have gone out, Mr. Preston took his little car when he went—"

"Is that the late chauffeur?"

"Well, sir, the head mechanic he's called usually. His car's gone, but whether he took it himself I can't say. I heard him moving about before I got up, and the car was gone when I got down to breakfast."

"You sleep here?"

"Up there, sir." He nodded at the upper story of the garage. "We have our meals in the house. Mr. Preston, he used to have his with the butler when we was down here."

"And no other car's gone?"

"Miss Allard took hers about half an hour ago."

"Then why the hell didn't you say so at once?" exploded the super. He turned to Travers. "How'd she get out? Is there another door?"

Travers shrugged his shoulders. "Mason's the man to ask about that. Shall we move on? Perhaps the mechanic'll come too. He might able to tell us something."

The four got in, and the Bentley shot off along the drive. Where the paved road turned left to the greenhouses they turned right, where a grassy track hugged the edge of the woods. The other constable was waiting with the gate open and Travers drew the car in. "Just a moment!" he said, as the guide began to move on ahead. "Is there any way out except this for the car you people found?"

"No other way at all," the constable told him. "It just had room to get in and no more."

Travers looked at the super. "Then something's gone wrong—unless the car was brought here overnight. Look over there at that grass. The dew hasn't been disturbed. No car's been brought in there this morning."

"Very funny," said the super, and rubbed his chin. "If he brought it in last night, where did he spend the night?"

Travers took refuge in another shrug. "Lord knows! Still, let's go and see the sights."

The car was a small Austin sedan, drawn in close to the evergreen clump, where it might have stayed for days except for the chance search. Travers had a good look round, but the leaf-mould hid every trace of feet.

"Suppose you haven't seen it before?" he asked the mechanic.

"Not that I know of, sir. At least it's never been in our garage."

"Start her up," said Travers. "We might judge how long she's been here."

The mechanic had her going over in no time. When he ran off a little water he reported an antifreeze mixture present. The gauge showed three gallons in the tank.

"How long'd you say she'd been here?" Travers asked.

The man shook his head. "I wouldn't like to say, sir. I shouldn't think it was longer than last night. It froze pretty hard the night before, and she wouldn't have started up as easy as all that."

Travers nodded. "Right oh, then. Shut her off and we'll leave her here as she was. There might be some fingerprints inside and there might not, in any case we hadn't better interfere with her any more. And where should we have gone to if we hadn't turned in here?"

"You'd have got to a road, sir."

"And where's it go to?"

"I'll show you, sir, as soon as we get out of here."

Outside the wood the mechanic showed them the road. To the left it went back to Marbury, and half a mile along to the right it joined the main London road. The four moved off slowly. In a couple of minutes the track of the wheels was found in a soft patch of ground; a few yards on was another wheel mark on a bare patch.

"Seems pretty conclusive," said Travers. "All the same, if the car was brought in the back way last night, I don't quite see the point of it."

"Most likely the man was on the watch all night," suggested the superintendent. "My men choked him off and he didn't get a chance to do what he came for."

"That may be it," said Travers. "Still, to make it more difficult, we might try to discover some tracks the way we came."

The mechanic took the Bentley back to the garage and the other three walked slowly back. But there was no further sign of the Austin or of any other car. Then when they got in sight of the house again, there was a large sedan drawn up at the front door.

"The Chief Constable for a fiver!" exclaimed the super, and made off at once and the policeman with him.

Travers turned towards the greenhouses in search of the head gardener, and found him in the potting-shed. He introduced himself, and they had a word over the tragedy before Travers put his question.

"Do any of your men live over by that back road?"

The gardener shook his head.

"Any of them been working there recently?"

"Now that's funny you should have asked that, sir. I was thinking of setting a man or two on to clearing up them paths and trimming the shrubs, only Mr. Allard, he come along—on Monday, I think it was—and, 'Finch,' he says, 'I don't want any men to go in the woods yet. Nobody's to go in without my special orders,' he says. So I says, 'Very good, sir,' and we just didn't go and that was all."

A couple of minutes' small talk and Travers moved on again, his head full of all sorts of unanswered questions. He still, for the life of him, couldn't see why that car had been left in the woods overnight instead of being brought there just before it was light. And unless Allard expected the car to be brought where it was, and wanted the matter kept secret, he didn't see why he should have seen his head gardener and interfered with something of which he must have been profoundly ignorant.

A chauffeur was at the wheel of the car and the policeman was still on duty at the door when he reached the front porch. Inside the hall there was no sign of anyone except a footman.

"Where's Mason?" Travers asked.

"Upstairs with the gentlemen, sir."

"Then would you mind finding my man and sending him to the library at once."

He had a peep in the lounge to see who was there, and found Spence alone.

"Hello!" he said. "What's happened to everybody?"

"Don't know," said Spence. "First one drifted out and then another. Any more news?"

Travers told him about the Austin, and made him promise to keep it dark. And if he got through to his paper again he was on no account to say a word about Allard's hint that the murder of Crewe ought to have been a fake.

Palmer was waiting in the library and he had with him what Travers wanted—the plan of the bedrooms. They went over it together.

"Something I thought you might like to know, sir," said Palmer. "From what I can gather there's some sort of a meeting taking place upstairs in Mr. Drew's room. Mr. Samuels is there, and Mr. Franks and Miss Hastings. You couldn't hear a sound as I came by, but they were all in there."

"Mr. Drew's room? That's a big bedroom, isn't it?"

"It's the only big one that's being used at present, sir, except Miss Allard's."

"Yes, but why has he got a state room? Why didn't they use that vacant room next to where Mr. Crewe was? Which reminds me. I'll speak to Mason about that. And if you get any more news about that upstair conference in Mr. Drew's room, let me know at once."

As soon as the man had gone Travers went across to the door by which Susan Allard had escaped that morning. The bolts were still drawn at top and bottom, and looked as if they had been recently oiled. And when he came to examine the lock, there was no doubt whatever that oil had been used. He found himself surveying the corner of the carpet and with a sudden movement stooped and lifted it. In the slight film of dust was still the mark where the key had been laid. He went across the room and looked at the desk, wondering what it was that Sue Allard had been hunting for so desperately.

Quite a body of people were in the hall. He heard Mason's voice, "Here *is* Mr. Travers, sir!" and saw an elderly gentleman making for him. The Chief Constable introduced himself, said he knew Travers well enough by repute, and he knew Travers' uncle very well indeed.

"I'm sure I've heard him speak of you, now I come to think of it," said Travers. "A deplorable business, this, don't you think?"

The other agreed. It was far too serious a thing for his own people to handle, and he was requesting the Yard to take action at once. He understood that Mr. Travers had a suggestion to make in that context.

Travers smiled diffidently. "I'm afraid it was rather premature on my part. I hope you won't think it grossly rude of me, only . . . well, you see, they'll send down a Chief Inspector, and while they're at it they might as well send Norris. I mean, I happen to know him pretty well—worked with him before and so on—and it might perhaps help."

A note was made at once. "See you later," said the Colonel, and moved off with his staff to the lounge.

Travers caught Mason's eye and retreated to the library. He closed the door and drew the butler away.

"Anybody tackled you yet about Miss Allard?"

"They asked me, sir," said Mason, "but I knew nothing."

"Stout fellow!" said Travers. "And I suppose you don't happen to know if Mr. Allard or anyone employed a private detective who patrolled the house at night?"

Mason's look of astonishment was sufficient answer.

"The reason I asked," explained Travers, "was that I saw a man in the corridor outside my room at dawn this morning. Quite a gentleman by the look of him. Tallish and well-set-up. Military appearance. Wearing a waterproof buttoned to his ears."

Mason shook his head. "Can't think who it was, sir. It must have been—" He broke off with a startled look. "Do you think, sir, it was the one who did it?"

"Don't know," said Travers, and then the butler looked startled again.

"Had he got a sort of hatchet face, sir? Tanned face—and smart appearance?"

"That's it."

"Well then, sir, it might have been Preston, the head mechanic—though what he was doing in the house is best known to himself."

"The head mechanic, eh? We'll see into that," said Travers. "Was he in to breakfast, by the way?"

"He was not, sir. He came across to the kitchen at about seven—so I'm told—and had a cup of tea. That's the last we saw of him."

Travers grunted. "Very strange. Very strange indeed. Oh! and something else I wanted to ask you about. That room next to where Mr. Crewe was. Why wasn't it occupied?"

"Well, sir, it was going to be occupied. In fact it probably *will* be occupied—to-night." Mason nodded like a man with a grievance. "There's something else, sir. After all those people we have in the house, who do you think the master was having down next?"

"Lord knows!" said Travers.

"A Chinaman, sir!"

"Good God!" said Travers, and then repeated lamely, "A Chinaman?"

"A Chinaman, sir!" echoed Mason. "He's due at the station at seven to-night, sir. Quite a gentleman he is, so the master said, and if it wasn't for his face you wouldn't know but what he was like ourselves. There was to be no special food, if you know what I mean, sir. No changes whatever."

"Do you know his name?"

Mason thought back. "The master did tell me, sir, but I didn't quite catch it."

"It wasn't, by any chance, Wen Ti?"

"That's it, sir." The butler's eyes opened wide. "How on earth did you know, sir?"

"I didn't know," said Travers. "I guessed."

CHAPTER VI
ARRIVAL OF AUTHORITY

THERE WERE NO other excitements that morning so far as Travers was concerned, though there was one happening that was rather inexplicable. No sooner did he get into the dining-room where Spence was now installed, and where he was hoping to compare notes, than Franks put in an appearance with, "Excuse me, but can I have a word with you, Mr. Spence?"

That was the last seen of the reporter till after lunch, and then what he said merely left Travers still more in the dark.

"As soon as the Yard get here, I'm going," was what he said to Travers. "Sorry I can't let you on to it but I've given my word. But you can take it from me that I've got a story that'll make people sit up and beg for more."

Travers angled delicately. "You're the first instance of a crime reporter who found himself in the very house with a murder and then wanted to get out of it."

"Maybe," said Spence. "What I know won't solve any murders, but it's a great little story all the same."

Spence was in a bit of a quandary, with the lounge out of bounds by the Chief Constable's orders, and a policeman sitting on duty at the 'phone.

Sue Allard had duly returned before lunch, so Mason said, and had had her meal upstairs. By her orders the new head mechanic, who was taking the place of the departed Preston, had been told to stand by. Preston, according to Mason, had left Allard's service on perfectly amicable terms, having given a month's notice. Allard, indeed, had been very annoyed that he was going, and had made him a good offer to stay on. There seemed, in other words, no possible reason for connecting Preston in any way with the murders.

Just before two o'clock Scotland Yard arrived in full force; platoons of them that crowded the hall till it looked like a meeting of the plain-clothes-men's union. Chief Inspector Norris's head had not swollen in the least since his promotion. Though his back was as much like a ramrod as ever, he was wearing the same old blue coat with the velvet collar, and he smiled just as modestly when he held out his hand to Travers. Then there was Lewis, his right-hand man, all energy and ideas, and as much unlike his steady-going, methodical chief as a man could be. There was Menzies, too, grizzled and hard-bitten, and about to examine, in company with the local doctor, what would surely be his thousandth corpse.

Travers smiled as he looked round. "The same old gang! Ghastly thing to say, but it makes one feel quite at home."

"Hope we shan't stay here long enough to call it that," said Norris. He looked round. "Shall we go up? You fellows stand by on the landing."

He led the way with Travers at his elbow, the other trailing behind. He stopped at the door, and Travers caught the look.

"It's all right, Norris," he said. "The handle's smothered with prints, from mine to the third footman's."

Norris peeped inside, then called for the camera men. When they came out the fingerprint men were turned loose, and Menzies got to work. Norris and Lewis stood just inside the door, and Travers carried on with what he knew of the murders. Menzies replaced the chalk with which he had made an outline of Allard's body, then began to examine his wound.

"Warm when you saw him?" he said to the doctor.

"He hadn't been dead ten minutes," he was told.

Menzies nodded as he rubbed the dead man's chin between his fingers. He pushed the head over and looked at the neck.

"Any point in trying this for prints?" he said to Norris. "He's had the hell of a scrap with someone—and just before they scored that bulls-eye on him."

The fingerprint man tried it and reported nothing.

"Right," said Menzies. "Let's have that dressing-gown off him, doctor. And the jacket. And now let's see his wrists. . . . As I thought."

Even from where he stood Travers could see the discoloration. Whatever else was faked there was nothing wrong about that. Then Lewis picked up the button which had been wrenched from the dressing-gown.

"What was the starting-point of the bullet?" Norris asked.

Menzies shrugged his shoulders. "Depends whether he was standing up or toppling over or actually down when the shot was fired. We can test that later. Mr. Travers will do very well. About the same height, I should think."

Travers suddenly came to life. "Sorry, Norris, but I'm afraid there's something I forgot. Do you mind?" He went over to the bed and gently lifted the pillow. "Isn't that the mark of a revolver?"

There wasn't much doubt about it. Norris had a photographer in at once, and Lewis took measurements.

"It's a remarkable thing," he said, "but here's another of those contradictory things you were mentioning, Mr. Travers. We get into our heads the idea that Crewe intended some sort of a fake, and Allard knew it, and yet we find Crewe with a revolver under his pillow all night."

"Local colour, sir," suggested Lewis. "If you're planning a fake you might as well plan it thoroughly while you're about it."

Norris shook his head. "There's never any need for a man to lie to himself. And about the revolver, Mr. Travers? No sign of it when you first saw him dead?"

"Not a thing," said Travers. "And as far as I remember—mind you, I wouldn't swear to it—the room wasn't so disordered as it is now. I mean, when I try to visualize the room as I saw it then, it seems different now."

"Exactly. And we're to assume, Allard was shot with Crewe's pistol. And since it wasn't visible to you, it wasn't visible to the other man—the murderer of Allard—and therefore he knew it was there."

Travers smiled deprecatingly. "I don't think I'd say that. You see, I was rather staggered at what I saw—and I'm bat-eyed, and I hadn't too much time to notice things."

"One thing I can definitely tell you," came Menzies' voice from behind. He had been dabbing at Allard's wound with a piece of lint soaked in some dope or other. "The shot wasn't fired farther off than three feet away. Looks as if it was fired from the window."

"How do you know?" asked Travers.

"Various ways," said Menzies dryly. "And look at the sleeve of this dressing-gown, how it's scorched. He probably knew the bullet was coming and put his arm up."

"I'd have ducked," said Lewis flippantly. Travers rather agreed with him.

"Wherever it was fired from, he was a good shot," said Norris. "Allard might have been looking out of the window. The angle looks like forty-five degrees from the ground level."

Menzies smiled ironically. "You and your angles! Why shouldn't it have been fired from the floor? Why shouldn't he have been falling when the bullet hit him? He might even have been lying on the ground." He pointed down to the body. "Do you want this chap any more? If not, we might as well clear him out of the way."

"Try the other first," said Norris. "I'd like to see them together a bit longer."

They chalked out Crewe's body, and Lewis took the measurements, then Menzies and the doctor got to work. The body was lying forward, and they leaned it back against the wall to the position in which Travers said he had first seen it. But as soon as the pyjama jacket was taken off Travers had a shock. He now saw what he had missed when he caught his first glimpse of the body just after the dagger had struck. On the wrists there were the clear traces of a struggle, and on the forearm and chest were little abrasions that might have come from the same dagger during the fight that preceded the thrust. Menzies squinted at them with his glass, then dabbed at them with the lint and squinted again.

"Any difference in the time of death?" he asked the doctor.

"Not much. Only a matter of minutes." He looked up questioningly at Travers. "As a matter of fact, if it hadn't been for what this gentleman saw, I very much doubt if I could have separated the times at all."

"What was the actual difference?" said Norris.

"Less than five minutes," said Travers. "Say four and you won't be far out."

"Keep him steady," said Menzies, "and we'll get this skewer out of him." He gripped with the pliers and drew the knife out straight. Norris held the box for it, and the fingerprint people tackled it straight away. The white powder showed no trace of a print.

Norris grunted. "That's bad luck. Still, let's have a look at it."

It was a cross between knife and dagger. The blade was six inches long and two-edged. A guard, which rather gave it the appearance of a toy bayonet, came next, then the handle shaped to a bulge at the top and made of a material which looked like ebony but which turned out to be wood coloured black. From the wear marks which the glass showed up it seemed to be a good many years old.

"You identify it all right?" asked Norris.

Travers nodded. "I may be bat-eyed, but that's the one I saw. You couldn't mistake that peculiar shape. You're not suggesting substitution of any kind?"

"Oh, no!" and Norris smiled. "Though I knew that happened once, as Menzies can bear me out." He passed the box over to Lewis. "Get a picture and accurate measurements for the Press, and send it to the Yard at once. Ask for Orrey to get on with the knife itself."

Menzies went over to the lavatory basin in the corner and began washing his hands. "Finished with them now?"

"In a minute," said Norris. He stood there looking down at the two bodies, then had another long look from the window. "I expect it's a damn silly question," he said to Menzies, "but if the murderer of Allard—or perhaps Allard and the murderer—knocked this body askew when they were struggling, oughtn't there to be some sort of mark or abrasion?"

The police surgeon shook his head. "All there might be is the mark of a muddy boot treading on the corpse or rubbing against it." He came over, holding the towel in his hand, and turned the body round and back, then shook his head again. "Nothing there, is there, doctor? Mind you, we might run across something when we get him on the table."

Norris nodded. "Well, get their clothes off and take them away. Then we'll go through the room."

No sooner were the bodies out than a length of wire and an electric bulb was fixed to the dressing-table lamp, and a couple of plain-clothes men got ready. In a quarter of an hour the floor and walls had been gone over with a small-toothed comb, and there was nothing worth putting in a container.

"Right," said Norris. "Take the bedclothes away just as they are and go over them in the next room." He marked the position of the feet and then had the bed taken out too. "Now we have room to look about us," he said to Travers.

Travers saw at once what he had been anxious to get at—the door which led through to the bedroom Allard had occupied. He looked at the pair of bolts, but concentrated most on the hinges. He must have spent five minutes over them with the glass before he was satisfied.

"You were quite right. That door hasn't been opened for some time. And that's a pity. Allard might easily have done Crewe in himself if the door'd been faked."

"You'll pardon me," said Travers, "but I don't quite agree there. Allard was actually talking to me when we heard the noise of the struggle."

Norris smiled enigmatically. "We'll take your word for it, Mr. Travers. And now this mud of yours in the wardrobe."

The photographers let off a couple of flashes before he and Lewis got to work. Then the bulb was played round the inside of the wardrobe and every inch gone over for marks and prints.

"It gives me the queerest sort of feeling when I think of it," said Travers to the company generally, "but do you realize that when Allard and I stood here looking at Crewe's body, the murderer was actually listening to us in there, not ten feet away. I passed so close that I might have heard him breathe."

"It's a pity he hadn't asthma, sir," said Lewis.

"Make it whooping-cough," said Norris. "But about these marks of what we suppose to be feet, Mr. Travers. Think very hard indeed. When you saw them, were they dry or wet?"

"Dry," said Travers, without a second's hesitation. "I know it, because it struck me that there was something else that ought to have been right—but wasn't."

"What do you mean by that exactly, sir," asked Lewis.

"Well; if the murderer came in from outside—as he must have done for his feet to be muddy—then the mud or dirt must have been wet. As an afterthought I may add that there was no clear impression of the soles of the boots."

"Yes, but you wouldn't rule out the fact that a man might have had his boots muddy—very muddy—while waiting about outside, and they might have dried by the time he had to get in here?"

Travers smiled. "I'd rule out nothing. Forgive me if I sounded dictatorial. What I said was merely a personal impression."

"That's all right, Mr. Travers," said Norris, unhooking the dressing-gown and handing it over to Lewis. "Don't you keep anything in that ought to come out. And now what about the prize exhibit?"

He took out the dutch hoe and had a look at it. It was of quite a common size and type, and seemed to have done several years of work. In the handle were stamped the letters C.A.

"Make a note to ask about that from the head gardener," said Norris. "It belongs to the estate, and they ought to know if they've lost one—and where. Let the print people go over it."

For the first time there was some luck. Almost as soon as the white powder had been dusted, two sets of prints—some clear, some blurred and interchangeable—stood well out. They belonged to both Crewe and Allard, and when the handle had been gone over in its full length there was not another print found.

Norris gave a non-committal grunt and had the hoe put aside. Lewis, who had been hunting round, suddenly produced the towel that Menzies had used, and which had been hanging by the side of the corner basin.

"I don't know if you noticed it after Doc. Menzies had been scrubbing himself with this," he said, "but I thought there was something funny. Have a look here. See the powder?"

Norris had a look and showed the towel to Travers. There was powder—plenty of it—still on the towel. Travers gave a modest smile.

"Allard wasn't shaved, but Crewe was," he said. "Perhaps the gentleman was fond of powder."

"Why'd he shave at all, and then get back to bed?" asked Norris quickly.

"Merely a suggestion," said Travers, and withdrew again.

Norris nodded to Lewis and the towel was laid aside with the hoe. Lewis put Allard's sleeping-suit and dressing-gown with them and made another discovery at the same time. In the dressing-gown pocket was a key of the ordinary mortice lock type. Norris made faces at it, then gave further orders.

"Go to that butler chap and find out what key it is. Bring him up here if he knows. And while you're about it, have orders sent round for everybody to stand by for interview. In the hall will do."

Norris heaved a sigh. "Well, we're getting on—if it's slow. What about tackling the dressing-table and drawers?"

The dressing-table produced nothing, unless it was a large tin of powder, its top pierced by holes that sent out a positive deluge when the tin was shaken.

"You'll notice that it wasn't kept on the table top with the other things," said Norris. "And I see he's got his shaving tackle still on the shelf above the basin. Now the drawers."

Travers had noticed, from some subtle knowledge of Norris's methods and certain changes already in his attitude, that he was beginning to form certain ideas. As soon as the chest of drawers was opened from top to bottom, he couldn't fail to notice that Norris was looking so pleased that he was finding it difficult to disguise the fact. Travers himself was flabbergasted. Each drawer had oddments in it, except the large one at the bottom, and in this was each article of clothing that the occupant of the room might have been expected to put on—and in order of donning: shirt, shorts, socks with garters attached, trousers with braces attached, collar, tie, waistcoat, jacket, and lastly, overcoat, and a tweed cap beneath it. Norris rubbed his hands.

"There we are! Everything ready for the getaway. He'd shaved and got back nicely into bed and was ready to bolt as soon as the footman got clear." He shook his head. "The trouble was somebody else got here first."

Travers was beginning to see things too. "Perhaps that's what Allard was alluding to when he told me the murder was all wrong," he ventured.

"Don't know," said Norris. "There's lots of things I'm not satisfied about where Allard is concerned. I didn't quite like his manner when he brought Crewe along to the Yard."

"You saw them at the Yard!" said Travers, really surprised. "You've been keeping that up your sleeve."

"I don't think I'd say that, sir," said Norris. "I just happened to drop in when they were there. I may say while I'm about it, that I hadn't anything to do with the decision to take no action, but I had a hunch all the same that everything wasn't what it appeared to be. They were a queer couple to be in double harness. Allard was a gentleman; the other-" He gestured the rest.

Lewis came in before Travers could carry on.

"Butler's outside. He says he'll show you the door."

"Right," said Norris. "You send a man round to that gardener with the hoe and ask him to make a statement, and arrange for ladders for that outside wall. Have the head gardener look at the broken twigs and hear what he says, and get samples of that blood from the wall and the ground sent to the Yard. I'll be in the lounge."

Mason was waiting on the landing. "This way, sir," he said, and led them past the main staircase along the corridor.

"Where's this go?" asked Norris.

As he spoke they arrived at a junction. "That part to the servants' rooms, sir, and this to the library," said Mason. "It's a most inconvenient sort of house, if I may say so, sir. I believe this staircase was made specially for one of the original owners to get up to bed without disturbing anybody."

"Very considerate of him," said Norris grimly.

Mason made no comment but continued in the lead. The door he opened brought them to the room which Travers had entered that morning in search of Sue Allard. In the corner opposite the door which she had probably used was a tall, folding screen, decorated in the Chinese manner. Travers suddenly thought of Wen Ti as Norris followed the butler over. Behind the screen was a door, leading to the same shrubbery which ran beneath the window of Crewe's room. Mason fitted the key and the door opened easily enough. Lock and key showed traces of oil.

Norris stepped out and looked about him. A few sniffs of the cold air and he was in again.

"This screen always here?" he asked the butler.

"Always—to my knowledge, sir."

"Right," said Norris laconically. "Let me have that key, will you? And say nothing about it. Give me your own key later."

"I'm sorry, sir," said Mason with a little bow. "I have no key, sir. As far as I know this is the only one there is. The master—the late master, I should say, sir—used this door and nobody else."

Norris nodded. "Thank you, Mason. Have everybody assembled in the dining-room, will you—except Miss Allard. I'll see her last."

He watched the butler disappear, then turned to Travers.

"There's something else that's wrong." He clicked his tongue. "The whole damn thing is wrong. Crewe should have had the key—not Allard." He stopped suddenly as if he were listening. "No! I'm the wrong one. All the same, it doesn't fit in."

"What doesn't fit in?" asked Travers quickly.

"Don't know yet," said Norris. "We'll see first what that head gardener has to say. But one thing I'm pretty sure of. That little hint of yours about this place being home, sweet home, looks like being true. We shan't get away from here for a day or two—or else I'm a Dutchman."

"Dutchman!" Travers looked at him. "I wonder. Does a Dutchman use a dutch hoe?"

Norris stared. "Dutchman and dutch hoe? What do you mean?"

Travers smiled lamely. "I don't quite know. It merely struck me, that's all. And if you think I was pulling your leg, put it down to April the First."

"April the First. All Fools' Day," said Norris. "So it is! That helps to fit in. No, it doesn't." He clicked his tongue again. "Damn the riddles! Let's go and see these people and hear a few more."

CHAPTER VII
ON PARADE

THE LOUNGE made an admirable headquarters. The table over which Henry Drew had so efficiently presided with the cock-tail-shaker was now the desk behind where Norris sat. Another table by the telephone was conveniently placed for the stenographer. A third had been brought in and was probably intended later on for the exhibits.

Travers had a seat behind the main table, and the easy chair in which he sat seemed a tactful intimation that he was not too official. What he was wondering was if Norris, who had been for years the right-hand man of Superintendent Wharton of the Yard, would exhibit on his first big case those histrionic touches, those subtleties of cross-examination, and the amusingly trivial deceptions that his former superior had found so profitable. But Norris was evidently determined at all costs to be himself. His method turned out to be the purely fatherly and credulous and crassly sympathetic. Variations, thought Travers, could come later when experience had suggested some elasticity of technique; but he liked the quiet transparency of Norris, and found it as intriguing in its way as the showmanship of old "General" Wharton.

Whatever had been discussed at that meeting which had been held upstairs in Drew's room, Norris was taking no chances on any further collaboration between the members of that peculiar house-party. The plain-clothes man at one door was to usher in the examinee, and another man was to usher out—not back to the dining-room but into the hall. Norris opened his case and spread out a few papers imposingly.

"Ladies first, I think?" he said to Travers, and to the man at the door, "Ask Miss Hastings to come this way, will you?"

He was on his feet before the table as she came in, and pushed forward a chair. His smile was an engaging one.

"Miss Hastings, isn't it? Sit down, will you? We shan't be keeping you long. Just the usual formality."

In a hard way she was a most attractive woman, though she was looking her age. On a stage she might easily have passed for sixteen, and flapper parts would have suited her to perfection. Her voice was rather different from what it had been the previous night, and she was giving that little affected trill to the liquids that seems so essential in musical comedy. But her lips were a shade too thin; there was something cat-like about her, and the claws looked as if they might be extraordinarily near the surface. She made a *moué* as she took the seat.

"You're not going to ask me all sorts of horrid questions?"

"My dear young lady!" protested Norris.

"And I shall be able to get away to-night?"

Norris rubbed his chin. "Well... we'll see. I hope you will be able to get away." His tone changed. "And now to this little matter of business. Full name, Miss Hastings?"

"Margaret—just Margaret." She leaned forward and peered as he wrote.

"Quite. And tell me, Miss Hastings, just how did you come to be spending a holiday here?"

"Court Allard invited me. I knew him, you see."

"Exactly. . . . Any business occupation or profession, or are you one of the lucky people I envy?"

She sat up briskly. "Oh, I'm an actress."

"Really! That's very exciting." His tone changed again. "Was I given to understand that you were engaged to be married, Miss Hastings?"

She bit her lip. "Yes ... I was going to marry Charlie Crewe."

Norris nodded. "You have my sympathies in this appalling affair. Perhaps you'll allow me to say that, being a man old enough to be your father." A touch of Wharton, that. "But we'd be more than grateful to you if you could tell us something about Mr. Crewe; what he is exactly and . . . well, all about him."

"He was what they call a producer." The answer came pat as ninepence. "You know, he did plays. He was ever so clever. He was going to do one here."

"A play here!"

She smiled. "Well, not a play exactly. A talkie. Wonderful, it was going to be. I was the leading lady; what you'd call a star."

"Well, now, that *is* interesting!" said Norris, and looked as if he meant it. "But coming back to this terrible business of this morning, Miss Hastings. The idea got about, I believe, that there was some sort of hoax arranged. Did you know anything about it?"

She coloured slightly. "No! We all thought it was real."

"You mean the threatening letters were real?"

"Mr. Crewe told me they were real. I was awfully worried and I asked him."

"Quite!" nodded Norris. "Naturally he'd have told you the truth." He looked round at Travers. "Need we keep Miss Hastings any longer now?"

Travers leaned forward. As far as he could judge the lady's feelings were by no means lacerated at the tragedy, and in any case he saw no reason why she should get away with a story so extraordinary.

"Miss Hastings," he said, "there is one thing that has been puzzling me ever since last night. Two things, perhaps, but we'll take them one at a time. Last night at dinner. Had Mr. Allard given some of you people orders—or warnings—about what you said and how you said it?"

She had the answer all ready. "Oh, yes! You see he didn't want anything to get out about the picture. It was all to come as a surprise."

Travers nodded. "I see. That explains it perfectly. Now a more personal question. You seemed very surprised—I might even say alarmed—last night when Mr. Franks came into the room. You knew him?"

She coloured violently. "No, I didn't ... I mean, I thought he was somebody else. You know. I thought he was somebody who was dead. Somebody who was killed in the war."

Travers nodded again. "Quite. That would naturally be upsetting. And just one other piece of information you might give us, Miss Hastings. I think you know the answer. . . . Who is Wen Ti?"

She watched him warily, biting her lip; hesitated for a moment, then, "I didn't catch what you said."

"Never mind," smiled Travers, and left her to Norris.

The inspector smiled too. "That's all for the present Miss Hastings."

She hopped up at once. "Thanks awfully. And may I go now?"

"Go where?" asked Norris, still smiling paternally.

"Well, back to town. Anywhere."

He shook his head. "Not at present. To-morrow, perhaps. And if you should think of anything you'd like to tell us further, or anything you'd like to modify, come here at once."

He turned away and began to scribble on the pad. The plain-clothes man touched her on the arm and, rather bewildered, she was shown out at the hall door.

"Anything in that picture business?" asked Norris.

"I'd say no," said Travers. "Frankly it's too preposterous for words. There are no facilities here for that sort of thing. There were other lies too. How could she think Franks was somebody who was killed in the war? He's about her age—round about thirty—and the war's been over thirteen years and more."

"Of course it has. What was that Wen Ti question about?"

Travers explained.

"Right!" said Norris. "We'll follow that up—and the picture business too. Ask Mr. Franks to come in, will you?"

It was a cold day and the room was none too warm, but when Franks came in one had the idea that his hands were hot and sticky. As he approached the table he pulled out his handker-chief, wiped his lips and twisted it in his hands.

Norris tried to put him at his ease and got him seated. "Just a matter of formality, Mr. Franks. We shan't keep you very long. Full name?"

"Percy Franks."

Norris went through the motions of writing on the pad. "And how did you happen to be here, Mr. Franks?"

He sat up, story all ready. "Well, you see it was like this. I'm an actor." A deprecatory shrug. "A singer, if you like. A tenor. Mr. Allard saw me at the Cap d'Or at Monte where I happened to be appearing, and he seemed to be very much struck. He saw me after the show and told me he might have something good for me. A talkie, so he said, that he was going to be interested in. A week ago he sent for me to come over as my engagement had ex-pired . . . so I came. Got here last night, as Mr. Travers knows."

"Do you happen to have the letter?" Norris asked mildly. He saw the violent flush that ran across the other's face. "No, I thought you wouldn't keep it. But do you happen to know just what the idea of this talkie was?"

Franks shook his head. "I don't. I understood from Mr. Allard last night that we'd talk everything over this morning. I know all the others were in it."

"Quite." He looked at what ought to have been the plan of the bedrooms. "I see your room was rather away from the scene of the tragedy this morning. But did you hear anything? Is there anything you can tell us?"

Franks looked remarkably serious. "I'm sorry, Inspector, but I didn't hear a thing. You could have knocked me down with a feather when I heard what'd happened."

"You knew Crewe?"

"Never heard of him before in my life."

Travers looked up quickly at that piece of insistence. "Know any of the others?"

"Before last night? No!"

"You'd never met Miss Hastings, for instance?"

He seemed quite amused at that. "Oh, that! You see, she mistook me for somebody else. Somebody she knew who was supposed to be killed in the war."

"A very natural mistake, if I may say so," said Norris, and leaned back in the chair. "I think that's all, Mr. Franks."

Before the tenor knew what was happening he was being shepherded to the door. He turned round at the last moment.

"Is there any reason why I shouldn't go back to town, Inspector?"

Norris rubbed his chin. "I don't think it would be advisable at present. To-morrow, perhaps. You might think of something you've left out—or want to alter."

"Want to alter?"

Norris waved his hand. "My little joke!" The door closed on Franks and he turned to Travers. "Working out well, isn't it? Before we've finished we'll know what happened at that meeting as well as if we had the minutes in front of us. Send Mr. Drew in, will you?"

Drew sauntered in gracefully, perfectly unconcerned, as was seen from the little smile that puckered on his lips. His eyes were wrinkled slightly, and Travers felt like smiling too—the atmosphere had immediately become so friendly.

"Guess you want me to sit down."

"That's right, Mr. Drew." Norris was smiling too. Drew's voice had been the friendliest in the world; just a trace of huskiness in it that gave it quality. If there was an ounce of vice in him, Norris was the most surprised man in England.

"Full name, Mr. Drew?"

"Just Henry."

"Nationality American?"

"Sure!"

"What State?"

Drew smiled gently. "Guess we'll make it Texas."

"I see." Norris found the joke. "You've been a bit of a wanderer in your time. Business or profession, Mr. Drew?"

"Movie actor when there's nobody better to take the job."

"Any particular parts?"

Drew's face wrinkled to a grin. "Bad man—hero—cow-hand. Once I was a gunman, but I didn't cut any ice in that part."

Norris laughed. "You arrived in England on Monday?"

Drew shook his head. His voice was all the time as gentle as if he were telling a bedtime story to a drowsy child. "Not Monday, Chief, Sunday. We stayed a night in the big town and then came on here."

"Quite. And how'd you happen to come to England at all?"

"Well, it was this way. Crewe and Samuels and myself were together out in Hollywood, where we had a dandy little act." He shook his head, still smiling. "Guess it wasn't hot enough for those Hollywood guys."

"It didn't go?"

"You said it. Then Crewe, who was sort of manager, had some news from over here and said he was liable to be sending for us as soon as he got the lowdown. Soon's he landed he sent Sam and me money enough to come over. Some big shot was making a picture and he reckoned he'd fit us in some-wheres." He gave a little shrug. "Guess that's all."

"You didn't know what this picture was precisely?"

"No sir. Not a thing. We were going to get the lowdown this morning—then something happened."

Norris nodded. "Yes. Something happened. You expected things to happen?"

"If you mean the letters, I'm saying nothing. Crewe was a great guy, and I'm not doing him dirt now. If the letters were all ballyhoo, I guess that's no business of mine."

"A most admirable spirit," was Norris's comment on that. "And this morning. You heard or saw—or suspected—nothing?"

Drew smiled. "I was sleeping so sound I didn't even hear that footman bring in the tray. I just rolled over and went to sleep again."

"An easy conscience," said Norris. "And with regard to those threatening letters. There was a reference in the papers to one or two men in America who'd have been glad to see Crewe dead. Do you know who they were?"

Drew smiled dryly. "Guess that all of Hollywood wouldn't have cried any if the three of us had been bumped off."

Norris turned to Travers. "Need we keep Mr. Drew any longer?"

"I don't think so," said Travers. "Unless he can tell us what he knows about Wen Ti."

Drew looked at him with a quick turn of the head.

"Guess I didn't get that, Mr. Travers."

"Forget it!" said Travers flippantly, and leaned back.

Drew was escorted deferentially to the door, where he looked back as if he wanted to say something. Then he thought better of it and the door closed.

"What about him?" asked Norris.

"I think he's a great fellow," said Travers. "Quite young too—not more than twenty-five, do you think?"

"You never know," said Norris, using Travers' own tag. "Ask Mr. Samuels to come in, will you?"

Samuels floated in quietly, with just one anxious glance at Norris. But he was at his ease in a second. As he moved the chair before sitting down he gave a little laugh.

"Guess I have to be mighty particular about where I deposit myself these days."

"You'll find that one all right," Norris told him. "And you won't be here very long, Mr. Samuels—at least I hope not. Just the usual formalities to run through. Full name?"

"Taylor Samuels."

"And how'd you come to cross the Atlantic, Mr. Samuels?"

Samuels told them the whole story in much the same words that Drew had used. Like Drew, too, he knew nothing about the picture for the making of which he had travelled thousands of miles.

"You were taking a big risk, surely!" remarked Norris.

"Maybe," said Samuels. "Only, you see, I happened to know Crewe, and any proposition that looked good to him kinda looked good to me."

Samuels, too, had thought there was some catch in the matter of the threatening letters. He had had no qualms himself about anything happening to Crewe. As for the events of the morning, he had heard nothing—not even the shot, though he was only two rooms away.

Norris looked puzzled. "You'll pardon me, Mr. Samuels, but surely you were dressing at the very moment the shot was fired. You went out of your room very soon afterwards."

Samuels looked at him. "Went out? Oh, yes, I get you. Went out for my walk."

"Yes," said Norris. "Again I must ask your forbearance, but why did you choose that particular morning to take a walk? I know you've said it's your custom, but you didn't take one yesterday or the morning before."

Samuels explained so gently that Norris felt positively ashamed at his own veiled suggestions.

"Well, you see, in another man's house—especially a swell house like this—you can't do what you'd do in your own. I just wanted to get the hang of things before I did anything different. This morning I thought I'd start."

Travers could see Samuels in carpet slippers, cigar in mouth, tuning in on his favourite radio station, cat purring away on the rug by the rocking-chair, and asking nothing better in life than reliable domesticity. And then a shadow passed across the American's face—the wind outside perhaps, stirring a branch—and as the changing light moved to give, in the fraction of a second, the appearance of a moustache, Travers suddenly sat up. He knew who Taylor Samuels really was—*and he wasn't Taylor Samuels!*

In the same moment he became aware that Norris was speaking to him, the old question about wanting Mr. Samuels any more.

"Just one thing," he said, and leaned across the table to catch the American's eye. "We've heard what the other people have had to say, Mr. Samuels, and frankly it isn't very much—about what I'd like to speak to you about, I mean. What can you tell us about Wen Ti?"

Samuels looked at him inquiringly. Travers repeated the question. He got a shake of the head for his pains.

"That's one on me." He smiled. "Who *is* this Wen What's-his-name, anyway?"

"That's what we hoped you would tell us," prevaricated Travers, and looked at Norris. "That's all, I think."

"That's all, Mr. Samuels," echoed Norris. "We may need you again later."

Samuels rose at once. "I guess you won't take it personal sir, but this third degree of yours has got ours beat." He looked around benevolently at the stenographer. "I hope that gentleman over there hasn't been takin' down all we've said?"

"A mere formality," Norris assured him airily. "If we want you again, Mr. Samuels, we'll let you know. And thank you very much."

At the door Samuels was pulled up short again by Norris's voice.

"Oh! Mr. Samuels! May I offer a suggestion?" He smiled ironically. "Well, not perhaps a suggestion. Just this. I have no objection whatever to your holding another meeting upstairs. I'd rather welcome it."

Samuels gave him a sudden, anxious look, then the door closed.

"Well, what about him?" Norris asked. "Too transparent?"

"Yes," said Travers slowly. "Yes. I think that's just the word. Yet I don't know." He thought for a moment. "No chance of anybody listening at keyholes?"

Norris smiled. "Why?"

"I'll tell you," said Travers, lowering his voice. "That wasn't his name he gave you. His name's Lem Shepherd."

"Lem Shepherd?" Norris frowned. "Where've I heard that before?"

"Go back to just after the war," said Travers. "Remember a rather fat chap who used to be in the movies? Took the part of parent generally, in the comics. Used to be full of wise-cracks, and his greatest asset was a look of dazed bewilderment he was always exhibiting. He had a straggly moustache in those days."

Norris clicked his tongue. "I've got him! Some sort of scandal, wasn't there?"

"As far as I remember it, it was like this," said Travers. "There was a poker game at his house and a small dinner affair after. Everybody got tight and a girl was pushed out of a window and broke her neck. Nobody knew who did it or how it happened, but Shepherd got the blame. There wasn't a producer who dared to employ him after that. A year or two ago there was a publicity campaign organized to get him into the talkies, but American womanhood wouldn't have it."

Norris nodded. "I'll get full information at once." He made a note on the pad. "You didn't like to tax him direct with what you knew?"

"I didn't," said Travers. "I mean I preferred to let you know in case you wanted a card up your sleeve. Just now when you gave him that nasty jolt about continuing the meeting upstairs, I almost thought you knew."

Norris shook his head. "It was news to me. . . . Funny thing, you know, but I liked the chap. I knew he was swindling me all the time, and yet I didn't resent it. I don't know what you'd call his manner. It isn't exactly plausible. Confidential, perhaps."

Travers fidgeted with his glasses. "Several things, you know, I'd like correct answers about from our friend Samuels. As I told you, I distinctly heard him mention the name of Wen Ti. What intrigues me more is why he was so anxious last night, when he rebelled against Allard's intention of keeping him where he couldn't talk, to find out all about a murder case that took place in England a good many years ago. You remember it well—the Mercer Case."

"Anxious to hear about the Mercer Case!" Norris didn't see it. "You mean he introduced the subject?"

"Introduced it?" Travers smiled. "He dragged it in by the scruff of the neck!"

Norris grunted. "Hm! We'll look it up and see if there's anything in it." He looked at the clock. "What about asking Miss Allard if she feels fit enough to see us for a minute?"

Before Travers could speak there was a tap at the door and the plain-clothes man poked his head outside for a moment, then shut the door again.

"Mason would like to see you for a moment, sir."

"Good," said Norris. "Show him in."

CHAPTER VIII
THE PLOT THICKENS

MASON HAD SOME interesting information, and he appeared to have come in for the special purpose of imparting it. His manner was extremely secretive. He would consider it most regrettable, he said, if the staff connected him with anything that went beyond the gossip of the servants' hall.

"The thing is this, sir," he told Norris. "George, the second footman, was on duty last night till everybody went to bed. He was in the hall when that Mr. Franks came out of the billiard-room, and he went up to George, sir, and asked him which was Miss Hastings' bedroom; not in any improper way, I should say, sir, but he said he had something of hers to give her most urgently—if she wasn't asleep. He was shown the room, sir, and tapped on the door and was told to come in. He then gave the footman half a crown, but shortly afterwards the footman made it his business to go past the door and he heard angry voices coming from the room. What was said, sir, he couldn't distinguish. I should say, sir, that George will probably be dismissed when the matter is reported to Miss Allard, because he was asked by Mr. Franks not to say anything, and he took the tip accordingly; a most discreditable breach of faith, sir, if I may refer to it as that."

"That fits in all right," said Travers. "He did make an excuse to leave the billiard-room early last night. By the way, Mason, while you're here; anything heard about the Chinese gentleman who's due at seven?"

"Nothing, sir. The chauffeur has already received his orders to meet the train, sir."

"Excellent!" said Norris. "There's something I'd like to check up, too, as you're here. There's no doubt whatever in your mind that every member of your staff is clear of all this business?"

"None whatever, sir," said Mason. "Those who were on duty upstairs came down together, and that was just before Mr. Crewe was killed, sir. When the shot was fired everybody was in the kitchen, with two exceptions, sir; myself, who was with Mr. Travers, and Preston, who had already gone, as far as I can gather, without waiting for breakfast."

"That's all right then," sighed Norris. "Miss Allard had tea yet?"

"I believe it's going up almost at once, sir. You and Mr. Travers would like tea here, sir?"

"That's good of you," said Norris. "I think I would. And will you give Miss Allard my compliments, and ask her if she'll join us down here for an informal chat?"

"And ask my man to come here at once, if you don't mind," added Travers.

Palmer came in most sedately—warily almost. On occasions like these, Travers was inclined to be the least bit exacting.

"You've heard that footman, George, talking about Mr. Franks going to Miss Hastings' room last night?" he was asked.

"Yes, sir. I did hear it mentioned, sir."

"Good," said Travers. "Get acquainted with George, if you can manage it, and find out if he really did hear any words that were being said inside. And tell Mason that you're to go with the chauffeur to meet a gentleman who's arriving to-night by the seven train. Pick up anything you can and try to see the ticket he or his man hands in." He looked at Norris. "I expect it'll be London, but there's no harm trying. Marbury's not such a small place that one couldn't book through from almost anywhere."

"No harm, certainly," said Norris. "And if Palmer could also manage to get on friendly terms—fatherly terms, if he'll permit me to say so—with Miss Allard's maid, he might get an inkling where she went this morning."

"Miss Allard has no maid, sir. I understand she sent her maid away for a month's holiday three weeks ago. One of the junior housemaids has been acting as her maid, sir. You see, she's only been here since Monday, sir, and she was going away to-day in any case."

"Any idea where?"

"The south of France, I believe, sir. That's the talk in the servants' hall."

Palmer had scarcely left the room when the tea arrived and Sue Allard with it. She was looking very subdued. It was not that she was knocked all to pieces by what had happened. Norris could see she was feeling that; but there was some other peculiar restraint about her. Norris thought he knew what it was and tried to get her to smile.

"Well, Mr. Travers, here's your truant!" He placed a chair for her by the fire, and when the footman had gone, resumed his raillery. "You know, young lady, you were committing contempt of court this morning?"

She looked at Travers. "You didn't give me away?"

"Of course he didn't!" cut in Norris. "The local police saw your car and asked at the garage. You wouldn't like to tell us why it was so urgent that you should leave the house?"

Her voice was perfectly cool. "Would it make all that difference?"

"No," said Norris, and looked down his nose. "I don't suppose it would. Toast, Miss Allard, or tea-cake?"

She smiled. "Neither, thanks. Just tea. But do help yourselves. I'm sure you must be famished."

"Frankly, I am," said Norris. "And referring to that stolen visit of yours for the very last time; might I suggest that you went to town, and to cancel the arrangements you had made for the train and so on?"

She was staring at him long before he had finished speaking. She was frightened, but at what it was impossible to guess.

"Who told you that?" Her eyes opened wide, then she collapsed into a kind of foolish smile. "How silly of me! Of course, that was what I went for. You see, I'd arranged to go with people, and so on."

"But why didn't you 'phone?" persisted Norris.

Then she rounded on him. "Just what are you trying to suggest? Do you mean that I'm concerned in some way with what happened this morning?"

"Miss Allard! Certainly not!" Norris was genuinely indignant. "No. Call it curiosity. Anything else would be unpardonable."

She was very quiet for a minute or two. Travers, who had been stirring his tea abstractedly, plunged into the breach.

"What we're really interested in, Miss Allard, is the people your brother asked to the house. We may tell you in confidence that they have all been questioned this afternoon and they agree on one story, that they came here to make a talking picture."

She looked at him in astonishment. "But how absurd!"

"That's what we thought. Would you like to tell us what you know about them?"

She made a little face. "Well, the first thing I heard was when I got a letter from my brother—I'd been staying in town at my flat—asking if I'd do him a very great favour by coming down on Monday, as it were, to spend the night and as much more time as I could. I told him I would but I'd have to be away to-day. He said that'd do. When I got here he told me he'd be very glad if

I'd be awfully decent to the people who were staying here. He said he had some big theatrical scheme on and they were going to be very useful to him. I gathered they were a very mixed lot." She smiled. "As it happened they were rather nice; at least Mr. Samuels was a dear; so was Mr. Drew."

"My own opinion entirely," said Travers. "And you knew nothing else about them?"

"Nothing at all. Courtney said he would tell me quite a lot this morning, before I left—and he took my promise in advance to keep quiet about it."

Norris leaned forward with a gesture that was perfect in its friendliness. "You were very fond of your brother, Miss Allard?"

She smiled at him with a gratitude that was obvious. "I'd have done more than that for him. . . . And he was very fond of me, though he never showed it."

"I know," said Norris. "Those things aren't always on the surface. And Mr. Crewe. He'd been here some time?"

"Yes." It was she who now showed the curiosity. "Where my brother picked him up I can't imagine. They were so different. I believe it was about two months ago he came here. I did ask something, but I was told he and my brother were interested in some matter of business. Do you know all about him?"

"Only that he was an actor or a manager or something like that—and he was responsible for Samuels and Drew coming here. Miss Hastings now. You know where your brother met her?"

Her lip curled slightly. "I'm afraid I don't. Men are rather strange about such things, don't you think?"

"Perhaps we are," said Norris. "And by the way, in strict confidence, you might be interested to know there was something decidedly fishy going on in her room last night after you went up to bed. Franks called on her, and we understand there was a bit of a row. Did you hear anything of it?"

"Oh, no!" She said it so hastily that Travers for a moment wondered just why. "You see, I go off to sleep very quickly."

"Then you weren't alarmed by all that talk about threatening letters?" asked Travers banteringly.

She gave a little laugh—and checked it as suddenly. "No . . . and now it all seems so dreadful. Do you think it was . . ."

"We know nothing," said Norris. "If we did, you should know it too. You didn't believe in those letters?"

She rose to go. "To tell you the truth I wasn't interested in Mr. Crewe sufficiently. I thought it was very foolish of my brother allowing his name to be mixed up with his—and with all that horrid gossip. . . . There's nothing else I can help you with?"

"At the moment—no," said Norris. "It's been extraordinarily good of you to come down like this. I would like the name of your brother's solicitors."

She smiled from the door. "I'll send it in by Mason."

Travers closed the door after her.

"Charming young woman!" said Norris. "What I call a perfect example of an English lady. Wonder what she really went to town for?"

Travers laughed. "What a gorgeous *non sequitur!* But she did seem a little bit anxious when you got her in a corner, didn't she? And there was the little matter of what she was hunting for in the library. Which reminds me. When are you going through his private papers? There might be quite a lot of things about . . . well, about our friends of this afternoon—and about Crewe."

Mason came in with the name of the solicitors, and Norris had the plain-clothes men back again.

"Where does Mr. Allard keep his private papers?" he asked.

"In the safe in the library, sir," Mason told him. "I have the combination if you want it."

"Any one else know it?"

"No, sir. Only the master and myself knew it. You'd like me to open it at once, sir?"

Norris looked at Travers. "Yes, in a minute or two. We'll let you know."

He called across to the stenographer. "Ring up for all this afternoon's and this evening's editions of the *Evening Record* to be sent along. Tell 'em to get 'em here quick." He turned to Travers. "That chap Spence was probably bluffing. Hallo! Lewis looks in a bit of a hurry."

Travers glanced round in time to see Lewis disappear past the window. In a minute he was bustling into the room.

"Can you spare a minute or two, sir?"

"Why not? Found something?"

Lewis grinned. "That'll be for you to say, sir." He consulted his notebook. "About that hoe. Sutton, the head gardener, says one of his men was using it round the shrubbery bushes under that window on the Tuesday, and left it there while he knocked off for lunch. When he came back it was gone."

Norris permitted himself a grunt, and no more.

"Then about those broken twigs," went on Lewis. "A man wouldn't have any trouble in getting up to the window—or down—holding on to that creeper, but Sutton says he can't tell when the twigs were broken. He says this time of year a broken twig wouldn't wither for quite a time. If it had been the summer it'd have been different. However, we've broken off some new pieces to make a comparison to-morrow, and we're going to do some more in the morning."

"Right," said Norris. "And what about the blood?"

"It's blood all right, sir. There isn't any doubt about that. I'd like you to have a look at it, sir, if you're not too busy. And there's some other things upstairs."

"Right," said Norris. "We'll go up straight away. What about the car? Got all that finished with?"

"We've sent the number off, sir. There wasn't a thing anywhere else except some prints, and whose they are we don't know. They've gone up to town."

"Not the ones those local men made?" asked Norris quickly.

But Lewis wasn't to be caught out. "Not theirs, sir. We checked theirs, all right. These are a couple of new ones."

Norris nodded. "Come along then. We'll see all these wonderful things you've got upstairs." He called to the stenographer from the door. "Get hold of those solicitors as soon as you can, and let me know at once. Give my name and ask for somebody in authority."

When Travers entered that room again he found it hard to remember what had been lying on the floor the last time he had been there. The room now had its bed replaced, and it had been swept from ceiling to floor and the carpet sweeper put over for a test of the dust, and altogether it seemed rather ridiculous to think of it with two dead men sprawling, one with eyes staring at the ceiling, and the other with eyes that almost touched the floor. Then he saw that the faint chalk-marks were still there, and everything came back again.

Lewis went straight across to the still open window. "Just have a look outside here, sir, and tell me what you make of that."

Travers saw what looked like an iron hook set in the wall just below the sill, and almost hidden by the stout, intertwining stems of the creeper.

"Now, sir," said Lewis, "I think you'll agree that that hasn't been up there very long. You'll have to lean out to look, but I think you'll see."

Norris had a look then drew back for Travers. The hook had certainly not been in position longer than a day or two, since the metal still glinted where the hammer had struck the wrought iron nails that held it to the beam below the sill. The whole was a tremendously strong affair, and a bullock might have dangled from it without the slightest danger.

"This is the fishy part about it, sir," Lewis told them. "This hook was the hook belonging to a large pulley arrangement which used to be in a loft in the old days for slinging up carts and things to be repainted. Sutton says he saw it only the other day, but just where he can't remember. The other thing is that on Monday, after the men had knocked off, Mr. Allard and Mr. Crewe were seen poking about the sheds. Sutton reckons that's where those heavy nails came from."

Norris nodded away. "Seems pretty conclusive. I suppose, by the way, you could nail the hook in from the room here?"

"Easy as winking, sir. You try it for yourself. Not only that, sir, whoever was doing it couldn't be seen, provided there weren't any gardeners about."

Norris made a note in his book. "Well, that's excellent work so far. Anything else up here?"

"Yes, sir. The blood. We've taken photos of it wherever we could, but I'd like you to have a look out of here. If you look straight down, sir, you'll see what I mean. Practically none has gone on the ground, and where you see it on the creeper there's too much of it. The man would have bled to death at that rate."

"Perhaps he did," said Norris, and had a look all the same.

Travers peered down too, after a preparatory polish of his glasses, and saw what Lewis meant.

"And what's the idea of it?" asked Norris, who evidently had his own mind made up about the whole thing.

"The idea, sir? Well, it didn't bleed naturally. I may be talking a bit wild, sir, but I wouldn't mind having a small bet that blood was thrown out of this window."

"Then it won't be human blood," was all Norris said. "Anything suspicious about the broken creeper?"

Lewis mumbled something and temporized. "Well, sir, that I wouldn't like to say. There aren't any twigs broken off within ten feet of the ground, but that might be because it's perfectly safe to jump from there. I mean, say a man was getting down from this window. When he grasped the main stem of the creeper, ten feet from the ground, his feet would be only about three feet off it."

"In other words, there are signs that somebody went down the creeper to the ground, but no signs whatever that anybody got into the room by means of the creeper."

Lewis didn't see it for a moment. "That's good reasoning," said Travers. "If anyone tried to climb the creeper from the ground he'd have broken the twigs near the ground trying to get a foothold."

"There's just one thing about that," added Norris. "Assuming there was no entry from the ground, it's rather harder to explain those footmarks in the wardrobe. Mud can only come from outside, and there wasn't a trace anywhere else."

Lewis smiled tentatively. "There's only a certain amount of mud to come off, sir. What was in the wardrobe couldn't be on the floor."

"True enough," said Norris. "But he had to get *in* the wardrobe. Still, we may be asking Mr. Drew to shed a little light on that."

Travers pricked his ears at that remark, but Norris had already switched to something else. "Did you find those clothes he wore last night?"

"In here, sir." Lewis led the way to Allard's bedroom, where a suit-case lay on the bed. Various garments, evidently taken from it, lay alongside. "There they are, sir," said Lewis, satisfied if not triumphant. "Hidden in the bottom of that big wardrobe there."

Travers' thoughts ran back in a flash. "I think I can see it now," he said, and began unhooking his glasses. "When we got up here last night, Crewe went into his room like a shot, and we others stood chatting outside there in the corridor. Allard kept hanging round in my room and fairly forced me to take the bathroom first. I then seem to remember him going to his own room. He must have collected the suit-case from Crewe just before. Not much doubt about the murder being intended for a fake, do you think?"

"Don't know," said Norris, and rubbed his chin. "We've got to let all this settle down. No use rushing to conclusions." He gave a "Come in!" as the tap came at the door. It was a plain-clothes man from downstairs.

"Those solicitors, sir. The head of the firm would like to speak to you."

Norris bustled off at once. As soon as he had gone, Lewis took out his pocket-book and handed Travers a paper.

"There's something else for him, sir, when he comes back. Found that in his dinner jacket."

Travers had a good look at it. The original sheet of paper, as Lewis had noticed, had probably been quarto, and of excellent quality, but a good third of the sheet—possibly a heading of some kind—had been neatly cut off; so neatly, indeed, that it was none too easy to see it at first glance.

You have exactly another day to live. You knew you couldn't get away, so say your prayers, because your time's up.

"Quite a polite little note," said Travers dryly. "Whoever wrote it didn't waste any time on elegancies. No fingerprints, I suppose?"

Lewis shook his head. "Not the kind you mean, sir. There were his own, and Allard's, and Spence's."

"Spence's! So he had a look at it, did he? And you took his prints?"

"We got his prints before we let him go," said Lewis. "He knew it was just a matter of routine. Mr. Allard showed him this paper yesterday morning." He handed Travers the glass. "Have a look at those letters, sir, and see if you can see anything wrong with those y's and v's."

Travers squinted through the glass. "They are a bit askew, aren't they? One one way and the other the other."

Lewis nodded as he put the paper carefully back again. "That'll have to go up at once. Don't suppose we shall ever find the machine it was written on, but we'll know the make and most of what there is to know about it." He cocked an ear. "Here he comes!"

Norris came in with just a faint air of excitement about him.

"Just been talking to those people about Allard's will. His sister gets the lot."

"Lucky for her!" said Lewis. "What'll it amount to, sir?"

"Don't know," Norris told him. "A pretty fat sum by all accounts. What's more important from our point of view is that there's a private letter for her, deposited by Allard only a week ago, and only to be opened in the event of his death."

CHAPTER IX
STILL MORE ABOUT WEN TI

WHEN THEY LEFT the bedroom Palmer was waiting outside. He was a fine figure of a man was Palmer, venerable as an archdeacon, and with a natural dignity that always spontaneously achieved for him a high seat in the hierarchy of whatever servants' hall he entered. As for Travers, he remembered him being born, in the remote days when the old Colonel was alive and Palmer himself was the Colonel's man. Not that Palmer ever took advantage of such service; he was deferential to an incredibly consistent degree, and often to the great amusement of Travers himself, who had as little use for the niceties as a frog has for feathers.

There was no wonder, however, that George the footman had been somewhat flattered at the unbending of one of as high standing as Palmer. He had confided that the less Mason knew about anything the better, but he didn't mind telling Mr. Palmer that he had heard one word coming from the room where Franks and Margaret Hastings were holding their nocturnal *tête-à-tête*, and that was the name. "Crewe." Of that he was sure, and it was all the more exasperating therefore that he knew no more.

Travers gave Norris a squint over his glasses. Norris nodded in a way that looked none too good for Franks and his lady friend.

"Well, there's two good liars to start with. Remember what Wharton always says? A lying witness is the cop's best friend."

"There's something in that," said Travers. "Any other news, Palmer?"

"Only that there's another meeting on upstairs, sir."

Travers smiled. "How very amusing! Pity we haven't a dictaphone planted."

"The next meeting they have, I'll be chairman," said Norris grimly. "Now what about having a look at his private papers."

When Mason swung open the doors of the safe there was precious little to see. When they got the assortment to the table the whole collection turned out to be mostly estate accounts as rendered by the agent and practically untouched by Allard, and of the rest there were the counterfoils of numerous checkbooks and communications from solicitors and various business firms—the latter chiefly about cars. The really interesting thing on which Travers pounced at once was a package of accounts and clip pings that dealt with the last theatrical venture with which Allard had been connected. With these was the draft of what seemed to be the talkie to which the morning's witnesses had referred. Travers showed it to Norris.

"Looks as if there might be some truth in their story after all. There's only the rough draft_" He broke off. "Looks more like a play than anything else. Mind if I take it to bed with me to have a good look at?"

"Why not?" said Norris. "Here's something, by the way, that concerns Miss Allard. I don't suppose it's what she was looking for so earnestly, but you never know."

The letter was still inside its envelope which had Brighton for postmark, and was dated March 26th.

> THE VIEWS,
> PAWLEY POINT,
> BEACHVILLE,
> *March 26th.*

DEAR COURT,

What an extraordinary request! It sounds as if you are having a perfectly alarming collection of freaks at The Covers. Still, I'll come down to please you—and only to please you—since you consider it so urgent, but it'll have to be on my terms, which are very simple ones.

You must send Preston all the way down here for me to bring me and my things along, and he must get here early on the Monday morning so as to fit in with the arrangements of the people with whom I'm staying. And I must in any case be away again on the morning of the 1st, as my arrangements are already made for France. I shall have to call in at town on the way, so don't be alarmed if I'm late. Send me a wire here if you agree.

Sorry your letter was sent on from town here. I didn't know I was coming here till I accepted the invitation.

> Yours affectionately,
> SUE.

P.S.—I left my car in town, as you gather. I won't have your second man—he's a horrid driver. You must send Preston, who always looks so distinguished.

"I shouldn't think that's the one," said Travers. "It seems too innocuous. You want it? If not I might try an experiment with it."

Lewis, meanwhile, had found nothing in the drawers of the desk, and while the papers were being replaced, in came one of the men to say Norris was wanted on the 'phone. Also a copy of the *Evening Record* had arrived, and Lewis went off for it at once. Travers, finding himself temporarily a free agent, went in search of the butler and asked if Miss Allard would be visible for a minute. He was shown upstairs to a cosy room which, though an annex to her bedroom, seemed the real drawing-room of the house.

She looked the least bit alarmed at Travers' entry, but he made it so diffidently that she must soon have been rather amused. He mentioned the weather and asked how her car was running these days, and said he thought The Covers was a wonderful place, before he came anywhere near the point. Also he wouldn't sit down. Hadn't a minute to spare, so he said, when at least five had gone.

Then he gave a little cough. "Something rather personal. I mean, I hope you won't be annoyed with me at. . . Well, you see, it's this."

She looked at him. "You're not making me a proposal of marriage!"

"No," said Travers quickly. "At least . . ." He laughed. "Look here, now. I happened to see you in the library this morning, as you know, and you seemed to me to be looking for some paper or other."

She stared—rather frightened. "Yes?"

"Well, I believe I've recovered it for you—at least I've gone through the papers in the safe and so on, and this is the only one about you."

"Yes?"

Travers hesitated. "Well, I want to make a bargain with you. Perfectly unpardonable of me, perhaps, but not if you see it with my eyes. If this is a private paper you don't want everybody to know about, then you shall have it, provided you keep it to yourself—secrecy and all that; and if you assure me it is the paper you were looking for. Otherwise I shall have to return it to where it was found. Er—this is it."

He knew at once it was the one. She gave one look at it then thrust it inside the neck of the jumper.

"Thank you. You're a dear!"

He backed to the door, gave a quick "That's all right then," and sidled out. Then his diffidence vanished by magic, and he made his way trippingly down the stairs. Norris was in the hall on his way to the lounge. Travers followed him in.

"Something I'd very much like you to do," he said. "It's for you to say, of course, but I do suggest it most seriously, seeing as how we'll probably be casting a pretty wide net before this case is over. Send someone down to this place—The Views, Pawley Point, Beachville—just to have a look round."

"It *was* the letter she was looking for?" asked Norris.

"It was," said Travers, "though remember you're not to know anything about it. The real point is that there's something in that letter about which she's rather scared. It might be up to us to find out in case it has some sort of bearing."

"Right!" said Norris. "I'll send a specially good man along at once."

He took off the receiver, and Travers waited while he got the message through. When he hung up again he heaved a sigh.

"I don't know. I seem to get most uncommonly hungry down here. We're having dinner in here, by the way. I thought you'd like to dodge the gang. You mightn't be any too popular as things are."

Travers grimaced. "And what time is it?"

"Seven-thirty, the butler said."

"Good Lord!" said Travers. "I must fly. Got a copy of the *Evening Record* handy? If so, I'll take it with me."

He glanced through it in the intervals of his toilet, there wasn't any reason to do much else since the *Record* had achieved such a scoop that its banner headlines shrieked till even he who ran at top speed might read. Spence's style, however, seemed to have been somewhat cramped by various embargoes that Norris had laid as the price of his departure, though to the man-in-the-street the story was thrilling enough. Travers' name had not been mentioned, but in column seven was something that was far more interesting.

DEAD MAN'S MOVIE VENTURE
COMPANY ALREADY AT SCENE OF TRAGEDY
GALAXY OF UNKNOWN TALENT

That was then the great secret which Spence had been unable to impart; the secret which had been revealed to him as a result of the first upstair meeting. The slogan was evidently—*Publicity or Bust*. Though whatever Courtney Allard had had in mind had now collapsed beyond repair, the Big Four were evidently going to make full use of the spotlight.

Unhappily, there was little in the brief biographies that was new, and, worse still, there was nothing that contradicted the information already supplied by the same Big Four to Norris. Franks, it was stated, was unknown to the English stage but had a tremendous reputation on the Continent as an operatic tenor. Margaret Hastings, it was said, had appeared as leading lady— under her stage name—in number one touring companies, and Courtney Allard was giving her her great chance in town. Taylor Samuels was described as the greatest purveyor of wisecracks that ever America had produced; a man, in fact, who had Will Rogers put in the Curfew-Shall-Not-Ring class. As for Henry Drew, he was a wizard with the rope; could illustrate the Curse of Scotland with nine knives at a distance of twenty feet; could play the banjo and croon, and had a repertoire of crazy danc- es—"Pain in the Neck" was his famous one—that were going to set London talking.

Having digested all that, Travers wandered down to dinner. Mason himself was in attendance in the lounge; Sue Allard was dining upstairs, and the Big Four were in the dining-room. Talk, with the butler there, was none too easy, and it was not till he had departed and Norris was blatantly stoking his pipe before sampling the port, that the work in hand was alluded to.

"Menzies rang up," Norris said, putting away the pouch. "They got a Colt forty-five out of Allard's head. That agrees with the marks on the pillow. The knife business was rather funny, so he says. I didn't get all the technicalities, but there were two distinct thrusts—one that sort of went in, and another that Menzies suggests drove it in further, probably when he fell on the floor and the handle struck it. The first thrust didn't kill him; the second did."

Travers tried to think that out and failed. "When's the inquest?" he asked, principally for the sake of saying something.

"Day after to-morrow," Norris told him. "There won't be anything in it, and you won't be wanted. Also, there's a nice little job of work for you to do. Little trip in your car for the sake of fresh air."

"Fresh air?" repeated Travers, and waited.

"Good port this," said Norris. "Wish I had the money and I'd have a tot every night of my life. What were we saying? Oh, yes, fresh air. I happened to mention Preston to Lewis here, and he remembered something he'd seen among the papers in the same. Have a look at it."

He took it out of his pocket-book and handed it over.

THE COTTAGE,
WRYFORD ABBAS,
Sept. 12th.

DEAR SIR,

In reply to yours of yesterday, I have much pleasure in stating that the chauffeur, Preston, has been in my employ as stated in the reference which he handed in. His conduct was always excellent, and his knowledge of cars was extraordinarily good. I am certain you will find him an able and loyal servant. Personally I never wish to employ a harder-working or more conscientious man.

Yours truly,
MARK RUSTON.
(Cap. Late Indian Army.)

Travers handed it back. "You mean you'd like me to run down to Wryford Abbas to see this Captain Ruston?"

"That's it," said Norris. "Provided, of course, we don't get anything in before. Where the chap's gone we don't know. He left no message with anybody here about sending letters on or anything like that. As far as we're concerned, he's gone into the blank. We're making inquiries and something may turn up."

"The sooner we get hold of him the better pleased I'll be," said Lewis. "If that was the chap you saw wandering about the house in the early hours of the morning, Mr. Travers, he's got a lot of explaining to do."

"Yes," said Norris. "He looks like fitting in. If the worst comes to the worst we'll try a broadcast S O S."

Travers was rubbing away at his glasses. "There was something you were saying about Menzies and the dagger that killed Crewe. I'm afraid I didn't take it all in at the moment. The dagger had made two traceable movements, I think you said, and it was the second that killed him—and when the dagger itself struck the ground; that is, when it made the second movement, so to speak, for itself. Was that it? Because if it was, then it seems a most amazing thing to me. It implies that when I saw him he was still alive—"

"Why not?" interpolated Norris.

"Well," said Travers, and then thought for a moment. "Yes, perhaps he might still have been alive—breathing his last—when I saw him, and when the murderer of Allard and Allard had that scrap so that Crewe's body was knocked endways, then he actually died."

"I don't think that's quite it," said Norris. "Now I come to think of it, I rather gather that this is what Menzies meant. The first movement of the dagger wasn't clean into a vital spot. We'll say it was just above the heart-"

Travers was horrified. "You mean that if I'd had the pluck to draw it out, his life might have been saved!"

Norris smiled tolerantly. "If you'd taken that knife out he'd have snuffed it at once. No. Possibly he was dead when you saw him. Possibly he wasn't. But when his body was kicked endways, the knife altered its course and penetrated the vital spot—say the heart. I don't know whether Menzies will be able to state for a certainty whether the second movement of the knife was made before death or after it, but I doubt it."

There was a tap at the door and Lewis got up to answer it.

"Tell our people we're ready to go on again while you're up," called Norris.

It was Mason who came in, and one of Norris's men—evidently with some news—came in behind.

"I thought you'd like to know, sir," the butler said, "that there wasn't any sign of the Chinese gentleman on the train. There was nobody even resembling such a gentleman, sir."

Norris pulled a face, then let it broaden to a smile. "Somebody's been pulling our legs, Mason. It's still the first of April, you know."

The butler shook his head, and Travers smiled somewhere inside at the quaintness of the remark. "I'm given to understand, sir, that April the First, and what people are accustomed to call 'the fooleries,' sir, actually expire at midday." He coughed. "I trust you will pardon the remark, sir, but I would also state that the late master was known to me very well, sir, and he was perfectly serious when he gave me the information and instructions about the gentleman's arrival."

Norris patted him on the back. "My mistake, Mason. Another train, is there?"

"Nine o'clock is the last, sir, and the chauffeur and Mr. Travers' man are already on the way."

"Capital!" said Norris. "Thank you, Mason. Anything else?"

There wasn't, and the butler withdrew.

The C.I.D. man came forward at once. "Mr. Spence of the *Evening Record* is outside, sir, with his car, and says you'll let him in."

"He's an optimist," said Norris. He looked at the others. "Worth while seeing him?"

"He had a large parcel with him, sir," added the man. "He's got it now—at the door."

"Bring him in here, parcel and all," said Norris. "He's not to communicate with a soul."

Almost at once the reporter was ushered in, looking nattier than ever in the plus fours and the same polka-dot tie. A brown paper parcel was under his arm. He sobered down a bit when he saw Norris at the judgment seat, and was told to take a chair. The inspector gave him a remarkably sharp look.

"This is an extraordinary proceeding, Mr. Spence. You of all people should know you've no right to be here once you've been permitted to leave. If you're after information, you know the procedure."

"Yes," said Spence. "That Press Bureau of yours," and he smiled. Then he gave a shrewd look. "What about exchanging some news, Inspector? I mean—"

"I don't think I'd mean anything if I were you," said Norris dryly. "There's no news for you here, and the sooner you make up your mind to that, the better. What's in that parcel?"

"This?" and Spence looked at it. "Oh, just a bundle of *Records* for some friends of mine here. Perhaps you'll let somebody send 'em along."

"I see," and Norris made another face. "Look them over, Lewis, will you. Any additions to that story of yours that appeared in the six-thirty?"

"What story?"

"The stories of your four friends upstairs."

"Oh, that!" Spence said airily. "Nothing new about that except that we got the pictures on the middle page. Another follow-up scoop for the *Record.*"

"Hm!" said Norris. "So they sent you out this morning armed with their pictures, did they?" He stretched out his hand and Lewis, who had already removed the brown paper, put an *Evening Record* in it. Norris had a look at the photographs. "Hm! Doesn't do any of 'em justice." He rose. "Well, you'd better make arrangements to retain your last night's room. We're going to be busy down here."

Spence scrambled up hastily and looked at him. "You mean I can't go back to town?"

"I'm afraid not," Norris told him. "Isn't there a fable or other about a man who stuck his head twice in the tiger's jaws?" Having foreshadowed that piece of blackmail, he hesitated. "You've nothing to tell us? Nothing of what those people told you more than you had printed?"

Spence made no bones about selling the pass. "I think I have. You see, they sort of asked me, in confidence, to act as their agent between the agents. I was to do all this publicity stuff and get in touch with one or two likely agents who couldn't 'phone here—"

"One or two have already," said Norris ironically. "They didn't do much business."

"Well, I'm getting in touch with the outside world on their behalf," went on Spence. "As soon as you let them leave here, things ought to be cut and dried."

"I see. And all you'll have to do is draw commission."

Spence flushed. "Nothing of the sort, Inspector. I'm simply obliging my paper's clients. They've already signed on the dotted line to write for us—and the *Sunday Record*—as soon as you turn them loose."

Norris gave the semblance of a smile. "In the words of your friend, Taylor Samuels, you're sure some great little go-getter. And all this when they're turned loose. Anything else?"

"Nothing else," said Spence, and shook his head. "I'm holding nothing back, I give you my word."

"Right," said Norris. "Mr. Spence may go back to wherever he came from. See him as far as the front gates, and if he shows up there again, hold him till I know it."

Spence grinned cheerfully and marched off under escort. The door that opened to let him out, let in Mason.

"The gentleman was not on the train, sir. I thought you might like to know."

"Thank you, Mason," said Norris. "Very good of you. I suppose you'll now give the gentleman up for good."

"Perhaps we shall, sir. Miss Allard will doubtless inform me, sir. If the gentleman reads English, sir, I take it he knows of the happenings here, and ordinary good taste would keep him away."

"That's probably it," said Norris. He picked up an *Evening Record* and gave it to Lewis. "Look through this and see if it's marked in any way."

Lewis held it to the light for pinpricks.

Norris turned to the butler. "An excellent dinner you gave us to-night. Very good of you."

"Thank you, sir." The butler bowed. "If I might venture to ask, sir, how long will the—er—other guests be staying?"

"It might be a week," said Norris. "Tell 'em so in confidence, Mason, will you? Tell 'em you heard me say they could go as soon as they told the truth. Let it out to them as a great favour. Will you do that?" He leaned over. "And between ourselves, they might be gone to-morrow."

The butler nodded knowingly. "You can rely on me, sir."

"I'm sure I can," said Norris. "Here! take this paper with you. You might like to see it."

He watched the door close. "So much for that. And the Chinese gentleman didn't turn up!"

"Or, still to quote the excellent Taylor Samuels," said Travers, "I guess that lets out Wen Ti."

CHAPTER X
THE REAL DOPE

BREAKFAST WAS OVER and Norris was going upstairs when Mason brought a message from Samuels. Would the inspector receive a deputation? And, failing that, would he receive Samuels himself as spokesman for the rest?

"Tell him to wait," said Norris curtly. "He's kept me waiting long enough." Then he thought better of it. "Just a minute, Mason. Perhaps you'd better say I'll be ready in about an hour. I'll decide then."

A couple of selected men went with them upstairs and waited outside the room for orders.

"Now," said Norris. "Before we discuss anything else, we've got to be sure about this matter of a hoax. Were there any threatening letters—real ones—or were there not?"

"I rather think it depends on what we find to fit in," said Travers. "Unless, of course, you're prepared to take hunches as evidence."

"Meaning?"

"Well, I'd lay ten to one the whole thing was meant originally to be a stunt. Either that, or Crewe and Allard knew who wrote the supposedly serious letters and knew the fellow, whoever he was, was himself working a stunt. In any case, whatever they pretended to be feeling about the letters, they weren't taking them as they ought to have been taken."

"Allard was plucky?"

"He was a dare-devil—at least in a racing car. He always struck me as a fool in most else—only a fool with a considerable vein of low cunning. You mean if he and Crewe were good-plucked 'uns, they'd not give a hoot for the letters?"

"Something of the sort," said Norris. "And the motive for this stunt?"

"Publicity," said Travers. "Roaring publicity for that show he was going to do and which all those people were here for. It was doled out to the Press, though only few of them bit."

"Well, I'll put it up to both of you," said Norris, "that we'll act on the assumption that a fake murder was all arranged. As we proceed we'll see if that theory fits in, and where it diverges. Call the first man in."

This was a stocky man, only a shade bigger than Crewe, and quite a different type from the other who was, like Travers, of the lamp-post family. He stripped to his waist while Lewis got ready the photographs, then he donned the sleeping jacket the dead man had worn.

"This is Crewe," said Norris. "Kindly place him, Mr. Travers, just where he was when you first came in the room."

"Right," said Norris. "Now get into the bed. We'll put the small table alongside, and here's the tray. The footman's just left the room. Now what does Crewe do?"

"Hops out of bed and locks the door," suggested Travers.

Norris shook his head. "You forget the door wasn't found locked. No, my idea's this. Tell me if you think I'm wrong. If there was a fake, where was it to be, and how? Well, I say the gun under his pillow was to be the thing. He was to let off a shot—out of the window. That all right?"

Both agreed.

"Then what was he to do next?"

"Get out of the room by means of a rope round that hook," said Lewis. "First he'd throw the blood on the sheets and the floor and give a few groans. Mr. Travers was to be the mutt who heard it all and swore to it. There'd have been the sound of a falling body, then he'd have grabbed those clothes out of the drawer, locked the door so that he'd have time to get away, and then he'd have climbed down the rope and got to the car which had been left all ready for him in the wood."

"I agree with all that," said Travers, "especially with that part about myself as mutt. As I told you, that was what I was asked here for. I might also add that Spence was asked here so that the necessary publicity could be flashed to his paper without loss of time."

Norris rubbed his chin. "There's undoubtedly a lot in it that's right. About the car, we'd better not commit ourselves till it's been gone into. I don't quite hold with the theory of the clothes. I don't quite see that he'd have had time to dress himself."

Travers smiled. "I think he would. Don't you see what else would have happened? I was the mutt—all ready in a nice room conveniently placed for me, just as Crewe was in the perfect room for him and all placed ready. And just how was I to be a mutt? Well, Allard would have pretended Crewe was playing a First of April trick. He wouldn't have tried to break into that room till he knew Crewe was gone. Then I'd have been shown the exhibits."

Norris looked pleased. "That's it for a fiver! Still, here's Crewe in bed and the footman's just gone. Zero hour's arrived. What happened, and how?"

There was silence for a minute or two.

Lewis spoke first. "One thing we've got to admit, sir, that he got out of bed. And he also saw his assailant, or he'd have begun to do the things he was supposed to do—loose off that shot, for instance."

Norris nodded. "And where was the murderer? Getting in the window or coming out of the wardrobe?"

"I thought you'd agreed that nobody could have got into the room from the ground," said Travers, "otherwise there'd have been marks on the creeper. Also, if the murderer was in the wardrobe, we might reasonably assume he got between Crewe and the door just when Crewe was bolting across to lock it."

Norris pulled a face. "Destructive criticism's an easy thing, but I must say I think that wardrobe was too risky a place. Last night—the night before the murder, I mean—Crewe came in here and got like lightning out of his clothes and put them in a bag which Allard soon after took over and transferred to his room—clear evidence of the fake, by the way. But Crewe almost certainly had his overcoat hanging in the wardrobe, and he put that in the drawer. Also, if the man was in the wardrobe then, why didn't he kill him? He could have got away twice as easy."

Travers hooked off his glasses. "I'm certainly with you there, but let's talk wildly for a bit. I don't believe for a moment that Crewe locked his door when he pretended to that night, and I believe therefore that he only pretended to open it in the morning when the footman arrived. If the door was open all night, there are three men in the house who haven't alibis—Franks, Drew, and Samuels. Any one of the three might have walked boldly in here to see Crewe about something and murdered him then—though he didn't. He certainly might have got in the wardrobe during the night—though he didn't."

"Why didn't he?" asked Lewis.

"Because he was in his room when the footman brought tea. It's been agreed that every member of the house was accounted for at the time tea was brought. No," and he blinked away as he rubbed the glasses vigorously, "my idea is this. A third man was the confederate of Crewe and Allard. Someone in the house was ready as soon as the footman left, to nip in here and lend a hand.

Say it was Franks or Drew or Samuels; whoever it was did nip in and then murdered Crewe in reality. *Then* he got into the wardrobe, and when Allard came to see where the snag was—after I'd gone down to 'phone—he stepped out and killed him too, *as he had to, since Allard knew who he was.*"

Norris looked interested. "Just what did he come in here to do?"

Travers shook his head and hooked the glasses on again. "I don't know. I should say it was his job to remove the dutch hoe for one thing, but there I'm not sure."

"What about the muddy boots?" asked Lewis. "If it was an inmate of the house he ought to have been in slippers."

Travers fumbled for the glasses again. "There I have another theory to put up. The mud in the wardrobe was faked. Suppose everything had gone according to schedule and Crewe fired the shot, splashed the blood and all the rest of it and disappeared. We'd have had to assume somebody fired the shot, and we'd have had to account for where the firer had been concealed. Allard would have suggested the wardrobe, and he'd have found the mud—planted mud—there. But when things went wrong, the man who stabbed Crewe knew about the wardrobe and used it himself because he hadn't the time to nip back to his room after he'd done the stabbing. Might I also add that there's something that remains to be explained about at least one of the three men I've named. Samuels went outside immediately after the murder, and though he was only a room away, he says he didn't hear the shot."

"And what do you think the dutch hoe was for, sir?" asked Lewis.

Travers smiled. "I think I'd rather hear what you or the inspector have got to say about that."

"My own idea's this," said Norris, without any finesse at all. "It was used to make those marks on the creeper. If you lean out of the window you can reach down just as far as they're made. They give the impression that someone got out this way. Right or wrong we've sent it to be put under the microscope for traces of what I might call plant life on it. You agree, Mr. Travers?"

"That's rather what I thought myself," said Travers. "If so, they were sticklers for accuracy. They must have known—or thought—the creeper mustn't be touched till just before the time when it was supposed to have been climbed down. Mind you, there was just one little snag about that dutch hoe, and that was the key in Allard's pocket. If the escape was to be by the window, with the door locked, why use the dutch hoe at all? And if the escape was to be out of the door and down the back stairs, why was the key in Allard's pocket and not in Crewe's? It doesn't make sense."

"You're right there," said Norris. "Still, we can't expect to put a jigsaw together in five minutes. Also"—and he gave a dry smile—"here's Crewe still in bed and nothing happening. We'll assume he gets out of bed."

The man got out.

"Now then, he goes to the door and Lewis comes in. They meet and Crewe sees something in Lewis's eyes that makes him back to the bed again. There is a struggle for the knife. Crewe gets pricked in places. The bedclothes are disarranged. Crewe is stabbed. He falls back against the wall. He slithers down. The murderer stands looking at him."

By some extraordinary cooperation of minds all this had been done. Lewis was looking down at the body which lay where it had been a few minutes before. With an incongruous touch, Norris stooped and rearranged the jacket of the sleeping suit.

"The next thing done was the throwing out of the blood?" asked Travers.

"Undoubtedly," said Norris. "It couldn't have been thrown out till the very last moment, and not by Crewe, who intended to put some of it on the floor here. Doing that—and perhaps other things we've still to discover—made the murderer late, and he was just going to the door when he heard voices—yours and Allard's—and hopped in the wardrobe. There he is now."

With Lewis inside the wardrobe, Norris called in the other man. "Now what's going to happen? Allard will certainly have to get between the wardrobe and the window before Lewis emerges, or else the struggle wouldn't have taken place so near the window. You come here, Allard. Lewis, you come out. Now there's a struggle, hand to hand, till the murderer—still you, Lewis!—gets near enough to the bed to grab the revolver. Allard grabs his arm when he sees it. The arm is held down. The bullet goes off at the required angle and catches Allard on the chin—"

"Excuse me, sir," said Lewis, pausing in the struggle. "We two ought to be over here by the window. What I do is thrust him away and then I fire as he falls. That makes the angle come right."

Norris nodded. "So it does. And you've got to kick Crewe's body over. You fall forward, Crewe, for a moment. You needn't stay like it. Now place Allard's body accurately."

Travers watched that being done. "I don't know what truth there is in the perseverance of expressions after death," he remarked, "but I don't think I ever saw anybody's face show so much surprise as his dead one did. That might, of course, mean that he was surprised at the man who shot him."

"You mean, who the man actually was?"

"That's it. And what's far more to the point—of course all this must have occurred to you already, but I just mention it in case—this murderer we're dealing with had had two struggles and they must have left marks and bruises on him. He may even have cuts or scratches."

"Just what do you suppose Samuels went out for, sir?" asked Lewis, who seemed to regard Travers as some kind of oracle.

"I haven't the faintest idea," Travers told him. "Unless it was that he knew he had to get the car away. He might have gone up there to try to start it, and have made a bad hand of it; not knowing the make or something like that." He waited till Lewis had made a note in his book; Norris was scribbling assiduously also. "Anything through about the car yet?"

"Plenty," said Norris. "They haven't got the prints at the Yard, but we've got the owner according to the registration." He consulted his notes. "Man called Spong, at Twentyford in Sussex. He's a small dealer. We're sending a man along there as soon as we get down. Only just got the news as I was coming up."

"If you like I'll do the two jobs at one go," said Travers. "I'd very much like to hear what Samuels is so anxious to get off his chest; after that—well, why shouldn't I get away this afternoon? I must call in at town some time too."

"Very glad if you will," said Norris. He contemplated the two dead men. "You two fellows get back into place. We'll have a good look and see if anything strikes us." He stood there for some time without saying a word, then nodded as if satisfied. "Everything all right?"

Travers made a wry face. "Do you know I can't help thinking that the body of Crewe is closer to the wall than it ought to be. I mean, if the body fell forward, or was merely knocked forward, only the upper part would move. The rump wouldn't shift."

Norris and Lewis consulted the photographs and Lewis had a look at his measurements and checked them.

"He's lying all right, Mr. Travers."

"That may be," said Travers. "The point is that when I saw him first he was propped up against the wall. May your man lean against the wall and then fall over naturally?"

They tried that, and Travers seemed to have reason on his side. Then Lewis and the plain-clothes man had a struggle round the body and dislodged it from the wall. The rump, as Travers said, still remained more adjacent than it should have been.

"You suggest the body was actually moved?" asked Norris.

"I don't know what I do suggest," smiled Travers. "I rather think I'm merely being a nuisance."

"No, no!" said Norris. "Say what's in your mind. As Wharton used to say, only fools don't make mistakes." He stood there again for some time, then made notes in his book. "All right, you fellows, you may go now. Sergeant Lewis will tell you what he wants."

Norris and Travers were left alone in the room, and the inspector was still shaking his head at the chalk mark where the body of Crewe had been. When he turned away he seemed to have made up his mind about something.

"According to present theories then, what we want is a man who was well in the know about that fake murder business; a man who certainly has bruises and who might have scratches from the knife. Samuels looks the most interesting, don't you think?"

"He has his possibilities," said Travers. "Franks looks rather out of it. I mean he couldn't very well have been in the know about the fake murder if he genuinely only arrived in England when he says he did. Drew doesn't strike me as the type. I don't know what you think?"

"Hard to say," was all Norris would admit. "The fact of the matter is that we're groping about in the dusk at the moment. Ask me what I think at this time to-morrow and it'll probably be very different from what I'm thinking now." He looked at Travers. "That chap Preston is worrying me a good deal. We've got something on him—that he was where he shouldn't have been. It isn't that that's worrying me so much as what he was up to when you saw him."

"My idea was that he'd lost his way," said Travers. "It wasn't properly light, you know, and I distinctly heard him come past my door before I got up, and saw him come back again."

"He was originally coming from the direction of Crewe's room?"

Travers nodded.

"I see. Then he might have been in there, collecting up extra things to take away for Crewe in his own car—luggage he couldn't get into the suit-case."

"You think Allard would have made a confidant of his own chauffeur?"

"By all accounts he was a superior sort of man," said Norris. "He didn't leave till about the time of Crewe's death. Even if he left the grounds, that's not saying he mightn't have nipped back again. He might be the man we're looking for—the third man in the know." He seemed to be liking the idea more and more. "Why! even all that about him leaving Allard's employ the last day of March might have been faked; arranged, if you like."

"He'll certainly bear looking up," Travers agreed.

Norris nodded. "If you don't get on his tracks this afternoon, we'll have the Press and an S O S on his heels. We'll see what happens by this time to-morrow. Now what about going down to see just what our friend Samuels wants to impart?"

When they got down to the hall, Samuels was there, having a word with one of the footmen. He made a beeline for them as soon as they reached the bottom stair.

Norris regarded him quizzically. "A cold morning, Mr. Samuels."

"Sure it's cold," said Samuels, and gave him a look which was that of a pet dog who's been scolded. "Look here, sir, aren't you goin' to hear what our little deputation's got to say? It's gettin' kinda tryin', all this hanging around. We'd like to get goin'."

"It's the truth you're going to tell me this time?"

A faint flush stole over the fat man's face. "You said it. I don't know if that goes for the whole bunch, but Henry and I are certainly handin' out the real dope this time."

"I hope you are," said Norris, and gave a look that made Samuels fidget nervously. "But I'm not seeing any deputation. I'll see you now—alone. After that I'll see the others and make the best I can out of it." He reached out for Samuels' arm as he turned away. "Why not now? I'll let the others know where you are."

Just then Mason came into the hall.

Norris called over. "Oh, Mason! Will you tell Miss Hastings and Mr. Franks and Mr. Drew that Mr. Samuels is with me in the lounge, and will they stand by to see me personally in a few minutes?" He thought of something else. "I suppose you haven't heard anything from that Chinaman?"

"Nothing at all, sir."

"Right," said Norris. "Let me know if anything should turn up." He turned towards the lounge, and slipped his arm under Samuels'. "You're rather anxious to get away, Mr. Samuels?"

"You said it!" and he shook his head emphatically. "And there's somethin' I'd like you to know right away. You was askin' the butler about a Chinaman who hadn't turned up." He gave Norris a shrewd look. "I don't aim to go butting into anybody's affairs, but were you referring to Wen Ti?"

Norris stopped short. "Why do you ask?"

Samuels shrugged his fat shoulders resignedly. "Well, if he was the guy you were interested in, I guess I'd forget it. There's nothing doing."

"What do you mean?"

"Mean?" Samuels shrugged again. "He's dead, Chief. Passed clean out. You see . . . well, Charlie Crewe was Wen Ti."

CHAPTER XI
SAMUELS TALKS

TRAVERS HAD NOT been surprised at that disclosure about the real identity of the elusive Wen Ti. What was puzzling him was the mass of implications that arose—the connection, for instance, with all that publicity business with which London had been regaled for many days. If Crewe was Wen Ti, then who were Peg Lorne and Zona Fox? Sam Leppard looked like being Taylor Samuels if one bore in mind his further alias—or was it his real name?—Lem Shepherd; and from the name Franks and the association with France, one might reasonably assume some connection with the tenor and Francis Perolles.

What Norris was thinking Travers didn't know. The inspector evidently determined that Samuels should see that his efforts in the cause of death were being met halfway, for he abandoned his official seat behind the table and drew the easy chairs up in front of the fire. Then he balanced on his knee the typescript of the remarks that Samuels had uttered on the last occasion.

"The name *is* Taylor Samuels?" he asked mildly.

"Sure," said Samuels. "That's what they wrote in the family Bible."

Norris smiled. "They didn't by any chance write Lemuel Shepherd?"

Samuels looked at him as if rather hurt. "So you're wise to that, are you?"

Norris waved his hand. "What's it matter so long as you're going to speak the truth? Your real name is Taylor Samuels."

"That's right. The other was kinda homely. You see, they always cast me as a homely feller."

"I see," said Norris. "Well, Mr. Samuels, I propose you should begin all over again and tell us just how you got here, and then what you know. Take your time and don't leave anything out. You don't mind notes being taken?"

Samuels gave a quick glance round at the stenographer. "That's O.K. with me, Chief. I guess this is kinda confidential anyhow?"

"That's right."

"And you'd like me to begin way back at Lem Shepherd?"

"That's entirely up to you," Norris told him.

Samuels bit his lip. "It was a tough break, but all the same I guess I had it comin' to me. You see, I got in with a bunch of fast steppers . . ." He broke off. "But I didn't do it, sir. They knew that as well as I did, but the cops had to make some sort of a show." He smiled. "Guess I was the show."

"And you've more or less been unemployed ever since," suggested Norris.

Samuels said that was so. He'd even tried small town shows until a too efficient Women's Organization got wise to who he was and ran him out of town, and then proceeded to follow him up wherever he went. Before that, and after, he had actually got a job in a cafeteria, and it was there that he ran up against Henry Drew.

"Real name?" asked Norris.

Samuels looked surprised. "Sure it's his real name."

"Any stage name?" asked Travers.

"Well, Arizona was what the boys always called him. Zona for short."

"And why the 'Fox'?"

Samuels looked startled, then gave a dry smile. "I guess there ain't much you don't know, Mr. Travers. Zona used to be in the Fox Studios, you see, so Crewe re-christened him when we landed."

He went on with his story. Zona had fallen on hard times too; living on what he could make in the crowd. He had had his chance and had fallen foul of the director, and that was the end of him. A sort of quiet, reminiscent twinkle came into Samuels' eyes when he began to talk about Zona Drew, who seemed to have been accepted by him as a kind of kid brother. Give him an even break on Broadway, and he'd make good. He could do all the old corner stuff—knife-throwing, roping, fancy shooting—better than any of the old-timers, and he had all the modern stuff besides.

Then Samuels ran across Charlie Crewe—and that, by the way, seemed to be his real name; at least Samuels had heard of no other. He had been in the States for years and, as far as Samuels knew, had been in the show business all his life. For the two years before Samuels had met him he had been the right-hand man of a Jap called Kimoto, who had been very well known for a spectacular show of magic and mystery. Then Kimoto died, and Crewe knew so much and no more. He tried to carry on the show with himself as chief faker, but it had been a flop, and Crewe tried Hollywood. The rest of the story was as he had previously given it: the formation of a kind of triumvirate; the haunting of studios; the attempt at a road act which was crippled from the start by lack of money for the purchase of scenery to put across Crewe's big act, and which was finally ruined by the persecution of Samuels himself, though the other two carried on for a bit and sent Samuels a share of what the show made. Then Crewe's father died, and it was after that that he announced that he was going back home.

"If I might interrupt you for a moment," said Travers, "I would like you to be very explicit about that. Tell us all you know. You see, it strikes me as a very peculiar thing that a man like Crewe should be able to say he was coming to England to make good, and that as soon as he got here he should be able to command the capital of a man like Allard. It isn't as if Crewe were a well-known man; a man with a reputation that would recommend him immediately to Allard."

"I get you," said Samuels, and began to think back. "Who his father was, Mr. Travers, I don't know for sure. I know he was a mighty sick man, because I heard Crewe say so just before he was called away to New Orleans, which was where the old man lived. When he got back to Hollywood I could see he was all het-up over some new scheme or other. He was goin' back home and he was sendin' for Zona and me. And he did."

"He never let anything else out about these wonderful prospects of his in England? Didn't say he was coming into money, for instance?"

Samuels shook his head. "Not a word, and that goes for Zona too. All I said when he was talkin' so confident was, 'Can you make it?' 'Sure,' he says, 'I can make it! Another coupla months or less and you and Zona'll be hittin' the high spots in good old London.'"

Norris leaned forward. "Tell me, what in your considered opinion were the relationships between Crewe and Allard? Did you ever get the idea that there was any sort of blackmail going on?"

Samuels stared at him; then his face flushed. "You're crazy to talk that way, sir. What sort of a guy do you think Crewe was? Didn't I tell you what he was like with Zona and me?" His eyes fell and he fidgeted with his necktie. He looked up timidly. "Guess I hadn't ought to talk like that to you, but I got kinda raw hearin' you . . ." The words wouldn't come.

"That's all right," said Norris. "I know what you think about Crewe, and perhaps I shouldn't have said what I did. Go on with your story. Tell us what happened when you two landed."

Samuels went on. Crewe met them in London and announced that he had interested a very important man in a show that was going to be put on in town. The name Courtney Allard conveyed nothing to Samuels, but Crewe said he was going to be the big noise in the theatrical world and had already financed one show. That admittedly had been a flop, but principally because the publicity work had been so bad. That was to be altered now; indeed, much of it was already being done, and Crewe chartered a taxi and took the new arrivals round to see their names on the signs. Perolles, he said, was a fine tenor Allard had discovered in France, and Peggy Lorne was the find of the century. He himself had picked her up at a show in Hastings where she was doing songs at the piano. According to Crewe, she was going over big.

"Hastings?" said Travers reminiscently. "That'd be the Margaret Hastings who's in the house here."

"Sure!" said Samuels. "That was the *nom de plume* Allard picked out specially while you and Mr. Spence were stayin' here."

"All mixed up with that fake murder publicity business," Norris told Travers. "Carry on, Mr. Samuels."

Samuels said the show certainly looked like a wow. The leading lady was to be Marie Lang, and everybody knew who *she* was. The principal comedian was Tom Basnet, and those two alone ought to fill any theatre in town.

Travers looked at Norris. "Allard was certainly plunging in pretty deep. Those two were the ones that almost put over his last show—the one that flopped—if you remember. And why wasn't there any publicity about them, Mr. Samuels?"

That was all coming along as soon as the contracts were signed, Samuels said. The show itself had been drafted to give Crewe himself and Drew and Samuels their big chance. It was to be a play with music rather than a musical comedy. The scene was to be at a ranch.

Crewe was to be a Chinese cook called Wen Ti. He made up so excellently as a Chinaman that he could explode a cracker by looking at it. He was to be brought in from the kitchen to amuse the guests, having owned up to being by way of a magician. Zona was to be a cow-hand called in for the same purpose, and he was to cut out Perolles in the affections of Marie Lang, who was one of a dude party staying at the ranch. Peg Lorne was the daughter of Samuels, the owner of the ranch and whose business it was to furnish the dry humour. Tom Basnet was to be the comic villain—sub-plot of the discovery of oil on the ranch and some trouble over the deeds—and he was to get shot in the last big scene. Everybody was to be in a state of panic. Then—enter Wen Ti. By some cunning arrangement of mirrors he was to make the body disappear; doing, in fact, what had been the great feature of Kimoto's big show. The sheriff was to be perfectly flabbergasted at a corpse disappearing under his very nose. Samuels confessed that he had the whole thing very muddled up, but those were the high spots as he remembered them. If everything had gone right, Allard—who had never seen Samuels or Drew perform—should have given them the once-over the morning he was killed. The book was to be gone over the same night, when Basnet was coming down, and Marie Lang too.

Travers saw the idea of the posters. "So Crewe was really to be the sensation of the play," he said to Samuels.

"Sure," said Samuels, and showed no surprise at all. "Right at the end—I forgot to tell you this—he turns out not to be a Chink at all. He's some sort of detective that's been sent to get the goods on Perolles, who's in some oil racket or other."

"Then you knew those threatening letters were all a fake?" suggested Norris.

Samuels admitted it. He added that as publicity he thought it a bum idea, and he'd told Crewe so, but Crewe seemed set on it.

Travers hooked off his glasses. "I wonder if I know why he was set on it. Admit that as publicity material it had whiskers on it as long as Noah's grandfather's, as Mr. Samuels said, but don't you think Crewe wanted it to fit in? I mean, was his own body to disappear when the fake murder took place? Imagine the sensation if the Press bit the bait. 'Man murdered and mysterious disappearance of the body,' and all that. Then later on it would turn out that it had all been a gorgeous April Fool's Day joke, and the play was to have a similar motif, and, best of all, Crewe—the supposedly murdered man—was the Wen Ti about whose identity the whole of London had been wondering for weeks."

"We'll go into it," said Norris. "Perhaps Mr. Samuels can give us some more information?"

But Samuels couldn't. All he had known and troubled about The Covers was that he and Drew were sitting pretty. Crewe had sent them passage money and expenses, and he'd handed them a couple of hundred dollars each when he met them.

"Anything you want to ask?" said Norris.

"I don't think so," said Travers, who had half a hundred questions ready. "Unless Mr. Samuels would care to tell us why Drew had that big bedroom?"

That was easily explained. Drew wanted room to keep his knife-throwing and rope-work up. He had had a stout board installed there, and kept it hidden away in a large trunk when he wasn't using it for the knives.

"And where did he do his revolver practice?" asked Norris, almost too quietly.

Samuels' eyes narrowed slightly. "He didn't have a gun, Chief. Maybe later on he'd have done some practicin' in the woods out there." He shook his head solemnly. "No, sir! Zona didn't have a gun."

"Thank you," said Norris, and got to his feet. "We can't let you get away just yet, Mr. Samuels, but we might be able to manage it some time to-night."

The fat man sat down again in the act of hoisting himself up.

"Zona and I are mighty glad to hear that. You see, some of the agents have been makin' inquiries, and we should hate to miss anything . . . after comin' all this way."

"I expect you would," said Norris. He glanced at the clock. "We've just time for a word or two with Mr. Drew, and if anything arises out of that we'll let you know." He smiled. "If you should want to ring up anybody in town about—er—the inquiries, you can use the 'phone here—provided one of us is here."

Samuels had hesitated rather curiously when Norris mentioned Drew's name, but he left the room with his tail wagging. Norris nodded amusedly at the broad back as the door closed on it.

"Don't think there's much vice in him, do you? No scratches or marks of a struggle—even if he *could* struggle, which I very much doubt."

"I'd hate him to roll on me," said Travers. "Still, as you say, I rather like him. And as he says himself, he's sure had a tough break. By the way, you didn't ask him why he went out that morning before breakfast."

"No," said Norris. "Several things I've got up my sleeve. Just when he and Drew think about leaving here, I might produce an awkward question or two and keep 'em on tenterhooks. Mind you, I think Samuels would lie through thick and thin for either Crewe or Drew."

"You think he's shielding Drew?"

Norris made a face. "If I knew what he had to shield him from I'd have a shot at an answer. I didn't like the way Drew was supposed to be so sleepy the morning the footman brought in the tea. He's supposed to have grunted and rolled over. What any ordinary person would have done would have been to gulp the tea and then get down to it again." He shook his head. "Yet it's all wrong. If there's any truth in Samuels' story—and I think there is—neither he nor Drew had the slightest interest in killing Crewe—or Allard. Just the contrary, in fact."

Travers nodded. "I think Samuels was telling the truth about the play business. What he said agreed with that rough draft of the book I took up last night. What I can't quite get at the moment is why Allard went into this show right up to the ears. He must have spent a small fortune already on advertising."

"You saw what I was driving at about blackmail?" asked Norris. "That's another snag. Here's this chap Crewe turns up from nowhere and induces Allard to spend all that money and to launch out into a grandiose and highly speculative scheme. Then there's the money Allard gave him—or advanced to him—which he sent to the other two in America, and the four hundred dollars he gave them when they got here. It doesn't sound right. Where was the appeal? What did Allard see in him?"

"Perhaps he had the gift of the gab," smiled Travers. "If the right-hand man to a modern magician can't talk, who can?"

"Then there was that virtual collaring of the whole show," went on Norris. "From what I can see, he *was* the show, and he was running it for the convenience of himself and his two pals. Still," and he shrugged, "if I had a million I shouldn't mind chucking it about a bit. If Allard was a bit of a fool and Crewe got round him, that's no business of ours. We'll have Drew in, shall we?"

The chairs still remained at the fire. Drew came in with the same grave young manner that was characteristic of him, and he was to make Travers think of a nicely mannered pup that quietly watches a thorn taken out of its pad, except that there was always a little smile hovering somewhere about his mouth.

"Sit down, Mr. Drew," said Norris. "We've been hearing a lot of nice things about you from Mr. Samuels."

"Is that so?" He smiled slightly. "Guess Sam is a natural-born talker."

"Better at that game than Crewe was?"

Drew shook his head slowly. "Charlie was no talker, Chief; he was a dead sure mesmerizer. You'd have been tickled to hear him handing out all the bunk that he used to use with Kimoto." He gave a quick look. "Guess Sam told you all about that, Chief?"

"He did say something about it," Norris ventured, and spread rather ostentatiously on his knees the typescript of Drew's original statement. "I take it, Mr. Drew, there are a few things you'd like to correct, or amplify, shall we say. Perhaps you'd like me to read to you—entirely without prejudice—what Mr. Samuels has told us."

Norris proceeded to read extracts, pausing every now and again to look questioningly at Drew. When it was over, Drew said he'd nothing to add. Pressed by Norris he insisted that he had no idea what was in Crewe's mind when he was so anxious to get to England and so confident of making good.

"It's an amazing thing, you know, Mr. Drew," said Norris, "but he seems to have had Allard in mind all along. You never heard him mention the name? You can't think of any hint he dropped?"

Drew could think of nothing.

Norris nodded resignedly, then suddenly changed his tone.

"Now a direct question that concerns yourself primarily. Your room was used for the purpose of a committee meeting at which you four people decided to tell me certain things which were untrue and to keep back certain things that were true. We don't mind that once in a while, but we'd be sorry to have it repeated. You and Mr. Samuels are anxious, for instance, to get away to town. You wouldn't like to be requested to remain here. Perhaps you'll tell me, therefore"—he smiled engagingly—"since you were the host at the meeting, just why you decided to say what you all did. What was the reason for the lies?"

Drew's version rang true. He and Samuels were strangers in a strange land and unused to police methods. The last thing Samuels wanted was notoriety and the old scandal raked up, and what went with him went with Drew. Franks was also a newcomer, and for some reason or other he seemed pretty scared at what had happened. Margaret Hastings was also scared a bit, and he didn't know why. All the same the four did not see why they should lose everything because of what had happened. They were entitled to a certain amount of publicity, and they determined to use it. The talkies seemed to present better openings than the stage, and that was why Allard's show had been slightly tampered with. And surely there was no harm in getting Spence to act for the party? And in any case, said Drew, there never had been unanimity, even at the first meeting. Nobody knew quite what he wanted, and when something was done, everybody was scared stiff that it had been done. The only thing the four were agreed on was that the sooner they got away with a clean bill of health, the better for them.

Norris appeared to accept all that unconditionally. "You're a performer with the rope, Mr. Drew? What we used to call the lasso when we were boys."

Drew modestly admitted that he was.

"I wonder if you'd perform an experiment for me," Norris asked. "There's a hook outside the window of that room where the deaths took place, and I'd like to know if a rope could be thrown so as to catch on it."

Drew said he'd certainly have a try, but there was some vague change that came over him as soon as Norris had mentioned ropes at all.

"Then we'll try it straight away," Norris said. "Perhaps you'll fetch one of your ropes, and Mr. Travers will go up to the room and point out to you when we're outside, just where the hook is."

He stooped at the side table as they passed it and handed Travers a piece of chalk.

"Perhaps if you mark the hook with that, Mr. Drew'll be able to see it better."

He still lingered at the table, then all at once picked up one of the photographs.

"You have knives for your knife throwing work, too, Mr. Drew, don't you?"

"Sure," said Drew, and watched him as he spoke.

"Anything like this," said Norris, and handed him the photograph of the knife that had killed Crewe.

Travers could see that Drew knew what was on the photograph before he looked at it. He gave it the merest glance, then his face took on a queer, twisted smile.

"Gosh! I wish you hadn't asked me that question. You're goin' to have me in all wrong."

"You mean you've seen the knife before?"

"Sure I've seen it," said Drew, with the same wry smile. "It's one of my knives. Somebody borrowed it and forgot to bring it back."

CHAPTER XII
CAPTAIN MARK RUSTON

TRAVERS FOLLOWED the experiment with interest. From the window he missed the finer points of Drew's preparations. Drew missed for five times running, and each time grinned cheerfully and blamed nobody but himself. The trouble was that between that hook and the sill was only a bare two inches, and the edge of the spinning circle had to fall to a nicety. Then at the sixth attempt he got it.

What Norris was saying to him Travers couldn't hear, but the inspector looked pleased. Then with a dexterous flick Drew made the rope leap loose and down it went again. Travers went down too, and Drew stood back when the inspector went over.

"Extraordinarily clever," said Travers. "Didn't you think so?"

"Amazing!" agreed Norris. "It fits in too well, that's the trouble. What I was wondering was, if a man really used a rope to escape from that window, how he'd manage not to leave it there to tell the tale. What I thought was that he'd have a rope double over the hook so that he'd merely have to pull one end when he got to the ground and down the rope'd come. Then this chap does something with his wrist and the rope hops off the hook as if it were alive." He looked round for Drew. "Come over a minute, Mr. Drew, will you?"

"That was a remarkably clever effort of yours," Travers told him.

Drew smiled. "Well, it wasn't any too easy. Not much room to operate."

"I suppose you couldn't put one of those knives of yours into that wooden sill?" asked Norris casually.

Drew looked at him as if he'd been asked to do a dirty trick. The old wry smile flickered over his face.

"Seein' as how you're askin', I guess I might. You're not suggestin' that I'd kill a man that way, are you, sir?"

"No, no!" Norris told him hastily. "It isn't you I'm inquiring about. But you'll admit that what you can do another man might have done."

Drew nodded, then took a look at the window. "Guess she'd spin a bit too much. She wouldn't strike true. She might . . ." He shook his head dubiously, then his eyes twinkled as he looked at Norris. "If you've got a hunch you'd like to try it and you'll just take a peek out of that window, I don't mind doin' my stuff from this end."

Norris shook his head. "Not this morning, thanks! But about that missing knife of yours. You sure you can't remember back to when you saw it last?"

"Nope," said Drew promptly. "I had five of them last Monday but on Wednesday I noticed one was gone. Being a guest I sort of hated to say anything."

"I understand." Norris gave his usual temporizing nod. "Well, Mr. Drew, I think that's all for the present. I hope you'll be able to get away this evening."

"Thanks," said Drew, and though it sounded a bit curt Travers could see he was uncommonly relieved.

He held out his hand. "Good-by, Mr. Drew. I mayn't be see-ing you again."

Drew looked at him, then smiled gently.

"I sure hate to say it, Mr. Travers, but there isn't anybody I'd like to see less of—unless it's the Chief here."

Travers laughed. Norris smiled as he watched the disappear-ing figure of the cowboy actor.

"Never a scratch—and he's as strong as an elephant, that young fellow. He'd have killed that flabby Crewe in a couple of seconds, and he'd have snapped that hop-pole Allard clean in two."

"Quite," said Travers. "And yet it doesn't fit in. There's too much of it. This fellow's tailor-made for the job. What you'd rather have is a suit of reach-me-downs. And what's the pro-gram now?"

Norris glanced at his watch. "Just time to see the rest of the Big Four. You coming in?"

Travers said he had a dozen things to do, much as he'd have liked it. As it was Norris was half-way through the meal when Travers drew the Bentley up ready at the front and came in to lunch. What with the footman hovering round there was no time for a talk till Travers had finished, and then it was time to go.

"Get anything out of that couple?" he asked.

"Precious little," said Norris. "They had it all worked out to the very last syllable. She was sitting up reading in her room—so she says—and he called in about that mistaken identity busi-ness. Both swear their voices never rose above the conversation-al, and Franks swore on the four gospels that Crewe's name was never mentioned. Oh! there was something else. She says she never was engaged to marry Crewe. She was leading him up the orchard. He took a great fancy to her—I'm quoting the lady, of course—and she saw where her bread was buttered. As soon as she got comfortably settled in this great show of Allard's, she was going to send Crewe about his business."

"You didn't believe it," remarked Travers.

Norris shrugged his shoulders. "Some of it was true all right. All I know for certain is that she and Franks know something.

They're both scared, as Drew said. By the way, she owned up to having been at Hastings and having chosen that as a convenient name down here."

"You've got a hard-bitten one to handle there," said Travers consolingly. He sighed. "Well, I'd better be pushing off. This my packet of photographs and things?"

"That's right. We couldn't get anything of Crewe except the post-mortem one, but he doesn't look too bad. Ring up if you get hold of anything important."

"I will," said Travers, "and I'll be back late tomorrow in any case."

Norris went with him to the car. "I'm putting a man on at the agencies," he said, "and sending another down to Hastings to follow up our lady friend. Headquarters are getting in touch with New Orleans through New York, so we might have some news by the time you get back. Needle in a haystack business, but we might get something about Crewe's father."

With only four hours of daylight to rely on, Travers pushed the car on across country. It was almost four o'clock when he arrived at the little town of Twentyford and asked for the where-abouts of Spong's garage. Spong himself was on the premises, and he seemed considerably surprised when Travers, after the tank had had ten gallons in, told him his real business. In the seclusion of the office Spong produced a copy of the *Evening Record* in which he had advertised the Austin for sale. Travers produced the photographs of Crewe and Allard.

"Were these the two gentlemen who came here and bought the car?"

Spong put on his spectacles and had a look. Allard he spotted at once; the other he wasn't quite sure about, though it was he who had driven the Austin off behind the Rolls they'd both arrived in.

"That's all right then," said Travers, and having secured a set of Spong's prints on the trade card he accepted, he pushed on towards Wryford Abbas, another thirty miles. A short cut led him rather astray, and it was getting on towards dusk when he reached the village.

It was Palmer who noticed on the front of a white gate that led to a small house back from the road the words "The Cottage." Travers stopped the car just past and got out. When he looked over the gate he knew there was something wrong. The brick path was overgrown with weeds, and the house beyond it was so small and unpretentious that it might have been a labourer's dwelling. The garden was neglected, too, and at one time there seemed to have been fowls in the tiny paddock that surrounded the house, for one fowl-house lay overturned and rotting and a coop or two seemed falling to pieces. True there was a garage of sorts at the side, but it looked just large enough to take a Morris and no more, and the garage could have done with a couple of coats of paint.

Before he knocked at the door he knew there would be nobody at home; the house had a feeling of desertion about it. When he had knocked at back and front he went out again by the white gate, and as he turned he saw a thin spiral of smoke against the dark background of woods. The house was not wholly deserted then, and yet it couldn't be the one he was looking for. The Captain Mark Ruston who kept cars and a chauffeur would have something rather different from a tumble-down cottage like that.

As he started the car off again Travers realized he was feeling remarkably hungry. An attractive-looking inn by the village green caught his eye and he pulled the car up. In a quarter of an hour he was confronting a dish of bacon and eggs and a pot of tea, and Palmer elsewhere was undoubtedly doing much the same.

The last post, he learned, went at seven, so he scribbled a note to Norris telling him about Spong and suggesting a call at Allard's bank for a look at the check which was probably still in the bank's possession since it had not been found at The Covers. He also enclosed the card that carried Spong's prints, in case they should be the unknown ones found in the Austin. Then he pushed the bell for someone to take the letter to the post. The landlord himself came in.

"By the way," Travers said to him when he'd taken over the letter, "I'm looking up my old friend Captain Ruston who lives somewhere about here. Place called The Cottage, I believe it is."

"That's right, sir," the landlord told him, "a little place on the left-hand side as you came in."

Travers raised his eyebrows. "Little place, is it? Mind you, I haven't seen him for years, but I rather expected he had a pretty big place down here."

The man glanced at the clock; there was plenty of time for the post. "I reckon he's come down in the world since you saw him then, sir."

"Really? How did that happen?"

"Well, sir, I only know what they say about here, but when Captain Ruston first came out of the Army—that'd be just after the war—they reckoned he had a lot o' money. Then he got in with a farming company what started about here. Going to do wonders, they were. Got people to put their money into it and made a rare fuss. You know what farming was like just after the war, sir; everybody thought they was going to make their fortune. Captain Ruston, he was a great man in it, and then they went bust and they say he lost the lot. All I know is he started poultry farming and didn't do any too well at it, and then about a year ago he went abroad—to France or somewhere, so they said—and now they tell me he's back again. Got money, so they reckon; at any rate a man I know went up to see him yesterday about buying his house and he reckoned he didn't want to sell it. 'When I would have sold it, nobody didn't want it,' he says, 'and now you want it, I don't want to sell.'"

Travers nodded comprehendingly. "I must go and see him before I leave. Did you know his man? Preston, I think his name was."

The landlord smiled. "Did I know him, sir! Extraordinary old character he was. We shan't get another like him about these parts again."

Travers was wondering what was the exact connotation of that word "old." He put out a feeler.

"He was a bit of a character, as you say. How old would you put him at?"

"How old? Well, not less than fifty, sir. An old regular, he was. Used to be the Captain's batman in the war—as you probably know, sir."

Travers nodded again. "So I believe. But he knew a good bit about the Captain's cars, didn't he?"

A look of utter bewilderment spread over the other's face. "Cars, sir? He never had no cars, except one he used to drive himself when he first come here. Then he sold it—just before Preston went away, that was—and later on he bought one o' them little Austins at an auction."

Travers took refuge in yet another nod. "And Preston didn't act as chauffeur, then."

Whatever Preston had or had not been, the landlord seemed immensely tickled at the idea. "I'd have liked to see him driving a car, sir." Then a thought suddenly struck him. "I've got a photo of the Captain, sir, if you'd like to see it." He caught Travers' glance at the clock. "I'll send my daughter with your letter, sir."

He came back with a framed photograph of what looked like the village cricket team, and pointed to himself first.

"There's me, sir, at the end, as you see. That's Captain Ruston with the pads on. Rare fine wicket-keeper he was. And a rare nice gentleman too, sir."

Travers had a look, then gave his glasses a polish. Something about the face of Captain Ruston seemed vaguely familiar—and then he dismissed the idea. It was the regular type of army face—set of jaw, keen eyes, clipped moustache—that led him to think that.

"Taken two years ago, sir," said the landlord, and had another look at it himself. Then, "You'll excuse me asking, sir, but were you thinking of staying the night, because we'd have to get the rooms ready."

Travers thought rapidly. "Yes, I think we'll stay. Ask my man to come in, will you."

Half an hour later he set out again to call at that diminutive building which was aptly named The Cottage. The whole business was extraordinarily puzzling, and in the words of his old nurse, there was some jiggery-pokery somewhere. Nothing was right about Captain Mark Ruston except his name. House, cars, chauffeur, the letter to Allard—everything was wrong. Travers even found his heart beginning to beat rather quickly as he entered the white gate and saw a light in a downstair room.

The door opened hard on his knock and he saw a tall, well set-up man, wearing a tweed jacket and light grey flannel trousers of quite good cut. He carried himself like a gentleman and he spoke like one. And let it be understood about Travers, whatever his eccentricities and his don't-give-a-damn attitude towards the conventions, and whatever the hilarity of the garb he chose to assume, there was always a something about him that told you he was a somebody. Ruston, used to summing men up, must have seen all that at once, and as soon as his strange visitor spoke he could have had no doubt about it.

"You're Captain Ruston?" asked Travers.

"Yes," said the other, and looked at him. "You want to see me?"

"If I may," said Travers.

Ruston waved him into a tiny sitting-room with one or two very nice pieces and quite a lot of books. On the gate-leg table was a drawing-board with paper and drawing materials. He drew the windsor chair to the fire.

"Sit down, won't you? And may I give you a drink? A spot of whisky?"

"Thanks. Just a spot," said Travers. He took out his pocket-book and found the credential chit that Norris had provided. "My name's Travers—Ludovic Travers. This sort of explains what I'm here for."

Ruston nodded, holding the siphon. "That enough for you? Say when."

Travers duly said when and took the drink. Then as Ruston poured out his own and the light fell on his face, and the ribbon of black that would soon be a moustache, he knew where he had seen Captain Ruston before—or was it his brother?

"Here's how!" said Ruston, then took a swig, and the chit. "Did I understand you to say 'Ludovic Travers'? You're not the man who wrote 'The Economics of a Spendthrift'?"

"I'm afraid I am."

"How perfectly wonderful!" He looked hard at Travers, then down at the chit. He frowned as he read it. "I don't quite see what this means—I mean, how it refers to me."

Travers replaced the chit in his pocket-book. "This is how it is. You've read about those murders at The Covers, Marbury? Where your former chauffeur, Preston, was employed?"

Ruston's eyes narrowed. "Yes?"

"Well, Preston has disappeared. He left his employment quite normally on the expiration of his notice, at the end of March—"

"Just a moment," broke in Ruston. "I take it you're associating Preston with these murders—in a direct capacity, shall we say?"

Travers looked profound. "I'm afraid I mustn't answer that."

"I see. Well, tell me at what time precisely the man Crewe was killed?"

"Say eight-fifteen," said Travers.

Ruston nodded. "Right. That's good enough. I happen to know that Preston has been rather worried about being connected with the affair, and he tells me that if you inquire at the garage on the London Road, Marbury, the proprietor will tell you that he was filling up his car there when the town clock struck eight. After that he drove on away from the town."

"Splendid!" said Travers. "We'll inquire, as you say. Merely the necessary elimination of people who might possibly be affected," he explained.

"Quite," said Ruston, and took another swig at the drink. "Just how could Preston be involved?"

Travers looked even more profound. "Well, between ourselves, we happen to have implicitly reliable information that Preston did not spend the whole of the night where he should have spent it—in his room at the garage. In short, he was seen wandering about the upstair corridors in the early hours of the morning."

Ruston's eyes narrowed again. He hesitated slightly, then finished off the drink—very slowly. He rose.

"Won't you have another?"

"Thanks, no," said Travers. "Bit too early for me."

Ruston poured himself out another small tot and sat down.

"So Preston was seen wandering about upstairs. What on earth did he do that for?"

"Lord knows," said Travers. "Unless he was enamoured of one of the maids—a perfectly unpardonable suggestion on my part. Tell me," and he suddenly smiled and leaned confidentially forward, "have you a brother, Captain Ruston?"

"A brother? Heavens, no!"

"No cousin or anybody who closely resembles you?"

Ruston smiled as he shook his head.

Travers sank back again in the chair. "Then that settles it."

"Settles what?"

"That it was you I saw that morning, just as it was getting light, in the corridor outside my room."

Ruston stared at him. "You must be mad."

"Possibly," said Travers. "All the same I'm telling the truth—and you know it."

"Preposterous!"

Travers shrugged his shoulders. "Have it your own way." He leaned forward again. "What was your regiment?"

"Regiment? Punjabis—Indian Army, of course. Axed in nineteen-twenty."

Travers smiled inscrutably. "I wonder if you'd mind my having a few shots in the dark. You were axed; came home with quite a lot of compensation money, therefore, in your pocket. You were unlucky. The farming company didn't turn out to be what it promised. You lost most of what you had—except this cottage. You even had to get rid of Preston, your old batman. Finally, you tried chicken-farming, and that didn't pay too well either. You were getting desperate, then perhaps you saw an advertisement—or perhaps a friend told you. You'd always been fond of cars. You knew a lot about them. I know a bit myself, and I spotted what that drawing there on the table was as soon as I set my bat eyes on it. Well, you had to live or go under. You applied for the post of chauffeur-mechanic to Courtney Allard, and you wrote your own testimonial and reference, using Preston's name." He paused. "Am I right?"

"You seem to know a hell of a lot," was all Ruston said.

"That's not the point," said Travers. "The thing is, am I right?"

"And suppose you are?"

Travers smiled. "If I am right, I'm not blaming you for the deception. I won't say it's quite what everybody'd have done; only, so long as you lived up to what you said you were, Allard was the only one concerned."

Ruston nodded grimly. "I think he got his money's worth."

"I expect he did," said Travers, then laughed. "It must have been great fun. What was it like feeding with old Mason?"

The tenseness disappeared at once. Ruston smiled. "Mason's a damn good feller." He shook his head reminiscently. "It was a curious life—in some ways—but I enjoyed it."

"Exactly," agreed Travers, and fumbled for his glasses. "And to get back to business. Just what were you doing that morning in the corridor upstairs?"

Ruston's face set. "You're on the wrong tack. Sorry and all that, but I wasn't upstairs. You can question me till doomsday, bring the whole of Scotland Yard here if you like, and I can only say what I know. The rest of what you said is right—I own up to that, reprehensible or not—but I wasn't inside that house." He rose with an air of finality. "There you are. Take it or leave it."

Travers blinked at him. "And it's true?"

Ruston glared. "What do you mean? Do you question my word? Of course it's true."

"Right," said Travers feebly. "Then perhaps we'd better leave it."

CHAPTER XIII
TRAVERS HAS AN IDEA

IT WAS A wholly puzzled Travers who drove back to town the following morning. That business of Ruston was beyond him entirely. He had struck Travers as a sahib from crown to sole, and it was impossible to believe he was lying. True there was that awkward matter of his writing out his own reference, but to judge a man who is on his beam ends by the standards of everyday life, was scarcely fair or logical. And if he definitely was not in the house that morning, then who was it that Travers had seen? To think of impersonation was to add yet another complication to a case that was already tortuous enough. And yet Travers was not prepared to dismiss that solution. Crewe and Allard seemed to have involved themselves in such sinuosities of preparation for their flamboyant murder stunt that one more subtlety hardly mattered.

Back in town again, Travers put in an hour in his room at Durango House, and even there his thoughts still ran back to what had happened the previous evening. He wondered just what Ruston now proposed to do with himself. Presumably he now had money, though what he had saved in Allard's service couldn't last him long. Then the thought of Ruston and money produced another idea. Crewe had got money from Allard. Samuels and Drew had got money from Crewe. Had Ruston also been in the swim, and had he got money too? The fact that he was who he was, made it now extremely probable that Allard might have chosen him as some sort of confidant. There were things—if one only knew them—that he might have done, and as for that alibi he'd produced, it was no alibi at all unless a witness could be found to say precisely where he was when the murder of Crewe actually took place. Nothing would have been easier for a man who knew the roads as Ruston did than to have doubled back—after establishing that pseudo-alibi.

Travers sat there, chewing the cud on that, and then his eyes fell on the typewriter he had just been using. Curious, he thought, how each individual machine had peculiarities that set it apart even among those of its own make. The machine on which the supposedly threatening letter had been written to Crewe, for instance, with its wobbly v's and y's. That machine there must have some peculiarities, thought Travers. He ran off a line or two—the words of that last letter as far as he remembered them—and then surveyed the result. Then he polished his glasses and had another look. Most amusing—and one in the eye for Norris! Fingerprints might be infallible, but typewriters certainly were not; his own machine also had those wobbly v's and y's. Then suddenly he fingered the texture of the quarto sheet of paper and began to wonder if he had done Norris an injustice. After lunch in his own rooms Travers was sitting comfortably before the fire wondering whether or not to get back to The Covers in case Norris should have returned from the inquest, when the telephone bell rang—Durango House passing on a message from Norris himself, asking Travers to go round to the Yard as soon as he could. Travers grabbed hat and overcoat and set off at the double.

Norris was in his room and greeted him as if he'd been away for weeks. As soon as he got Travers seated, and before he heard a word of what had happened, he explained the urgency.

"We want you to do something for us," he said. "I know you've only just got back, but something has turned up which may want careful handling, and I'd rather you did it than one of my own men. It's about that Beachville business and Miss Allard."

Travers raised his eyebrows.

"Something's wrong somewhere," went on Norris. "If you remember the famous letter she was so anxious to have, and what she told us, she was supposed to have been spending a long week-end with friends down there. It turns out she was doing nothing of the sort. That place—The Views—is only a small cottage which is let furnished. Somebody took it for three weeks, expiring the end of March, and now some more people have it. What I'd like to know is if the lady who took it from the agents for those three weeks was Miss Allard, and if she took it, just what she was doing there that had to be lied about."

"Did the description agree with how the agents described the lady?"

"That's the trouble," said Norris. "My man went down there to make general inquiries; a sort of confirmation of what she said in the letter. We didn't anticipate anything like this, and naturally he didn't have a photograph or description. The thing is this. Lewis will go down with you—he'll be ready at four o'clock, and you can take quite a good photo we've managed to dig up out of the *Tatler*. I know it sounds rather absurd going to all this fuss about something which doesn't seem immediately connected, but you never know."

"As you say," said Travers. "Four o'clock then, outside here. Anything special you've got in mind for my particular brand of beauty?"

"I don't think so," said Norris, with never a trace of a smile. "Unless you see the agents on the excuse of taking the house, and so find out who was down there exactly. Agents always nose out those things. The rest I'll leave to you. And now, what happened yesterday?"

Travers told him all about it, and pleaded the cause of Captain Ruston as if he were his brother. Norris heard it all—even the suggestion of impersonation—without much comment.

"Won't do any harm to ask him to make a statement some time," was his final verdict.

"And what's been happening at your end?" Travers asked. "The Big Four gone at last?"

Norris smiled grudgingly. "Yes; we let 'em loose last night—the whole gang of 'em. We know where they are and they're being looked after. The two Americans are at the Porlock in Harries Street; Franks is at an hotel in Southampton Row, and Miss Hastings is with friends in Maida Vale. We had a most exciting time after you left."

"Really? Do tell me all about it?"

Norris, methodical as ever, consulted his notes. "Well, first we tried letting off the gun in Crewe's room and listening where Samuels was, two rooms away. I had Samuels in with me. When the gun went off and I heard it distinctly, he put up a very good case. He said he did hear something, but in his room on the outskirts of Hollywood he overlooked a main street where cars were always crowding by and backfiring and so on, and he accepted the noise—from habit—as a matter of course. Also, he says he suffers in the early morning from catarrh, which brings on a certain deafness, and that's why he wanted to go out as usual, to clear his pipes in the open air before breakfast. Mind you, I'll give him this credit, the sound could be heard much more distinctly where you were downstairs than in his room."

"I shouldn't be surprised," said Travers. "There's no accounting for sounds. And what happened then?"

"The next thing was Miss Hastings, *alias* Peg Lorne, *alias* Margaret Laws. She got hold of Mason and very delicately asked if she might see Mr. Allard's private papers, as there was something among them which belonged to her and which she ought to have. Did Mason know where the papers were kept? So saying," went on Norris, as if he were giving evidence, "she toyed with her little bag and showed the edge of a pound note. Mason—the fool—told her very courteously there was nothing doing. If I'd known I'd have given her the run of the lot, provided I got hold of what she wanted."

"What do you think she was after?"

Norris clicked his tongue. "Damned if I know. I wish I did. I do know she's scared about something. She was like a cat on hot bricks, walking delicately like that bloke in the Bible; you know, trying to be very gentle and patient and coy as if butter had never melted in her mouth. I could have slapped her face."

Travers laughed. "And you a married man! Still, she is a bit of a hussy, as you say. And what about that disappearing body theory? Do anything at it?"

"Did I not!" said Norris. "I stood in that room for half an hour, waiting for inspiration." He shook his head. "Couldn't see a thing. For instance, in that proposed play the Chink makes a body disappear by an optical illusion, an arrangement of mirrors or something like that. There weren't any mirrors in that bedroom. If Crewe's body was supposed to disappear, it could only have been carried down the rope attached to the hook. I mean, that's what people would have been led to believe. Actually, as we know, a live man would have gone down the rope, or out by the back door with the key Allard had, after marking the creeper and throwing down the blood."

"I think you've gone rather beyond what I outlined," said Travers. "All I was thinking of was the strange coincidence of two disappearing bodies—one on the stage, and the other that preceded it for publicity purposes. I didn't suggest that the same methods might be followed." He suddenly began to fumble in his inside pocket. "Oh! here's something I'd like you to look at. Have you got that last letter Crewe received—the one that threatened death within twenty-four hours?"

Norris went over to the desk. "We got it back this morning. Here's the magnified version showing the peculiarities of type."

Travers offered him the quarto sheet he had typed in his room. "Compare it with this, will you? And try the paper."

Norris got his glass on it. In ten seconds he was looking up astonished. "It's the same machine. And the same paper or I'm a Dutchman!"

"Keep your nationality," said Travers. "It is the same machine—the one in my private room at Durango House. You got a conference later on today?"

"This evening," said Norris. "Why?"

Travers smiled. "If you want to make the Chief Constable's eye bulge, tell him you now know for an absolute certainty that those threatening letters were all bunkum. I reported to you, if you remember, that Crewe and Allard came to our place on business. Crewe happened to be left alone in the room for a time with my typewriter under his nose. Say that we had a brainwave and checked up on it, and show the result. The paper's ours and everything."

Norris's smile was non-committal, but he set the paper carefully aside for all that. He held out his hand.

"I shan't see you before you start. Ring up with anything you get hold of. I'm going along back to Marbury straight away."

"Anything special?" asked Travers.

Norris shook his head. "Routine work. We're combing that shrubbery to see if anything's lying about." He gave a sudden smile. "You might be interested to know, by the way, that that blood on the wall and the ground was probably pig's blood. I dare say we'd find where it was bought if it were worth the trouble. That couple must have been planning for days to fake all that business."

"Playing at Indians," said Travers. "But a rotten ending to the game. See you to-morrow perhaps. And don't go getting murdered yourself."

It was a Saturday, and normally Travers should have been down at his sister's place in Sussex, and Palmer with him. As it was, the man was due to stay on in town, and Travers sat ruminating by the fire while a bag was being packed. He was a generous-hearted soul, and somehow he felt sorry for those two Americans who had arrived in London only a week before. With all his heart he was hoping that the pair of them would get a good job. Capital thing for Samuels, he thought, if he could make good on this side under an assumed name and then get a fresh hold on things back home. Then an idea came to him—just that he himself had enough influence, if not to get the pair the necessary job, at least to give them the chance of showing their stuff. And when Travers had that sudden idea, and acted on it, he had no notion whatever that what he was doing was to solve the problem of what came to be known as The Case of the April Fools.

As he was in the act of taking off the receiver, he remembered it was Saturday, and Ronald du Fresne wouldn't be round at the studio. But he tried his private address at Hampstead, and got him there. Du Fresne said he'd heard all about the two guys in question. He'd held off himself because he was always rather suspicious of swimmers on the crest of notoriety. But he'd certainly have a look at them as Travers suggested. As a matter of fact, he was looking for a man of the type Samuels seemed to be. Travers gave the hotel and number, added a flippancy or two just to show that he wasn't too anxious, and then got hold of the Porlock.

Drew was out, but in five minutes he was listening to the husky voice of Samuels. He hadn't fixed up anything definite, he said, and from that Travers gathered that things weren't going any too well—publicity or no publicity. Travers broke the news about du Fresne and the International Associated Corporation, and gave him a few moments' advice on what to do and how to handle the producer himself.

"Gosh, Mr. Travers! I'll say that's good of you," came Samuels' voice, and as though he meant it.

"That's all right," Travers told him. "And keep quiet about Lem Shepherd. You don't know him and never did. If anything gets out, refer Mr. du Fresne to me for the reason. And be sure to keep me informed of what happens. You've got my address. Nothing to do with the police in any case. And you must come and have dinner with me here some night next week. Bring Drew as well." He smiled to himself as Samuels began to babble more thanks, then cut in with, "Well, good luck! I hope you muscle in on the film racket."

. . . .

Travers made no attempt to hustle the Bentley along; there would be plenty of time to survey the ground before dark and, unless a miraculous stroke of luck turned up, not enough to finish the job. He and Lewis chatted away, about the case mostly, without arriving anywhere in particular.

"Throwing the net pretty wide, isn't he, sir?" asked Lewis, referring to the interest Norris was taking in the affairs of Susan Allard.

"Depends what he ultimately gets in it," said Travers.

"What'd you think of her?" went on Lewis. "She didn't strike me as the sort to be up to anything shady. Quiet, pleasant-mannered little lady, I thought she was."

"You can't judge 'em by looks," said Travers, who knew as little about women as ducks do about dumplings. "Besides, she was asking for it. There was that slipping out of the house business she wouldn't explain, and that hunting about for the letter. Got that map handy? We ought to be getting pretty close now."

About five miles short of the town they took a side-road. A couple of miles on they came to an unspoilt ridge overlooking the sea. Lewis spotted a landmark which had been mentioned by the man Norris had sent down, and then they saw the house, standing in a quiet side-road with nothing near it but a brand-new bungalow across the way on the higher land. Travers pulled up on the side of the road.

"You get out and tinker with the radiator," he said to Lewis. "I'll sit tight and have a look round."

The Views was little more than a cottage, but a delightful one. It would have been just the place for a maiden lady with a maid and a couple of cats. The walls were covered with creeper, there was a flagged path to the front door and what looked like being an attractive garden, and altogether there was an air of peace and gentility about it. Hardly in keeping was the large garage with doors painted a vivid green.

Lewis came over to the door. "Just take a quiet look over at that bungalow, sir. There's an old dame keeps squinting round to see what we're up to. A regular nosy Parker."

Travers had a look at the sharp-featured woman who was peeping round the gate, not ten yards from where the car stood. As the Bentley went on slowly past, she was in the house again, but watching with the curtain pulled back—so Lewis reported. Travers stopped the car fifty yards on. He nodded back.

"She might know a thing or two, Lewis. I'll bet there isn't much going on across the road that she doesn't know."

"Then you go and try it, sir," said Lewis. "You're a better one with the ladies than I am."

"Heaven forbid!" said Travers piously, and got out. In the fifty yards of preparation time he hunted about for a reasonable excuse, and then decided to tell more or less the truth. After all, Sue Allard was never likely to hear of it.

The thin-faced woman opened the door.

Travers bowed gravely. "I don't know your name but I'd rather like to speak to you for a minute on a matter of importance. A confidential matter."

It took her very few seconds to decide that he was selling neither insurance nor vacuum cleaners, and curiosity probably did the rest. He was shown into a sitting-room with a, "Won't you take a seat?"

Travers told her she was obviously a woman of discretion, and let her catch a glimpse of his credential card with the words "Scotland Yard." It was to do with the disappearance of a young lady that he wanted her valuable assistance, and he showed her the *Tatler* picture, from beneath which the name had been removed.

"She's not the one they were asking about on the wireless!" She was immediately enthusiastic.

"No," said Travers ponderously. "I'm afraid not. We haven't got to that yet. You see, this is a wealthy young lady who's suddenly taken into her head that she wants to live her own life—greatly to the distress of her relatives."

"What's her name, may I ask?"

"Her name?" Travers was sure he'd blushed. "Oh—er—Travers; but that's in strictest confidence. She didn't use that name down here. The thing is," he went on hastily, "can you tell us what she did down here so that we can get some idea of the people she met and so on, to see if she dropped a hint of what she was going to do when she left here."

Susan Allard, he promptly learned, had apparently been in the house quite alone, except for an Alsatian dog. She had left every morning, sometimes early, sometimes late, but always before lunch, and she rarely returned before tea-time. The dog was nearly always left behind in the house. Sometimes she had books under her arm. The bus to the town, as Mrs. Cocks pointed out, passed the end of the lane, a hundred yards away.

Travers nodded away mysteriously. "We have definite information," he said, "that she left here last Monday. I suppose you didn't see her leave?"

But Mrs. Cocks had. At about ten o'clock a perfectly magnificent car had called up. Miss Travers had been on the look-out for it and had the gate open so that the car drove straight in. About half an hour later it drove out again, though Mrs. Cocks hadn't been able to see who was in it. An hour later it returned, and it was Miss Travers who got out to open the gate. She was wearing a brown costume and small felt hat. Whoever it was that had driven the car must have stayed to lunch, for it was not till three o'clock that the car finally went off. Again it was Miss Travers who opened and shut and locked the gate. The car took the direction of the town.

"That might be to give the keys up," said Travers. Five minutes' further stay produced no further information, and after the most profuse of farewells he went back to Lewis.

"Well, sir," said the sergeant, "was she a winner?"

"Don't know," said Travers. "We're not past the post yet."

Lewis heard all there was to hear and seemed rather disappointed.

"That doesn't get us much forrader, sir."

"I don't know," said Travers. "I've got the merest suggestion of an idea. Let's go along and see that house agent."

CHAPTER XIV
ONE USE OF CAKE

IT WAS quite dusk by the time they reached the town, and as soon as rooms were booked at the hotel they had a spot of tea. Travers was anxious to get on with the business; a jig-saw can be even more fascinating when you have to find the pieces first—or make your own. Lewis had been puzzling his wits, ever since he heard it, over that cryptic remark Travers had made after leaving Mrs. Cocks' bungalow, and at last he ventured to put the question.

"So you think you've got hold of something, do you, sir?"

"I won't say that," Travers told him, "but we seem to have got hold of a remarkably peculiar set of circumstances. Take Miss Allard, for a start; a woman who's never soiled her hands in her life, worth a couple of thousand a year, and going down to a solitary cottage by the sea—in March, mind you—and fending for herself; the maid, who might have been useful, having been meanwhile sent on a holiday for a month. And she lied to her brother about it all."

"Perhaps she thought she'd like to look after herself for a change," suggested Lewis. "You never know what people like her'll do next. Look at that queen, Marie Something of France, who used to milk cows. And not only that, sir, she wouldn't naturally like her brother to know about it because he might have been horrified."

"Perhaps you're right," said Travers. "But there's the other point, that she had no visitors; or more remarkable still, that if she had any, they came so secretively that even the lynx-eyed Mrs. Cocks saw nothing. And we can't get away from the point that she was uncommonly anxious to get hold of that letter she wrote to her brother, and that's peculiar in itself since the brother was dead. I mean she didn't need to give a cuss about him."

He rose to his feet and Lewis gave him an inquiring look. "What now, sir?"

"Think I'll find the private address of that house agent," said Travers. "You take my advice and treat yourself to the movies."

He got the address from the telephone directory and set off in one of the town busses after calling to say he was coming along. The visit turned out to be a waste of time as far as new information was concerned. True, the agent definitely identified Sue Allard from the picture, but there had been no reasonable doubt about that all along. She had taken the house under the name of Mason.

"I suppose you sent somebody along to clean up after she'd gone?" Travers asked.

"Oh, yes. We have a woman who does all our places for us."

"Nothing unusual left behind? No letters or anything?"

"I shouldn't think so," the agent told him. "All our employees have strict orders about reporting anything found. If there was anything else unusual she'd have been sure to mention it."

So much for that. At the station he looked at his watch and decided it was far too soon after tea to be thinking about dinner, and as there was no time like the present he took a taxi and set out for The Views. Quite a cheerful party seemed to be assembled inside judging by the sounds of revelry by night, but the maid soon brought along the head of the household to the room where Travers was waiting. An affluent, jolly sort of person he turned out to be, though his face straightened somewhat when he scanned the credentials. Travers told the same tale that he had poured into the ears of Mrs. Cocks. Once more the visit appeared to be time wasted, except for the whisky and soda which was courteously accepted.

"So it was all spotlessly clean, was it?" said Travers.

"Like a new pin," he was told. "Never a piece of paper or anything."

Travers nodded, then put the same question another way. "Tell me; suppose you hadn't known who had had this place before you, could you have guessed in any way from . . . well, from any impressions you gathered when you got here?"

The other laughed. "If I'd known it was a woman who'd had the place I'd have put her down as quite a good sort. There was an empty champagne bottle—half-bottle, I should say—in the ash-bin by the garage, and a damn good brand too."

That, thought Travers, was on the only occasion when she had lunched there, though what she had to celebrate was quite another thing. In any case that was all the information he had to chew on during the ride back to the hotel, and all the prospects for the next day, as far as he could see, were to discover where she had usually lunched and to ascertain if she had had wine regularly with her meals—though what use that information would be when it was obtained he couldn't quite see. Then there was that library of which she had apparently been a member, and there might be the conductor of the bus that ran by the end of her road; both very vague hopes and scarcely worth the trouble involved.

After dinner he and Lewis spent the night exploring the possible avenues of inquiry, and it was decided that Lewis should try to get hold of a bus conductor while Travers ferreted out the library.

It was not till well after nine that breakfast was over, and by the time the papers had been looked through over the first pipe of the morning, it was ten o'clock. The two set off together down King's Road. Not fifty yards from the hotel Travers stopped dead.

"Must have a look in here," he said to Lewis. "Antique shops have the same fascination for me as the millinery places have for women."

"A ham and beef shop'd be more in my line," said Lewis, and waited for a bit while Travers peered through the window. Something seemed to be interesting him enormously, and Lewis strolled on to the next window. A further couple of minutes passed before Travers rejoined him.

"A perfectly delightful little Queen Anne mirror there," he said. "I couldn't for the life of me tell if it was a reproduction or not."

"Have a look at that, sir," said Lewis, pointing to the confectioner's window. "Is that genuine or is it a dummy?"

Travers smiled. "That's about the last thing in the world I'm a judge of."

But he had a look at the cake. It was a superb piece of work, as the owner of the shop no doubt realized, for it occupied the precise centre of the window with a space all round it. The bottom layer was well over a foot in diameter, the last and seventh would be about three inches, and what with the immaculateness of the white icing and the trailing orange blossom and the silver pellets and the little silver Cupid, it was a handsome affair if somewhat ornate. Travers expressed the opinion that it was far too decorative to be real.

Lewis nodded. "That's what I thought, sir. Give me a plain sultana one like my old mother used to make."

Travers suddenly stared into space, then, at his viewpoint in the middle of the pavement, began fumbling at his glasses.

"Do you know," he said, "I've had the most preposterous idea. Excuse me just a moment."

Lewis wondered what on earth it was that was suddenly galvanizing him into such speed as he showed to the island where the policeman was directing traffic. He watched Travers make an inquiry, saw the policeman's arm moving in indication, and Travers bolting back again to the pavement.

"Come along," he said. "We'll make them open up."

Lewis moved on in Travers' wake. "Who?"

"The Registry Office," said Travers. "Don't you think that's the solution?"

Lewis chewed hard for a minute on his cold pipe. Then he nodded. "Do you know, sir, I believe you're right."

"Do you think so?" said Travers, his face lighting up. Then he shook his head. "I don't know. It sounds too easy. And yet it fits. Three weeks down here, Lewis, where nobody she knew would be likely to come. Ample time to fulfill the necessary statutory period required for residence of one of the parties." He stopped short. "And why should she allow a chauffeur to be alone with her in the house from before lunch till three o'clock?"

Lewis moved him on again. "We'll soon find out when we get there, sir, wherever it is."

"Over here," said Travers, and crossed the road.

The registrar could not be located but somebody responsible heard what Lewis had to say, and there was no difficulty whatever. Travers was bursting with excitement as the pages were flicked over.

"Here we are, sir," said Lewis, putting a dramatic finger on the sheet. "Susan Fairchild Allard, spinster, aged twenty-three, to Mark Colin Ruston, aged thirty-eight, late Indian Army."

Travers hooked his glasses on again and had a look for himself. "Who are these two witnesses?" he asked.

"Just casual ones," said the official. "When the parties don't bring their own we arrange to supply them. Do you want this any more? You know you can get a copy at Somerset House?"

On the pavement outside the office Travers smiled like a schoolboy. He couldn't have looked happier if somebody had presented him with the contents of a dozen antique shops.

"Great work, sir!" said Lewis. "This'll make 'em think a bit at headquarters." His face fell somewhat. "The thing is, how's it help us? What good can we make of it?"

"Plenty of time for that," Travers told him. "Let's get back to that hotel and 'phone it through. If we haven't done anything else we've eliminated something." He clicked his tongue. "Weren't we a couple of fools? Everything plain as a pikestaff and we couldn't see it. Asking specially for the chauffeur to be sent down; trying to get the letter back so that we shouldn't know; the half bottle to celebrate; all fits in like a glove."

"Rum sort of thing for her to go and do, wasn't it, sir?"

"You mean the marriage?" He smiled. "Oh, I don't know. I'd say they'd make an excellent couple. He's quite a good chap. And what happened exactly after the wedding? I suppose she went to her flat in town and then to The Covers, where he had to wait till his time was up. On the Thursday morning he went to town as arranged, to wait for her, ready to take the train together to the South of France for their honeymoon. That's why she had to leave the house that morning—to tell him what had happened and to say she couldn't come. That's why he went back to his cottage place, to wait till the funeral was over and everything was settled. How everything was to be explained later to her brother—I mean if things had gone normally and he hadn't been killed—she was probably leaving to chance. In any case, she had plenty of her own to live on."

"It also explains just what he was doing wandering about the corridors in the early hours of the morning," said Lewis. "And if you ask me, sir, that queers our pitch with him."

Travers smiled as he shook his head. "Don't you believe it! He's the first one we've got hold of with a motive."

"But what'd he want to kill Crewe for?"

"I'm not thinking about Crewe," said Travers. "He had motive enough to kill Allard if he saw a chance of getting away with it. What was Allard going to think about his sister marrying a man—disregard what that man was for the moment—who'd been having his meals in the butler's parlour. And not only that. Two thousand a year mayn't be so much these days when you've carved income tax and what not out of it. On the other hand, Allard's income, which is now his sister's, would have made many a man chance his arm."

Just short of the hotel office Travers stopped.

"Why shouldn't we finish up the job for good and all? I mean we've got heaps of time, and we can't get through to Norris direct. Why not send him a message that everything's going well, and we'll roll up at about tea-time. Then we'll push off now and see Ruston and hear what he's got to say."

"Best thing in the world," said Lewis. "I'd like to see Ruston's face when you tell him the news."

By eleven o'clock they were on the road again. At twelve-thirty, within striking distance of the village, they stopped for lunch, so as to catch Ruston just after his meal. It was half-past one when the car drew up before the white gate.

"Would you mind if I ran my eye over him, sir?" asked Lewis. "I've heard a lot about him, and I'd like to fix him in my mind."

"In five minutes or so," said Travers. "I'll make an excuse to bring him along."

As he spoke there was the barking of a dog, and Ruston appeared at the front door, holding a grey Alsatian back by the collar.

"So he's looking after the dog," said Lewis. "Bit of a toff, isn't he, sir?"

"He's a toff all right," said Travers. He gave some unnecessary orders in a loudish voice, and then opened the gate.

Ruston stood by the door, gravely regarding the unhurried approach.

"Morning!" said Travers genially. "Here I am again, as you see, like a bad penny."

"Yes," said Ruston, and Travers didn't like the straight way he looked at him. "What is it this time?"

Travers gave the ghost of a shrug. "Oh, nothing much. Just clearing up odds and ends."

Ruston still made no move to ask him in. The Alsatian thrust out his nose, and Travers fondled its ears. The dog nuzzled to him in the friendliest way in the world.

"Great dog you've got here! Reassuring sort of fellows—Alsatians—aren't they?" He looked away vaguely towards the end of the untidy garden, then bestowed on Ruston his own most friendly smile. "I expect this chap was none too pleased with himself, being in the house all day while his mistress was out."

Ruston's face, already tanned with weather to the colour of old tiles, flushed with a more vivid red.

"I wonder if I might have a word or two in confidence," said Travers, and almost before he had finished speaking, found the way cleared for his entry.

He took his hat off and dropped it on the table, then drew himself up a chair. He went on speaking as if the conversation, or the monologue, had never been interrupted.

"Talking of dogs and all that, I'd be the last person in the world to butt into your private affairs. It's no concern whatever of mine. The trouble is, of course, that the police aren't always so careful, and I gather that you two people aren't any too anxious to have your—er—affairs made public at the moment."

Ruston spoke crisply—almost rudely. "Look here! Stop all that chatter about my affairs. Just what is it you want?"

Travers bridled up in a flash. He rose from the chair. "I don't know that I want anything that other people can't get just as well. There's a sergeant of the C.I.D. waiting in my car. I'll send him in to you."

Ruston flushed again. "Sorry! Unpardonable of me. Do sit down again. You see, I was a bit . . . a bit taken aback."

Travers sat down again. "That's all right. I shan't keep you five minutes in any case. Between ourselves, you gathered that we know just what happened last Monday?"

"Yes," said Ruston, and his eyes narrowed again.

"It was you that Miss Allard was so anxious to see last Thursday morning? Pardon the apparent rudeness, but I want the absolute truth, please."

"Yes. She had to come to warn me off. We were going away, you know."

Travers nodded. "A pity you didn't see fit, the other night, to take me into your confidence somewhat. You *were* in the house that morning at daybreak? I mean, it was you I saw outside my room?"

"Yes," said Ruston. "I'm sorry about that."

"That's all right," Travers told him. "I think perhaps you had every reason for saying what you did. But you do realize, don't you, that as soon as we discovered this morning what we did discover, you became much more interesting from the point of view of the police." He smiled forgivingly. "I knew you were going to be annoyed when I said that. I don't think I'd bother if I were you, provided your alibi's copper-bottomed. Tell me, for instance, can you help us by saying what happened after you filled up at eight o'clock at that garage you mentioned?"

Ruston nodded. "I've been thinking of that. Just short of the eighth milestone on the London Road a Harridge's lorry had broken down, and I pulled up to lend a hand. They told me they were going to Brighton and were only putting tape round a couple of wires of the horn. They'd know the time if they were asked, but it must have been about a quarter past eight."

"Splendid!" said Travers. "We'll get that verified, and metaphorically speaking you'll be a free man." Probably as a sign of peace he pulled out his pipe. "Mind if I smoke? And what did you think to yourself about that ghastly business?"

Ruston shook his head. "I've no more ideas than the man in the moon—and that's God's truth. I've thought about it for hours, but I'm damned if I can see a thing. I'll tell you this. Everything was normal when I was in the house that morning. I went out by the library door and dodged the two coppers. When I left I hadn't the foggiest notion that everything wasn't normal. Mind you, I'd read that tripe in the papers about threatening letters and all that."

"You didn't take it seriously?"

"Good God, no. Did you?"

"I didn't know much about it," Travers told him. "You knew Allard fifty times better than I did. And you thought he was the sort of cove who descends to stunts of that sort?"

"He was a queer mixture," said Ruston, and shook his head. "A damn queer mixture. Unbalanced, I think you'd call it. Sometimes he'd have the reserve of an old man, and then he'd go and do some damn silly thing that a schoolboy would fight shy of. You never knew how to take him. I must say I got along with him all right. I oughtn't to say it, but I think he was rather afraid of me—if you know what I mean."

Travers nodded. "And Crewe. What was your opinion of him?"

"Crewe," repeated Ruston, and grunted. Then he grunted some more and looked uncomfortable. "Well, I had intended to keep this to myself, but seeing as how you know what you do, I might as well spit it out. He and Allard hated each other like sin. I'm dead sure he knew something the other was damned scared of having let out." He stopped Travers' interruption. "No, it's no use asking me how I know it and what else I know. I don't know a thing—God's truth again—but I'd swear to that anywhere. Besides, it's plain for anybody to see. Crewe was a dirty little bounder, and there's no point in mincing matters because he happens to be dead."

"Quite. And there's nothing else you can tell us at all?" He got out of the chair and picked up his hat.

"Not a thing. Wish I could, in a way."

Travers looked at him. "For the last time; you're honestly holding nothing back?"

"Nothing at all. You've heard everything I know."

"Good," said Travers. "Then I don't think you need worry any more about us." He smiled. "I couldn't by any chance take a note for you? I'm just going to The Covers."

"Thanks." He flushed again. "That's very decent of you. I think I would like to scribble something—seeing as how." With his face towards the writing-desk he put the tentative question. "Will anything get out now? I mean will—er-"

"Not a word," Travers assured him. "The first 'phone we come to we'll make a start on that further alibi of yours, and then neither of you will exist as far as we're concerned."

He stood at the door regarding the monotonous landscape till the note was written. Ruston strolled with him to the white gate.

"Come and have a look at my car," Travers said. "There's no time to vet it, but you might like to have a look at the innards—being an interested sort of bloke."

Ruston smiled somewhat sheepishly. "As a matter of fact, I didn't know a Bentley any too well. If it hadn't been for that car of yours I'd have been away from the garage an hour earlier that morning. It was looking at the innards, as you call 'em that kept me there till nearly eight and sent me off without breakfast."

CHAPTER XV
STILL DREDGING

NORRIS'S CONFERENCE passed off very well, though nothing new came from the galaxy of brains that attended it. The only suggestion that was made—and Chief Constable Scott himself made it—was that since the revolver was missing and since it was too dangerous a thing for the murderer to keep in his possession, it had been thrown away. If, therefore, the woods produced nothing, it might be as well to search the lake.

Norris had had just the same ideas himself, but he was far too tactful to be other than grateful for the suggestion. The lake had quite a clear bottom since it was dredged every other spring. Some parts of it were actually concreted for the growing of special varieties of water plants. In any case the necessary apparatus accompanied him to The Covers that night, the first thing in the morning the work was begun from a boat after a test had been made to see how far from the bank the revolver might be expected to fall. In the meanwhile the search of the shrubberies and woods continued.

Norris was prowling round watching the progress of the various operations when one of his men came from the house. There was a message from Travers that he and Lewis would be there that afternoon. Also a Lady Wendley had called from London. She had some information concerning the case and would Mr. Norris either call or send a representative to see her.

Just after two o'clock he was rung up by Travers with the news about Ruston and the second alibi that was to be tested. If Susan Allard hadn't been away at the funeral he might have had a few words with her; as it was he got hold of the Yard and set the alibi business moving. Then as he left by the front door he thought of something—the furtive way Samuels, according to the butler, had sneaked out that morning. He sent for Mason at once. The butler came out with him and showed the route Samuels had probably taken, if he had wished to avoid being seen.

It led straight to the lake, and at the nearest point, between lake and house, was a gigantic clump of rhododendrons.

In five minutes the boat had been shifted from the other side of the lake to work in the likelier spot. Norris watched for a bit then moved on restlessly to the woods. Almost as soon as he reached the slowly moving line of searchers, he was overtaken by one of the men from the lake. The pistol had been found!

Norris rubbed his hands as the equivalent of an, "I told you so," and set off back at almost a jogtrot. He held the revolver in his hand as if it had been a diamond.

"Hm! A Colt. Nothing else with it?"

"Nothing else at all," they told him.

"Never mind," said Norris. "Go on searching round the spot. If anything turns up let me know at once."

He rang up the Yard and sent the revolver off on the heels of the message. Then he treated himself to a pipe and began to think hard, and all his thoughts were directed to Taylor Samuels. A quarter of an hour later, the pipe not yet out, Travers and Lewis rolled up. Over tea they had a miniature conference.

"I don't think I'd be certain it was Samuels if I were you," said Travers. "Do any of those bedrooms, for instance, look over the lake?"

They had a look at the plan. Susan Allard's and Drew's were the only ones, and as it seemed little use looking at the former, they went up to the room Drew had occupied. One glance out of the window and Norris pulled a long face. Had the revolver been thrown from where they stood it would have comfortably cleared the rhododendron clump and landed in the water just where it was found. Norris scowled at the lake as if it had done him an injury, then his face cleared.

"Samuels or Drew," he said. "What's it matter which. From what we know of 'em they're one and the same person. Get something on one and you've got it on the other."

Just what he was proposing to do he didn't at the moment say.

Travers opened his mouth to speak, then closed it just as rapidly.

"Got something to suggest?" asked Norris.

"I don't think it's worth mentioning," said Travers. "All I was going to say was that we don't even know for certain that either Samuels or Drew threw the gun into the water. After all, if we believe that someone stole Drew's knife and carved Crewe with it, we can reasonably include in our suspicions the one that the knife—that particular knife—was used to throw suspicion on Drew. Which means eliminating both Samuels and Drew, since the same person might have continued to cast suspicion on either or both of them by using this window to throw the gun from." He smiled deprecatingly. "Bit vague, but there we are."

"There's something in it," said Norris, though none too enthusiastically.

As if to test what he had in mind he leaned out of the window. Below him a man came running round the path from the lake.

"Hallo!" shouted Norris. "Want me?"

The man stopped dead. "They want you round at the lake, sir. They've just fished out another gun and a packet of ammunition."

Norris was so surprised that his face was perfectly comical. "Good God! Did you hear that?"

Without waiting for a reply he bolted out of the door, Travers and Lewis at his heels. Round at the lake the boat was drawn in to the bank, and the two men were waiting expectantly. Norris made for the gun at once and opened the breech.

"Six cartridges in it!" He tipped them out into his palm one by one. "One empty shell—the rest all right. This is the one that did the trick or I'm a Dutchman."

Travers took the Colt and had a look at it, probably for the sake of holding the weapon that had caused all the trouble, since guns conveyed nothing to him as guns.

"What was in the other Colt?" he asked.

"Nothing at all," said Norris. He exhibited the small, cardboard box that held the ammunition. "Just holds four dozen, and six are gone. Here's the string the box was tied up with. What's more, look at the trade name on the box. Those shells were bought in Hollywood!"

"That seems unanswerable," said Travers, staring at the label.

Lewis was particularly pleased. "We know who we're to look for now. There were only three of them, and one's dead."

"Not so fast," said Norris, "or you'll have Mr. Travers reminding you that all this might have been done to cast suspicions on the two you're referring to. Still, let's get this off to the Yard."

They moved off slowly to the lounge. "Amazing thing!" remarked Norris, like a man with a grievance. "Can't make it out. Why two guns?" He looked round with the same comically aggrieved look on his face. "Damn it all, they may find another!"

Travers laughed. "Then you'd better go back to the lake and stop the dredging. All the same"—and his face straightened—"I don't see why you shouldn't find another. Three men from Hollywood and three guns; nothing unusual in that."

That remark kept Norris busy thinking till they entered the room. Then, in the act of taking off the receiver, he suddenly remembered something and took his hand away.

"When did you think of going back to town?"

"Well, I thought a spot of tea and then I'd get along," said Travers. "I just brought Lewis back in case you wanted to see me. Anything I can do?"

"You might take this gun and the ammunition along," said Norris. "Lewis, pack it up for Mr. Travers. Tell 'em what's happened, and say we're still dredging." He hesitated rather curiously, and Travers wondered what was coming. "I suppose you don't know a Lady Wendley, do you?"

A faint smile enlivened Travers' face. "Not the Nunc Dimittis?"

"The what?"

"Sorry!" said Travers. "Just a name my sister and I had for her when we were very young—I mean, if it's the one you're referring to. Lives at Plantagenet Square? Husband owns racehorses. Fickle Fanny, second in this year's National, if you remember."

"I don't," said Norris, "but it's the one all right. She wants to see us. Says she has something confidential relating to this business here. Suppose you wouldn't care to go along?"

"I'd love it," said Travers. "I haven't seen the . . . Lady Wendley for ages." His eyes opened. "I say, there may be something in it. Remember what I told you happened that afternoon at Fragoli's? Just before I left, Allard was dancing with the elder Wendley girl. Maud, that'd be; the younger one's Blanche."

"Right," said Norris. "You interview the whole family. What time'll suit you?"

"You push the bell for Mason," said Travers, "and we'll settle it over that spot of tea."

Norris had duly rung through, and at nine o'clock that evening Travers was admitted by Lady Wendley's butler into the drawing-room of her ladyship's town house. Lady Wendley herself, erect as a telegraph pole, swept into the room a minute later. The beam with which she greeted him faded delicately into a look of regret.

"Ludovic Travers! What on earth are you doing here? Years since you've troubled about me. And now I can't talk to you. Maud'll have to do that. How's Ursula?"

"Ursula? Oh, she's very fit. Delightful to see you again."

She nodded. "Do sit down. I'll send Maud in. It's the police, you know. Something very confidential about that Courtney Allard affair. Too dreadful, wasn't it?"

Travers cleared his throat with an almost inaudible cough. "As a matter of fact, I'm the police myself."

She stared. He explained at some length and managed to get the wind back to her sails; in fact she smiled with all her old aplomb.

"Of course. Your uncle's Chief Magistrate, or whatever it is. How *is* Sir George?"

"He was in great fettle when I saw him last," Travers told her. "And now might I presume to ask what it is you want us to know?"

The chesterfield on which she sat was back to the door, and Travers couldn't help but notice how she glanced round involuntarily, as if afraid, even in her own house, of being overheard. Her voice lowered to a sort of gurgle.

"It's Maud really. She and Courtney Allard were engaged; that is, they weren't really engaged, they were just on the point of it, if you follow me. I mean, everything was arranged and we were just about to send the notices to the Press. Quite an excellent young man in many ways, don't you think?"

Travers gathered that he was expected to agree, and promptly did so.

"Harry was very pleased about it," she went on. Harry was her husband, and Travers was not surprised at the information. "Then the most amazing thing happened. Not myself, of course; I mean, young people aren't what they were in my day, though that's not so long ago as you'd think."

Travers managed to interpolate the conviction that he was sure it wasn't.

"No; they arranged it together, and then we were told about it. He said everything was all right—or words to that effect—but he didn't want the engagement announced for a bit—"

"Pardon me," said Travers, "but just how long ago was this?"

"How long ago?" She thought furiously. "Time does fly, doesn't it! But I remember. It was just after he took up with that terrible Crewe person." She glanced round quickly. "Tell me, between ourselves, didn't he have something to do with it?"

"You mean the murder?"

"Of course!" She broke off. "Ah! Here is Maud. She'll tell you all about it. Come and sit down, darling."

Maud Wendley was wearing a scarlet gown that suited her dark complexion to admiration, but scarcely suited one who had had a narrow escape from widowhood. She seemed cheerful enough as she came across to Travers.

"Hallo! What are you doing here. And you haven't got a drink!"

Travers shook hands with a certain amount of embarrassment. The whisky was in before he had time to refuse it.

"You've been talking about me," said Maud Wendley accusingly. "You'd better own up, mother darling. What's she been saying, Ludo?"

Travers explained again at some considerable length.

"You didn't mind, darling?" asked her mother warily.

"Lord, no! The police'd have found out in any case. They always do. Bad luck on old Court, wasn't it?"

Travers said it was, added that the police had hopes and little else, and asked if she had any idea of the motive behind the peculiar attitude of Allard in deferring the public engagement.

"I haven't the foggiest," she said. "It was all right with me, you see, and I knew he was frightfully keen and all that. Mother told you what happened after?"

"I don't think she did," said Travers.

"Well, that's what we thought the police ought to know. We talked it over, didn't we, darling? Over a month ago, it'd be. Court said everything'd be all right in another month—"

"You mean the engagement might be announced?"

"That's right. Then, a fortnight ago, he said something was going to happen. He was rather excited at the time—we'd been to Pugnani's, you know—and he wanted me to promise that whatever happened I'd marry him inside a month. He was hinting at the most extraordinary things, and if it hadn't been for the others moving on—we were with the Quaines, Tommy and all that crowd—I'd have heard a lot more. One thing he did say, that either he'd get somebody or they'd get him. Those were the very words."

"I see." Travers thought, and thought hard. "Just tell me if I'm right. Did you get the idea that somebody or other was making things awkward for Courtney and he hoped to be free of their attentions inside a fortnight, and then not only could your engagement be announced, but you'd also get married practically straight away?"

"That's it. I think that's what the poor darling meant."

"Hm! Now an impolite question. He wasn't cooling off?"

"Heavens, no!"

"And you never had the idea that he was entangled with some woman? That he might actually be married to one?"

It was typical of her generation that she never turned a hair.

"Was he?"

Travers blushed, he didn't know why. "Well, no, not as far as I know, that is. You didn't ever think it?"

She smiled as she shook her head.

"And he didn't refer to it again after saying what he did that particular night?"

"Not a word. I knew if he had anything to say he'd say it. Frightfully bourgeois and all that."

"Quite. And when there was all that talk about threatening letters, what did you think then?"

"But they weren't threatening Courtney," broke in Lady Wendley. "It was that other man. What was his name—"

"Do be quiet, darling!" she was told. "Not that you're wrong, because you're not. You see," she explained to Travers, "I was frightfully annoyed about all that, and I told Court so. All he said was it wasn't anything to do with him, and there wasn't anything in it in any case."

"Quite. And what were the relationships between him and Crewe, do you think?"

"A poisonous little person! I just told Court I wasn't to see him. A positive emetic."

"Darling!" came the protesting voice.

Travers, having enough to digest for one evening, began to make his excuses, though it was an hour later before he managed to escape from the reminiscences of his childhood and the ramifications of a couple of families.

As he strolled back towards his rooms he tried to make some sort of sense of what he had heard that evening; something that would fit in. Crewe had definitely altered the course of Allard's life; that was one thing about which there could be no doubt. Moreover, Allard either had an infatuation for the man or was under his thumb; there seemed no reasonable doubt about that. If Crewe was blackmailing Allard, then the information he possessed was such as to be a bar to the engagement, and therefore might be assumed to be something about a woman. And if so, what woman? Surely not Margaret Laws, or whatever her name was? And yet ... he frowned to himself as he walked on. Crewe it was who brought her to the house. And if she stood in the way of the engagement, was it because Allard was married to her? But that would mean she was the one who should have been murdered. And if she knew all about it, why wasn't she blackmailing Allard too? Then, in the act of collision with another pedestrian, he had a brainwave. She *was* blackmailing Allard. Her price was a part in that show of his, just as Crewe's price was to run the show for the benefit of himself and his friends.

And yet that didn't quite fit in either. If it was Crewe that Allard hoped to eliminate, he'd be no better off if anybody else was left alive with the blackmailing information. If the noises he and Travers had heard together in Travers' room were not, after all, the sounds of Crewe's death, yet the fact remained that there was no means of entry. Allard couldn't have entered Crewe's room; Norris had been sure about that. And that, thought Travers, was a pity. Surely if anybody wanted Crewe out of the way it was Allard.

He was still feeling rather restless when he reached Trafalgar Square, and decided to walk on to the Embankment and 'phone Norris from the Yard instead of from his own rooms. An inspector whom he knew told him, to his amazement, that Lewis had just been in and had gone again.

"Do you know what for?" asked Travers.

The other didn't, but he got Travers his number. It was quite pleasant to hear Mason's voice at the other end of the line. Inspector Norris was upstairs, he said, but he'd send for him at once. When he came he made Travers repeat his story very slowly, and his voice could be heard methodically repeating it to the stenographer.

"That the lot?" he asked, when it seemed to be all over.

"Unless you'd like me to tell you a bedtime story," said Travers flippantly. "And how're things at your end? Fished up any more guns yet?"

"Not yet," came Norris's imperturbable voice. "We haven't got any guns but we did get one of those lasso things, like the one Drew used on our little window experiment. It was tied in a coil with a stone on the end."

Travers was too taken aback to say anything.

"And what's more," went on Norris, "we're still dredging."

CHAPTER XVI
ALL THE LATEST

THOUGH TRAVERS put in the whole of the following day at his own affairs, there were a good many minutes that he spent from time to time reviewing various aspects of the Case of the April Fools. The information that Norris had given about the discovery of the rope was indeed a facer. It now looked as if the marks on the creeper had not, after all, been made by the dutch hoe, and that the rope had been used by the murderer in escaping from the room. That meant that really there were two sets of marks on the creeper, so Travers finally decided: those made as a false trail by Crewe some time before he was killed, and made therefore by the dutch hoe; and those made by the murderer afterwards. The rope had doubtless been doubled over the hook, as Norris had suggested, and on reaching the ground the murderer had pulled it free and then hurled it and the gun into the lake. Whose the second gun was, and what it was doing there, Travers hadn't the faintest notion.

As for who the murderer was, that, he decided, was no longer problematic. It must have been Drew or Samuels or Franks—and he wished somehow he could have included Ruston. Those four alone might have been admitted to the secret of the fake murder, and those four alone might have known about the hook on which a rope could be put. It was while thinking of that, that he had a tremendous inspiration. That second gun; surely that was the one that Crewe had beneath his pillow, and the first gun was the murderer's own. Once the guns had been tested it would be known which one fired the shot that killed Allard, and that would be the murderer's gun. The other—Crewe's own—had been seen by the murderer, and he had slipped it into his pocket as he escaped, and had thrown it into the lake with his own gun and the rope.

Ruston, it seemed almost certain, could be eliminated straight away, but when it came to the other three, Travers couldn't for the life of him see rhyme or reason in it. Franks surely could be left out, since it was surely impossible that he could have been—for no apparent reason whatever—suddenly let into the secret of the stunt murder the very night he arrived at The Covers. And as for the other two, as Norris had admitted the previous night over the 'phone, he was up against a brick wall. If he threatened arrest they might call his bluff and laugh at him. Norris had already got hold of Drew and asked for information about the rope. Drew merely said that it had been lost at the same time as the knife, and what was more, he had told Samuels about the loss, and Samuels was prepared to swear to it on anything from a Bible to the *War Cry*.

"What are you going to make of it?" Norris' voice had come plaintively over the 'phone. All that Travers had been able to stammer was something about gum-trees.

The whole business was so puzzling that Travers determined to get some sort of order and logic out of it, and after tea that afternoon he set to work with paper and pen. It was not till dinner-time that his memorandum was in a fit state to be submitted to Norris. Then, after the meal, he felt the case so getting on his nerves that he made up his mind to take in some sort of a show. He had got as far as the lift when Palmer came puffing along to say that Inspector Norris would like to see him round at the Yard. Memorandum in his pocket, Travers set off at once.

"The very thing I was going to ask you to be good enough to do for us," said Norris, as he took over the foolscap envelope. "I'll put in an hour on it when we get back. I thought perhaps you'd like to go along with me."

The prospects sounded interesting. Among the other agencies approached by the Yard had been Finkelheims of Shaftesbury Avenue, who handled a considerable amount of booking for three of the principal cinema circuits. That morning they had been visited by a client who was disengaged, and this client had happened to mention that he knew very well two people who had been in the news of late—Margaret Laws and Percy

Franks. Finkelheims had asked no questions but had reported the matter to the Yard.

"Tony Street is the chap," said Norris. "Do you know him?"

"Good Lord, yes!" said Travers. "Used to be on the halls a lot. Did a kind of lazy juggler act. I wondered what had happened to him. Where's he been? The Provinces?"

"That's it," said Norris. "He had a bit of an illness, so they tell me, and dropped out. High-class movie theatres he's been doing mostly. Lives at Camden Town."

"Will he be in?"

"He'll be in all right," said Norris. "We got a message to him that someone was coming round at about nine on important business. It was on the Finkelheims' note-paper."

Street himself came to the door, and Travers recognized him at once from his elongated jaws, which seemed more suited to Hamlet than a minor Cinquevalli. He showed them into the sitting-room, chock-a-block with furniture and photographs and framed programs. Norris introduced himself and Travers, and at the same time produced three really first-class cigars. Travers contributed the pleasure he had often received from Street's act—one of the most original.

Ten minutes' reminiscence and circumlocution and Norris came to the point.

"Strictly between ourselves," he said, "a little bird has whispered that you're acquainted with two people we're interested in. We know 'em as Margaret or Peg Lorne and Francis Perolles. You may have other names for them." He noticed the way Street pricked his ears up. "They're not wanted for anything. Just routine work, as they happened to be down at Marbury when that murder happened. I expect you've read all that."

"Read it!" said Street. "Blimey! you could have knocked me down with a feather. Coming along in the world, thinks I, staying with the nobs. And all them posters all over the place. Have you seen 'em?"

Norris admitted that he had. More reminiscence followed.

"And that's how I first met up with them two," concluded Street.

"A smart little double turn it was. Wait a minute; I'll show you the bill. The Old Ranelagh at Shorefleet. Know it?"

"I can't say I do," said Norris.

"One of the best houses in the North. Always was. And clean. Lumme, you wasn't allowed to say damn." He stopped rummaging in the bottom of the cupboard to indulge in still further experiences, and when the search was resumed the bill failed to come to light. He stuck his head round the door.

"Ma! Where's that bundle of programs I was showing you the other day?"

Something was heard in the distance, and he closed the door.

"She don't know. Not that it matters. Still, I'd a liked you to have seen it. Something funny happened that night. Peg and Perce had a room booked up with Ma Leaper. Everybody knows about Ma. Don't matter where you go, anybody happens to mention Shorefleet, blow me if somebody don't start talking about old Ma Leaper, my name's not Street. You see these two rolled up on the Sunday night from Manchester, and Ma showed 'em two bedrooms. 'What's this?' says Perce. 'What d'you mean giving us two rooms. Peg and Perce,' he says, 'refined musical act. Ain't you never heard of us?' 'Oh, yes!' says Ma. 'I know them double turns. Hamley and George tried it on the last time they was here. What d'you think I am? A flapper?' And believe me or believe me not, poor old Perce had to wander round all the pubs in Shorefleet, that time o'night, till he found me to go along and tell Ma they was really married, so'd she'd let 'em have one room!"

Norris was suitably amused. Then, when he'd finished laughing:

"And how'd you come to know they were really married?"

"How?" Street winked. "Because I was witness at the Registry Office in Manchester where they got spliced the week before. That's why Perce had to find me, see?"

"And how long ago did you say that was?"

"How long?" He made strange noises for a moment or two. "Three years ago come next week. The way I know is because . . ."

When that was over Norris asked another question. "If this show was as good as you say it was, how'd it come to bust up?"

"The same old tale," said Street. "He got a bit swollen headed and she got temperamental, and from what I gathered at the time, he left her. About a couple of years ago that'd be."

"Hm!" said Norris. "So that little romance didn't last long. Perhaps you saw he's been singing in opera. How'd he come to know languages and all that?"

"Blimey! he always was a one for that," said Street. "In their act he always did something in French or Italian. Brings down the house every time if you've got a voice like his." He suddenly gave a surprised look. "You know who his mother was, don't you? La Belle Amy, she used to call herself. Did them extracts from opera with old Harry Finch; then did a solo act. Used to appear a lot at the Old Middlesex."

Norris nodded. "I remember her. She wasn't a fake, was she? She was really French?"

"She was French all right," said Street. "Now I remember . . ."

The reminiscences were ultimately continued at the nearest pub, to which Norris suggested an adjournment just before closing time. Then he and Norris took a prosaic bus at the Priory and climbed up on top.

"Satisfied?" he asked.

"Well," temporized Norris, "we knew most of it before—about that act of theirs for instance. It doesn't do to be too knowing when you're with a man like Street. I own we didn't know they were married. You see what she was scared of now, don't you?"

"I'm afraid I don't—unless it was of committing bigamy."

"That's it," said Norris. "That's why she tried to kid me with that yarn about not being serious over Crewe. She wanted to head me off from making inquiries."

"And what was she anxious to get hold of among Allard's papers?" asked Travers. "Not her marriage lines!"

Norris smiled enigmatically. "You never know with women. You bet she knew Allard made inquiries of some sort about her. All she wanted to know was what he knew. Why he drafted Franks into the show, for instance."

"And what are you going to do about it?"

"Nothing at present," said Norris. "You always want something up your sleeve with people like that. We might want to make her talk about something else one of these days. Franks now; we might have a quiet word with him when we see which way the cat's going to jump. Only for information, of course."

Travers was surprised. "You mean you don't think he had sufficient motive for killing Crewe?"

"Depends on what he thought of his wife," said Norris dryly. "He hadn't worried overmuch about her the last year or so. All he was probably scared of was the scandal it'd make—or it would have made rather—being dragged along to a police court to give evidence in a bigamy case. He didn't kill anyone. He hasn't the guts for one thing, and it wasn't he who borrowed Drew's knife and rope for another."

They were still arguing that out when they reached the Yard. One of Norris's men was waiting rather anxiously in his room.

"We didn't know where you were, sir, or we'd have got hold of you. Two or three things have come in."

"Right," said Norris. "Let's have a look at 'em." He took off his overcoat and stirred up the fire. Travers made himself comfortable in the one easy chair.

First came the statement of one of Harridge's men, who said he identified from the photograph submitted the gentleman who had spoken to him and his mate. He also described the car and gave the gist of the conversation and where it took place.

"Hm!" said Norris. "That's the end of him."

"Where'd you raise the photograph?" asked Travers.

"Miss Allard gave me one. I rather fancy he mentioned it in that note you brought. By the way, she should have left The Covers last night again. Staying in town for a bit." He gave a sudden "Hallo! This looks more like business."

Travers hopped up to inspect. It was a cable from New Orleans *via* New York.

Charles Crewe settled here nineteen-twelve, living
with married sister and accompanied by son, also Charles

Crewe. Believed to have been butler in English family but no occupation here. Son ran away from home but returned some years later. Sister dead nineteen-twenty; her husband nineteen-fourteen. Inquiries on lines suggested proceeding.

"What are you going to make of that?" said Norris, and regarded the cable at arm's length. "Butler over here. Made a bit evidently and thought he'd retire. Probably too high-toned for the son, who liked the look of the bright lights better. Then the son returned home, all forgiven; but went on with the theatrical game all the same." He grunted. "Reads like a tuppney novelette—and about as much use."

"I don't know if there's such a thing as a butler's society," said Travers helpfully, "but we might do worse than ask Mason if he ever heard of a butler by the name of Charles Crewe."

"Hm! Yes," said Norris, who evidently hadn't the least intention of doing anything of the sort. He put the cablegram on one side. "We'll wait to see if anything comes from New Orleans to-morrow, and if not we might do worse than try an S O S for information. What we're going to do with it if we get it is quite a different thing. We don't know that the father's death really had anything to do with the son returning to England. In any case I don't see the connection between either of 'em and Allard. Mason's always been the Allards' butler. If he knew the father he also knew the son, and he showed no signs of that."

"That's true enough," said Travers. "By the way, are you going down there to-morrow? If so I'll drive you. I'd rather like to look over the ground again if you don't mind."

"That's an idea," said Norris. "Say outside here at nine. Talking about butlers, what do you make of this?"

He passed over a half sheet of note-paper from his pocket-book. Travers took it to the light.

To my butler, Clifford Thomas Mason, the sum of five thousand pounds free of tax, as a mark of gratitude for services most loyally rendered and responsibilities willingly incurred, in the hope that he will still continue to render those services to my nephew aforesaid.

"Extraordinary business, don't you think so?"

"I don't know," said Norris, rubbing his chin. "It was old Allard he'd served and old Allard left him the money. He couldn't have been sure that Courtney Allard would pension the old fellow off when his time came. Also Mason was almost certain to die long before Courtney Allard in the natural order of things."

Travers smiled. "I know all that, but why's he still a butler? What's the special thing he's got to look after, that any other butler couldn't see to just as well?"

"To use one of your own terms, ask me another."

"But there'd be no harm in asking Mason himself to throw a little light on the matter," persisted Travers.

Norris sighed patiently. "If he tells us what an ordinary butler could tell us, it won't be worth hearing. If he's got something extraordinary tucked away in that head of his, then you can take it from me he's been paid five thousand Jimmy-o'goblins to keep his mouth shut, and neither you nor me'll pry it open."

"Yes . . . but what are you going to do?"

Norris waved his hand resignedly. "What is there to do? If we ask him anything intending to use it, we're enjoined strictly by the regulations to warn him first that he needn't say anything at all! If we want anything we've got to go on digging for ourselves."

Travers was aghast. "But that means you've got to go inquiring into Mason's past life and the Lord knows what." He made a gesture of humorous exasperation. "There's one thing about this case, from what I can see. It's turning out a geometrical progression. You'll never need another as long as you live."

"I wouldn't say that," said Norris imperturbably. "We know a lot about Mason. He told me a lot himself, for that matter. He was out in India and China with old Allard, for one thing." He got up from the desk and fished for his pipe. "I think I'll put in an hour at that summary of yours."

Travers, remembering that there was only one easy chair, began to make his excuses.

"See you here at nine, then," said Norris, helping him on with his coat. The question came rather too incidentally. "What's your opinion of Mason, by the way?"

"Mason? I don't know. I think perhaps he's a damn good chap. I like him. If you mean what's he like as a butler, I'd say he's a top-notcher."

Norris went over to the fire and bent down to light his spill.

"You don't think Mason might have killed Crewe?"

"Mason!" He laughed. "Good Lord, no!"

"Perhaps you're right," said Norris. "But it's curious how you—we all, that is—accept alibis. You'll remember that Mason vouched for all the staff being visible at the moment Crewe was killed. But who's to vouch for Mason?"

"But I saw him coming from the direction of the servants' hall when I went to the lounge door after I'd been trying to find a doctor's number!"

"That's nothing to go by," said Norris calmly. "That was a minute or two after the murder. Mason doesn't feed in the servants' hall, but he was there just as the last of the staff arrived, that is, just before Crewe was killed. After that he wasn't seen till you saw him."

"Funny!" said Travers. "What do you think he was doing?"

Norris shrugged his shoulders. "Don't know. He might have been rendering those loyal services we read about in that will of old Allard's. He might have been protecting his comparatively young master from the clutches of Crewe, whom, you may remember, he didn't like in the least. In other words," said Norris, with the first suspicion of a smile he'd shown since entering the room, "he might have been doing his special job of work."

Travers frowned. "And what job of work was that?"

Norris shrugged his shoulders. "Earning that five thousand pounds!"

CHAPTER XVII
DREW COMES ACROSS

MASON RECEIVED them officially as they entered the hall. Travers, regarding the old man, his deferential aloofness and his air of reserve that was almost patrician, found it hard to think that he had ever had a hand in the killing of anything.

"Good morning, gentlemen. Typical April weather, if I may say so."

"Yes, Mason, it is," said Norris genially. From his manner it was hard to believe that the previous evening he had made the serious, if ostensibly reticent, suggestion that Mason was a murderer.

"You'd like coffee, gentlemen, perhaps," went on Mason, as the footman took the coats. "I'll send it to the lounge at once."

"Very good of you," said Norris.

"A breakfast cup for me if you don't mind, Mason," smiled Travers.

"A breakfast cup, sir? Very good, sir." He gave a little bow, then took what looked like a letter from his breast-pocket. "Miss Allard left this with me, sir. I was to hand it to you personally, sir."

Norris took a look at it. "Thank you, Mason. We'd like to have a word with you in about a quarter of an hour, if you can manage it."

Norris slit open the envelope of the letter as soon as he got inside the lounge door.

"More matter for a May morning?" Travers remarked interrogatively.

Norris was frowning away as he read. There seemed to be two letters, and he slipped one between his fingers while he tackled the second. He passed that one to Travers as soon as he'd read it.

"She says she had that private letter from the solicitors yesterday, and as it was so remarkable she thought we'd better see it in case it threw any light on matters. She doesn't understand a word of it. What's on that paper is an extract. The rest of it, she says, was nothing to do with it."

Travers was frowning too as he read.

As I shall not be here to answer any questions I can be as frank as I like. There are two or three instructions I want to give you. I call them that rather than pieces of advice, and I want you to believe most urgently that they're the only things to do.

The first is that if Crewe hangs round you or attempts to make any too free with you or the house, send him about his business at once.

The second is that if anybody whatever attempts to blackmail you, remember that the law allows the victim to conceal his or her identity. If an attempt of that sort is made, *acquaint Mason first*, and then get hold of the police. I believe I have taken sufficient steps to ensure that nothing of the sort will happen, but if it does you will be prepared.

Above everything, whatever you do must be done to avoid any scandal. That is why I think the actions I have outlined are the best to cope with the situations if they *ever* arrive.

"Pretty conclusive, don't you think?" said Norris, as he put the letters in his bulging pocket-book.

"Yes. Perhaps it is," said Travers slowly. "He was being blackmailed by Crewe, as we suspected."

"There's more than that to it," said Norris, far more excited than was ever usual with him. "I was disposed to agree with what you said in that memorandum of yours, but we were both wrong. Crewe wasn't blackmailing Allard for something he'd done. Whatever the blackmail was for was something that affected both Allard *and his sister*. As I read it, Allard took the whole thing on his own shoulders while he was alive, but he knew once he'd gone, her turn would come to be threatened. Now then; what is there that fits that?"

Travers stretched his long legs to the fire and looked up at the ceiling. "I don't know—offhand. On the face of it, it must have something to do with what's common to them both, and the only thing I can think of there is parentage. If that means you've got to go casting your net wide enough to find the history of them, all I can say is what I said last night—that this case'll take you the rest of your natural life." He smiled. "But I don't think we need be quite so pessimistic as that. I don't mean that Mason will probably tell us what we want to know about their parents—"

"Pardon me," cut in Norris. "I'll say what I said last night too. If it's anything worth hearing, Mason was paid five thousand quid to keep his mouth shut."

"Perhaps you're right," said Travers calmly. "That merely allows me to make in comfort the point I was going to make. Courtney Allard may have done something really discreditable or even criminal. What concerns his sister is his good name now he's gone. That's where the blackmailer would get his chance to blackmail her."

The coffee arrived in the middle of that and they got out their pipes.

"Tell you what I'll do," said Norris. "I'll write her a note just to put her mind at ease, and tell her that if anybody even hints at anything resembling blackmail she's to let us know at once, no matter what happens. Then we'll have Mason in. I'll do the talking and you do the watching."

When the butler came in, Norris made such elaborate preparations to put him at his ease that he was rather bewildered.

"Sit down, Mason, and make yourself at home. Just an informal chat. One or two things you might help us with. Have some coffee. There's plenty left."

Mason sat down gingerly. "Coffee I've already had, thank you, sir And anything I can do, sir, I'll be most happy to do."

"We knew that," said Norris amiably. "First of all, we ought to tell you that in cases of this kind we have to cast the net very wide and ask questions which may not seem very much to the purpose. Now, about the parents of Miss Allard and her late brother. Can you tell us anything about them?"

"They were the children of the old master's only brother, sir. I can't tell you more about them, sir, because I happened to be in India at the time of his death, and the two children joined the family there. I always understood he was something in Australia, sir; a gentleman farmer or something of the kind."

"The late Mr. Allard adopted the two children?"

"That's right, sir. They went to a private school in Calcutta, sir, and then they were both sent home to school in England. The old master, if you remember, sir, definitely retired in nineteen-twenty-two."

"Quite," said Norris, who saw nothing of interest in the statement. "And now an apparently foolish question. I suppose in the course of your life you've ran up against scores of butlers, and heard them talk about scores more. In the whole course of your service, did you ever hear of a butler by the name of Charles Crewe?"

"William!" the word came like a shot. It came so suddenly that the speaker must have spoken involuntarily. And no sooner was the word out than the butler's face, that had shown an almost startled interest, resumed its mask of suave deference. "I beg your pardon, sir. I was thinking of someone else. Charles Crewe, sir?" He shook his head. "No, sir. Nobody of that name has ever come within my experience."

There was a difference in the sudden look he now gave. Travers afterwards described it as an artificial surprise.

"Charles Crewe, sir? Why, that was the name of the murdered man!"

"I know," said Norris, still sucking his pipe abstractedly and gazing into the fire. "We've found out that his father used to be a butler and that's all we know about him—at the moment. We expect more news at any minute from America."

"From America, sir." The words were merely a polite repetition, but on their heels the butler rose. "Was there anything else you wished to ask me, sir?"

"Was there?" He looked at Travers.

"I don't think so," said Travers. "Unless Mason cares to answer a very confidential inquiry. Whether he knew that Mr. Allard was being blackmailed by Mr. Crewe."

Mason's mouth half opened and his breath came quickly. If ever a man was distressed—and alarmed—it was he.

Norris looked up at him and saw his shaking hands and the obvious signs of emotion on his face.

"What's the matter, Mason?"

The butler moistened his lips. "I'm sorry, sir. The allusion, sir, to what has taken place. It was too much for me."

"You look as though a tot of brandy would do you good," said Norris. "And you never heard a word about any blackmail?"

Mason pulled himself together with a visible effort. "Not a word, sir. It was a thing I could hardly expect the late master to mention to me, sir." His shoulders lowered and he leaned forward with an air of inquiry that was almost pathetic in its half-frightened interest. "*Was* he being blackmailed, sir?"

"We don't know for a certainty," said Norris, "but we fear it."

"And do you know what was the—er—cause of the black-mail?"

Norris shook his head. "I only wish we did. That's where we were hoping you could help us."

The old man's figure straightened with an obvious relief. "I wish I could have helped you, sir." He hesitated. "Anything I can do at any time, I'm at your service, sir."

When the door had closed after him, Norris uttered only one word.

"Well?"

"He knows," said Travers. "He knows that Crewe was black-mailing him, and I'll bet a thousand pounds he knows why. And he was remarkably strange over that question about a butler called Charles Crewe. What'd he mean by popping out that word 'William'?"

Norris pulled a long face. "Don't know. The problem is, how can we squeeze our friend Mason and make him talk? It's no use asking Miss Allard anything. She's obviously in the dark. Do you think it's any use asking her to use her influence to make Mason open his mouth?"

"I think that's a capital suggestion," said Travers. "What'll you do? Ring her up or go and see her when you get back?"

"The personal touch, I think," said Norris. "I'll give her this written note of instruction at the same time."

"By the way," said Travers quickly, "something's sudden-ly struck me. There's something wrong somewhere about this blackmailing business. His private letter to her tells her she needn't fear blackmail, and that the law allows identities to be concealed. If he knew all that, why didn't he take his own advice? Why'd he allow himself to be blackmailed?"

Norris stopped sucking his pipe and looked round. "That's an idea. It is curious when you come to look at it. Unless"— and he paused impressively—"Allard determined to deal with Crewe in his own way, and if that failed it meant that he'd lose his own life. That's why he wrote a letter to be opened in the event of his death."

Travers got up and began prowling restlessly about the room. "I know. That's the devil of it. The one man who ought to have killed Crewe was Allard—and Allard was the one man who we're dead sure *didn't* kill him."

"That doesn't say he didn't get someone else to do it for him," said Norris. "Money counts in this life. What would it have taken to bribe Samuels or Drew or Franks?"

Travers clicked his tongue. "And that doesn't help. We've got to find out—" He stopped. "Let's go upstairs and have another look at those rooms."

They spent quite half an hour up there altogether without getting any further and after that they went down again and stood for some time in the shrubbery under the window of Crewe's room. They argued there for several minutes, then went round to the special door which led from the library—the door of which Allard had had the key in the pocket of his dressing-gown. Still more argument and they moved on towards the front of the house. Norris, half-way across the lounge window, drew back quickly, then unashamedly put his ear to the wall. With his right hand he motioned Travers to keep in the background.

They stayed there for three or four minutes like that, then Norris straightened himself.

"Come on! Let's go back the way we came."

"What was it?" asked Travers, turning with him.

"Mason, ringing up Miss Allard. I couldn't catch what he said because he kept his voice down, but I heard my name and yours." He stopped in the shelter of a rhododendron clump.

"I've got an idea. Let's go in normally and hear if he's anything to tell us. I wouldn't mind betting he's warned her in some way to keep her mouth shut. If so he's queered our pitch about asking her to get him to speak."

Norris seemed to be dead right. As soon as they entered the hall the butler came over to them.

"I've been looking for you, sir. Miss Allard has rung up, sir, to say she's finished all her—er—duties in London, sir, and she's leaving for France for her holiday—her interrupted holiday, sir—by the eleven-thirty train."

Norris's eye ran instinctively to the clock. It was already a quarter to twelve. He turned to Travers.

"Shall we have her stopped at Dover?"

Mason was watching like a hawk. Then all at once his hands began to tremble again.

Norris's eyes narrowed. "All right, Mason. I guess she can do with a holiday. You go and have that tot of brandy you ought to have had an hour ago."

"Thank you, sir." The butler moved off with an air of what certainly looked to Travers like exaggerated dejectedness.

Norris saluted his disappearing back with a grunt. "What about getting back to town? One or two things I want to do."

They sent word to Mason that they would not be staying to lunch, and in ten minutes were clear of the little town and eating up the miles on the London road. The case was left to look after itself till they came to Westminster Bridge, and then in a traffic halt Travers told Norris, most apologetically, what he'd tried to do for Samuels and Drew.

"I thought it wouldn't do any harm," he said. "It might keep them in touch without making them too aware of it. I haven't had any news yet as to how they're getting on."

"They were both down at Elstree yesterday," said Norris, in his most matter-of-fact tone.

Travers blushed slightly as he moved the car on. "What I was wondering was this," he said. "I don't want to queer your pitch, but I'd rather like to have them round at my place for a non-ceremonial meal and a yarn. Anything, for instance, that you'd like me to hint at?"

"Hint at?" Norris snorted. "I'd like you to stand 'em both on end and shake some truth out of 'em."

"Well, I'll try," said Travers modestly, "though I'm going to find it rather difficult with Samuels."

. . . .

That was why Travers did not dine alone that night. He had called at the hotel, but neither Samuels nor Drew was in, so he left a message. He was out himself when Palmer took the return call, to the effect that Samuels wasn't any too fit, but Drew would be glad to come round alone at seven o'clock as Travers had suggested. When he arrived, with the same grave shyness he had generally exhibited at The Covers, Travers felt a sudden glow of something remarkably like affection.

"Extraordinarily good of you," he said, as Palmer took the coat and hat. "Make yourself at home—and have a short drink. And what's all this about Samuels?"

Drew sidled to the easy chair after a long look round, which suggested the fear that Norris might be hidden beneath the table or the flap of the open bureau.

"Sam's had a tough break," he drawled. "When he got to that studio you were good enough to give us an introduction to, he found it full of people from the States. The first thing, one of the camera men came across and shook hands with him. So everybody in the studio knows who he is." He left the rest of the story to the imagination. "Sam wasn't feelin' any too good after that, and he's taking it easy back at the hotel."

"I got a letter about it to-night," said Travers. "I think that can be arranged all right. You might tell him I said so, will you?"

Drew looked at him. "Sam'll be glad to hear that, Mr. Travers." He shook his head, smiled to himself, and finished off the drink.

Then dinner arrived and the two ate and yarned. Travers got his man talking about his earlier experiences and how he came to get into the show business, and it was not till the meal was over and they'd drawn up to the fire again, Drew with a cigar and Travers with a pipe, that Drew himself made the first mention of the case.

"I guess Sam and I are in a pretty tight jam," he remarked reflectively. "That rope and knife business of mine doesn't sound any too good to"—he almost said "you," but stopped in time—"to Scotland Yard."

"I don't think I'd worry too much about that if I were you," Travers told him. "And by the way, please don't include me with the police—at least tonight. This is a friendly affair. What you say here is for you and me. That all right?"

"Sure. That's O.K. with me."

"For instance," smiled Travers, "you'll now understand what I mean when I tell you unofficially that you and Samuels have nothing whatever to worry about—provided you've told the truth and kept nothing back. If, between ourselves, you have doctored what you know to suit yourselves, then if they discover it, it's apt to be rather awkward for you."

"I get you," said Drew.

He made one or two motions to speak before he got off his mind what was troubling him.

"Sam and I have been thinking. Perhaps you'd break it gently to the Chief. We held back on him about the reason Charlie came over here. Sam and I thought it was something he saw in a paper. As things happened, we thought it better not to lay that before the court."

"I see." Travers nodded gravely. "Don't tell me if you don't feel like it, but just what was it you saw him excited about in the paper?"

"Well, it was like this. It was after he got back from burying his old man, and soon's he saw Sam and me he showed us this story in the paper about Allard who'd been spendin' a hundred thousand dollars on a show in London here."

"An English paper, was it?"

"Sure it was! Charlie brought it back with him. Said his old man used to have 'em sent to him regular. He said: 'That guy is goin' to put us three on the map,' and when we asked him to explain he shut up closer'n a clam. We figured—Sam and me—that he had some kind of a hunch." The wry smile hovered at the corner of his mouth. "Guess we were wrong."

Travers nodded. "Tell me just one thing. I know what that paragraph was. I may remember the paper it was in. It was about that last show—his first really—that Allard put on in town. It probably cost him twenty thousand pounds. But what I want to know is this. Was it a paper Crewe had, or a cutting?"

"A paper."

"Then was the paragraph marked in any way? With a cross, for instance?"

"Sure. It was about that long"—he indicated with his hands apart—"and there was a red cross at the corners."

He volunteered no more information, and Travers asked for none and tried no circumlocutions. It was ten o'clock when Drew rose to go. He said he'd had a great evening—and he had. Also he had to be up in the morning and down at the studio early. Du Fresne, he said, was a great fellow, and if things didn't break too badly he was sure of making good. At the lift he nearly broke Travers' fingers with his handshake.

Travers poured himself out a very weak drink and drew his chair up to the fire again. Drew's one disclosure seemed to him to be of the most tremendous importance—especially when linked up with the other events of the day. *If* old Crewe had marked that paper with a cross it showed he took an interest in the affairs of the Allard family. *If* Crewe found that paper among his father's effects after his death and immediately proclaimed that Allard was the man to make the fortunes of the three men, it showed that the father, before his death, had confided to the son some secret about the Allards—the secret, in fact, which Crewe had found so profitable. And *if* Mason was really acquainted with a butler of the name of Charles Crewe, then Mason knew what that secret was—and if not that, at least who old Charles Crewe was, and what his relationships had been to the Allard family that made him take an interest in the nephew's doings.

Before Travers' ruminations had lasted out the drink, the telephone bell rang. It was Norris, ringing up from the Yard.

"I knew you'd be up," he said, "till at least midnight."

"You haven't rung me up to tell me that old tag about wealthy and wise," retorted Travers. "What's the news?"

"What I had a suspicion of this morning," said Norris. "Susan Allard never set a foot near France. I left two men on watch and sent another to Ruston's place. She went straight to Marbury during the afternoon—as soon as we got away, in fact. Apparently she went on to Ruston after that. She was still there half an hour ago."

"What's the idea? Been having a conference with Mason?"

Travers heard a grunt over the 'phone.

"That's it. About time that bloke did something to earn that five thousand pounds."

CHAPTER XVIII
ONE NAIL ON THE HEAD

TRAVERS WOKE EARLY the following morning, his brain working at full blast. He had gone to sleep with the previous day's events chasing each other through his mind, and now he was resuming where a scant six hours' sleep had cut him off. With that newspaper extract specially worrying him, he called up the Yard before he had his breakfast, and managed to get hold of Lewis.

"Morning, Lewis. Any more news?"

"Not from this end, sir," said Lewis. "Mrs. What's-her-name spent the night down there as far as we know. That's the lot from this end. You got anything?"

"Not at the moment," Travers told him. "Still, we're hoping, you know. Nothing from New Orleans?"

"There was something, but not much use. They're still carrying on inquiries, but the old boy seems to have kept his mouth shut tight about everything in England. . . . You there?"

"I'm here all right," Travers assured him. "He and Mason seem very much on a par, what? By the way, there *is* one piece of information you can give me. Did Crewe have any effects?"

"Didn't you know, sir?" Lewis seemed genuinely surprised. "He had quite a lot of professional stuff in one of those rooms above the garages. Few private things as well."

"Good! Can you tell me if he had any newspapers or newspaper clippings among 'em?"

There was a pause at the other end of the line. "Well, sir, I went through the lot myself, and I don't remember anything of the kind. Between ourselves, after what you told him over the 'phone last night, I rather fancy the Old Man's going down there this morning to have a look-see for himself." He gave a little chuckle that had something questioning about it. "Working on the same lines as yourself, sir."

So much for that. After breakfast Travers got his pipe alight and settled himself before the fire. The problem, as he now saw it, was to get behind the mentality of Samuels; to see the kind of thing he might still be holding back. It would be something that was likely to bring into disrepute those good qualities with which Samuels, who doubtless owed Crewe much, had endowed him; and something, moreover, that was not likely to do Samuels himself much good in the eyes of the police.

The first conclusion at which Travers arrived was that Samuels need no longer be afraid of notoriety for himself. He had been recognized at Elstree, where his story was well known. If, therefore, he had been keeping something back because it might draw attention to himself, there was now no need for secretiveness. The second conclusion Travers reached was that if Samuels had been keeping quiet because he felt himself indebted to Crewe and had a considerable respect for the good name of the dead man, that drawback to freedom of action and speech was now removed, since once Samuels could be convinced that Crewe had been that lowest form of skunk—the blackmailer—mere indignation would make him open his mouth.

Travers even went further than that. Why should not Samuels be shown that Crewe had even tried to incriminate Drew? What was Samuels' code? Was it that of the man who is befriended by a killer and outlaw and who thereafter, whatever the deeds and reputation of that killer, refuses to give him away?

Did the allegiance and gratitude of Samuels stretch to that quix-otic point?

Half-past nine arrived and Travers had got no further for-ward. He lighted another pipe and shifted his ground. Moment by moment he went over Samuels from the first second he had clapped eyes on him. Was there anything he had done, anything he had let fall, that might be profitably interpreted? And be-fore Travers had spent five minutes on that line of research, he gave a little grunt. Then he hoisted himself up in the chair and began polishing his glasses. There was one thing Samuels had mentioned; more than that, he had dragged it into the conversa-tion by the scruff of the neck. That too offhand question he had asked about the Mercer Case!

In under half an hour he was in Bouverie Street and sitting on a high stool with a score of issues of the *Sunday Worker* piled before him.

He found the exploration a matter of difficulty. It was not as if the Mercer Case had been a normal murder, with full reports of the trials. It was not that Mercer himself had died, and one had nothing to do but read the account of the inquest. It was far different from that. Even at the death of Mrs. Mercer there had been no extended inquest, since the police were fully cogni-zant of the murderer. What information, therefore, that Travers obtained had to be sifted from a mass of chatty and irrelevant material, and at the end of two hours, what he had accumulated was merely this.

Stuart Mercer was an extraordinarily brilliant doctor, with several books to his name that made definite and important contributions to medical science. His name first came into no-tice in an oblique way when he was called on to give evidence in the case of the inquest on that patient of his who had committed suicide after, and as a result of, the wrong diagnosis Mercer had made. Mercer's conduct and speech in the coroner's court had given rise to much comment.

The next thing was when another patient brought an action against him for diagnosis and treatment that had been fantas-tically absurd. Mercer then did a most indiscreet thing, which only his madness explained—he fulminated in the Press against patients generally, and laid down some new and wholly Gilbertian theory that even though a patient was not at the moment suffering from a particular complaint, it was the doctor's province to forecast whether he might, even in the remotest future, suffer from that particular disease or complaint, and proceed to give him such treatment as would make the complaint innocuous. Some other big gun thundered a reply; Mercer promptly counterblasted; the Press called for action by the B.M.C., and then the real sensation occurred. Mrs. Mercer was found dead by one of the maids, and the police were called in at once. Mercer, then almost gibbering mad, calmly owned that he had injected prussic acid. After that, as Travers had told Samuels at the time, there had been panic among the numerous clientele of Stuart Mercer, since none of them knew if his diagnoses in their cases had been correct or were also fantastic.

So much for the case as it concerned Mercer himself. The two amazing things that Travers' inquiry elicited were these. Mrs. Mercer, before her marriage, had been the Hon. Alysia Fairchild—and the name of the new Mrs. Ruston had been Susan Fairchild Allard. And called to give evidence—formal evidence—on the death of Mrs. Mercer had been Mercer's butler—Charles Crewe! whose full name was Charles *William* Crewe.

Travers felt much like a man who has heard about diamonds, and read about them, and never having seen them, nevertheless holds two in his hand. He looked at his diamonds and wondered if they were real—and what could be done with them. But Norris would decide about that, and as soon as he could he called up the Yard. Neither Norris nor Lewis was there, but he got hold of the inspector at The Covers. He heard Norris's gasp when the news was told him over the wire.

"Right!" he said. "That's about all we want. Can you get down here at once, and in the meanwhile I'll work out a scheme for making our friend speak."

"An hour and a half and I'll be with you," Travers told him.

. . . .

And as soon as Travers did arrive at The Covers, Norris took him aside for a short council of war. The facts were gone over, the leading questions prepared, and the decks cleared for action—at least the table was set out in the lounge, and Norris took his seat officially behind it, with Travers just below the salt, and Mason's chair in the lone limelight.

It was curious how on such occasions Travers always felt his heart beginning to beat a little faster. When the butler entered the room and closed the door gently after him, Travers' heart began to race as if in the presence of some dramatic and intensely personal likelihood. Somehow, too, whatever happened, he felt overwhelmingly sorry for Mason. In his heart of hearts, too, he was hoping that Norris would not be too severe.

Norris fingered his papers before he spoke at all. Mason stood there, watching quietly, as if all eternity was time enough for him, then Norris suddenly looked up.

"Sit down, Mason, will you. Just a few questions we must ask you. And no recriminations."

"Recriminations, sir?"

"That's what I said. We agree to forget various things you've told us already, and we do that only because we believe that it's occasionally part of every man's creed that to do wrong that good may come of it is not an offense at all. You've lied to us, Mason, and you know it. Luckily for you, we know why." He waved his hand. "But that's all past. We're starting afresh. You'd like to do a service—a very great service—to Mrs. Ruston?"

The butler couldn't find words. He merely looked the answer.

Norris leaned back in his chair and wagged the pencil he was holding.

"A year or two ago a certain man refused to give me information which I asked for in confidence. He preferred not to talk because the law says he needn't talk unless he likes. You, for instance, needn't answer a single question I put to you or volunteer any information. But I wouldn't like to have happen to you what happened to the man I mentioned. We found out what we wanted to know, and it consequently had to become public—with results that were, for him, disastrous. You can give us certain information here and now, and I give you my word in advance that never a word of it will ever get out." He leaned forward. "The secret you've kept all these years will still be a secret. Now, Mason, what about it?"

Mason was disturbed—Travers could see that—but he still made a fight of it.

"If you would give me some clue, sir, as to the nature of the information you require?"

Norris smiled. "Drop the 'sir' and let's be three men together. We'll talk as men to men. Loosen yourself up, and don't sit there watching us as if we're trying to do harm either to yourself or anybody else. We're here to help. What you tell us is as safe as it'd be with your doctor or a priest." He turned to Travers. "Mr. Travers here and myself could tell you some things, if we were free to do so, that would set all London talking."

"Quite so, sir." But he still hesitated.

"What I'm getting at is this," went on Norris. "You mayn't understand why, but it's always better for information to come from somebody like yourself than for it to come from us—though we know it already. You don't see the point? Well, it's this. We know perhaps what we ask you to tell us. But you tell us on the condition that nothing's said to a living soul, and therefore the secret information remains secret, whereas if we used it ourselves we'd make such use of it as looked like being most good, without caring two pins about anybody's feelings." He leaned forward again, speaking very distinctly. "If, for instance, we want various details about Charles William Crewe, who was the butler of that poor chap Mercer, or want details about Alysia Fairchild before she was married . . ." He shrugged his shoulders and left the rest to Mason.

Before that last sentence of Norris had finished, the butler was twitching his fingers nervously. He tried to speak, but the words refused to come, and he moistened his lips. Then at last he got something out.

"Don't, sir! For God's sake don't do that!"

"It's the last thing I want to do," said Norris. "We want to spare everybody." He almost risked saying 'Mrs. Ruston,' but stopped short in time. He turned to Travers again. "What Mason had better do is to begin at where he entered the story; don't you think so?"

"Yes, I think so," Travers contributed gallantly.

"And nothing is to be said about . . . about anything I may have felt it my duty to tell you before?"

Norris made a large gesture. "Forget it. Didn't I say no recriminations?"

There were times in Mason's story where both Norris and Travers lost the thread, but the story was allowed to come in its own way, without more interruptions than were absolutely necessary. And to indicate in some small way that the talk was private and informal, Norris got out his pipe. Travers followed suit.

"You see, sir, I happened to be in England at the time," began the butler. There was a certain old-fashioned stiltedness about his language that went admirably with his natural dignity. "I had been unwell for some time, and the old master—I call him that, sir, to distinguish him from Mr. Courtney—the old master, I was saying, sir, sent me home for six months from Calcutta, where we then were, sir. He had always been good to me, sir, and he trusted me with affairs that were an honour to undertake, sir, though I was a younger man then than I am now. But that's not quite the point, sir.

"The old master wished me to consult Dr. Mercer, sir, since the doctor knew me very well, and of course I knew Miss Alysia. She was the old master's half-sister, as you doubtless know, sir, their mother having been twice married. The doctor prescribed for me, sir—that being while the poor gentleman was . . ." He broke off with a quick, "You know all about the tragedy, sir?"

"Most of it," said Norris. "But tell the story in your own way."

"Well, sir, the doctor did me a lot of good, and I hoped to return to India before my time was up. I met Mr. Crewe several times, sir, but he was always known as William, sir. That's what he was called in the house, and that's why I saw no connection between him and ... and the unfortunate man who was killed in this house, sir. I knew also, sir, for reasons which you'll hear in a moment, that he had a son who was living with his grandmother in the country, but I never had occasion to inquire after that son's name. Also, while I was in England, I often went down to the cottage Miss Alysia had at Richmond. The two children were always there, sir. She had an objection to them coming to town. At that time, sir, Miss Susan could just prattle and Master Courtney was quite a boy; I mean he had left, the baby stage, sir."

He shook his head solemnly. "I can remember how I felt when the tragedy occurred, sir, as if it was this very moment. The first thing I thought about was the children, sir, and I got permission from the solicitors to have them taken away at once to my own mother's home in Hampshire. She knew about everything, sir, and when she died, it died with her. Also I'd cabled to the master, sir, and I got instructions from him from time to time. You see it all fell like a thunderclap, sir, and there wasn't time for him to get to England. Then what I did, sir, was to engage a nurse for the children and take them back with me as the master instructed."

Norris made his first interruption. "Pardon me, Mason, but weren't there any relatives at all?"

"Not one, sir. It may sound strange, sir, but there wasn't a soul—except some cousins of his, sir, and they were only too anxious not to have their names associated with anything."

"And the nurse? She knew the secret?"

"She did, sir, but she was chosen for certain qualities." There was an underlying and justifiable pride in the way he said it. "She must have learned the secret in any case, sir, because the children naturally knew their own names. But they soon forgot those—their surname, I mean, sir—after the master changed them to his own. Nobody out there had the least suspicion, and quite a lot of money was spent here, sir, to keep it out of the papers so that the children should never have any scandal attached to their names. Both forgot everything, sir. Both were kept at school in India, and neither came home till we all came. The nurse—Elizabeth—died when the children were still young."

He was still shaking his head reminiscently when Travers coughed quietly.

"And Crewe?"

"Crewe, sir? He was paid handsomely, sir, to keep his mouth shut, and I believe he lived honourably up to his promise, sir. He received his allowance monthly through the bank, and after the old master died, sir, so that Mr. Courtney shouldn't have any suspicions, a capital sum was left to draw on. The grandmother had died by that time, sir, and he had taken his boy to America with him. The boy, needless to say, sir, had no knowledge of what had happened, neither had the sister—I believe it was, to whom he went. Personally, I have never heard of him, sir, from that day to this."

"And you did all that?" asked Norris in admiration.

"Well, sir, somebody had to do something. I may tell you, sir, that when I reached Calcutta I was in a state of alarm, sir, for fear I had done anything wrong or exceeded my instructions." He smiled gently. "I am glad to say, sir, the master was quite satisfied."

Norris nodded heavily for quite a long time, then he got to his feet and held out his hand.

"I'd like to shake hands with you, Mason. If there were more servants like you there'd be less talk of ..." The thread trailed away with the handshake.

Mason seemed very upset. "Thank you, sir. It's very good of you, sir."

"Nonsense," said Norris, and clapped him on the shoulder before he sat down again. "And you understand, don't you, Mason, that not a word of this becomes public? And now for a further confidence. Did you ever suspect that Mr. Courtney was being blackmailed?"

"No, sir," said Mason frankly. "How could I, sir? I saw no connection between . . . between that man and the William Crewe I'd known twenty years ago."

"Exactly." He seemed to be casting about in his mind for something further to ask, then shook his head. "There's no point in asking you for the why and wherefore of this and that. All that matters is that this and that happened. Have you anything to ask, Mr. Travers?"

"Something desperately important—from the point of view of two people," said Travers, as he fumbled at his glasses. "You had a confidential talk with Mrs. Ruston after we left here the last time, Mason. You didn't reveal to her who she was?"

The butler's eyes opened in horror. "That, sir! I'd rather have cut my tongue out, sir."

"You merely sounded her to see what she might know."

"That's what I did, sir." He flushed slightly. "To tell the truth, sir, I'm afraid I fabricated something to account for my questions." He gave a little bow. "She knew nothing, sir, nothing whatever."

"I'm glad of that," said Norris. "It'd have been pretty hard lines on you, Mason, after hanging on to the secret all those years, to have to give it up." He saw the other point, and gave a quick, apprehensive look at Travers. "And, of course, she'd have been in a fearful state. She never ought to have married. She oughtn't to have children!"

"That part's all right," said Travers. "It wasn't insanity as such—if I may put it that way. I don't think it could be transmitted. He'd been doing three men's work for years. No brain could stand it. It was total collapse—not lunacy."

Mason gave him an appealing look. "But she mustn't know, sir."

Travers nodded gravely as he got to his feet. "No, Mason, she oughtn't to know—whether it matters or not. To be the daughter of a murderer is no nice legacy. And tongues are cruel things."

"It's no wedding present either," added Norris.

Mason was shaking his head as if not knowing what to say. Then all at once his face took on a look of bewilderment.

"Then if it wasn't lunacy, sir, and Mr. Courtney had found out, he needn't have worried about it at all."

"If he'd known all the facts he certainly needn't," said Travers.

Mason was still staring. "Then he needn't have killed him, sir."

Norris clutched his arm. "My God, Mason! What do you mean by that?"

CHAPTER XIX
A NIGHT'S SIMMERING

MASON FREED HIMSELF with dignity. "I mean nothing, sir. I only repeat what has been said in the servants' hall."

"And what *has* been said in the servants' hall?"

"Well, sir, there was a considerable amount of comment when Mr. Crewe was made so free of the house. I will say he never took any great advantage of it. He never came down, for instance, when the master was away, but as Mr. Travers knows, sir, he wasn't the kind of man we expect to see here. After what happened, sir, there was bound to be gossip, and I own, sir, that the word 'blackmail' has been mentioned, though on the only occasion I heard it, I took immediate action."

"The opinion of the servants' hall is that Mr. Allard killed him?"

Mason pulled himself up with dignity. "I lay no claims, sir, to interpret the opinions of the servants' hall. I have my distance to keep. All I will say is that my impressions are that such a feeling exists. And, frankly, sir, I admit that knowing what I do now, I have the same feeling myself. If I'd been Mr. Allard, I'd have shot him like a dog."

"And a pretty fool you'd have been," said Norris curtly. "However, we're more than grateful to you, Mason. We can rely on you for anything else?"

"Implicitly, sir."

"By Jove! you did that extraordinarily well," said Travers, as soon as the door had closed on the butler. "I'd have laid a fiver he wouldn't have opened his mouth."

"And a pretty fool I'd have looked if the bluff hadn't worked," was Norris's answer. "All we had was those two names, and if he'd have stared blankly and put on that mute look of his, we'd have been a damn sight worse off than we were before. You didn't suspect there were any children, did you?"

"I certainly didn't," said Travers ruefully.

"Nor did I," added Norris. "Queer story, you know—and how it fits in! That business about Miss Wendley's engagement, for instance." He shook his head solemnly, then gave Travers a sudden glare. "Damn it all! Allard *must* have killed Crewe. He had to kill him! Do you realize that Allard's father is still alive and in Broadmoor? Do you think a man in Allard's position wouldn't commit murder to keep that from becoming public gossip? And there was the question of his own marriage, which would certainly have been off had anything got out. And there was his sister to look after. I tell you Allard must have murdered him!"

Travers recoiled slightly. "It's no use glaring at me. I say he didn't murder him. You've proved that for yourself. Allard couldn't work miracles."

"Hm!" went Norris. "I suppose he couldn't. But Crewe could. Why shouldn't he have taught Allard some of his conjuring tricks, and then have been caught in his own trap?"

"Ingenious," said Travers, "but that cock won't fight. Put Crewe in his room under the conditions that existed the morning he was killed, and the whole of Maskelyne and Devant's and the Royal and Ancient Society of African Wizards couldn't have killed him."

"But somebody might have done it for him."

"There I'm with you," said Travers. "As a matter of fact, all you're doing is to hurl at me lumps of my own memorandum."

Norris smiled dryly. "About time you wrote another, which'd be more than I can do." He looked round the room as he picked up his coat from the chair where he had thrown it. "Anything else you want here? If not, we might get back to town."

"As soon as you like," said Travers. "Got something special to do there?"

Norris nodded at him. "I'm not going to do a damn thing. I'm going to think. Something tells me we've got enough information to finish this case if only we can sort it out right. I'm going to have Lewis at the Yard to take the shocks, and I'm going to spend the night at home. You know the thing they always say in the cookery books? Simmer gently. That's the program for to-night with me."

Travers smiled. "Wonder what you'll find in the casserole or saucepan or whatever it is, to-morrow morning."

"It'll be something we can get our teeth into, I'll promise you that," said Norris, rearranging his metaphor with much more success than Travers had expected.

Travers laughed. "Good for you, Bill! The trouble will be when we try to get 'em out again."

Norris looked up quickly at the unexpected name. Somehow he felt that he and Travers were going to do something good. The nickname was an augury for it.

"I'll promise you that too," he said with his dry old smile. "You suffer from hunches, and I've got one now." He grabbed his hat. "We'll be getting along. I told my missis she might see me for tea and she nearly had a fit. It's best part of a week since I had a meal in the house."

It turned out to be nearer six than five when Norris eventually reached home. Though he would never have owned to it, he had somewhere inside him a taste for the artistic, and that was why he had bought himself a pre-war house in a pleasant backwater of one of the northern suburbs, with a fine old garden which, as he said ruefully, he had to get somebody else to dig; and quite a fine view across a valley towards Highgate. Mrs. Norris liked it too; so did the two children—a girl of ten and a boy of eight.

There was considerable excitement when he appeared that evening. Once on a job, a detective may be away from his home for weeks, but Mrs. Norris was used to that part of the contract, and it was the two children who ran a bit wild at the prospect of their father reappearing. While Norris had his meal they chattered so incessantly that their mother threatened to send them to bed early, though Norris knew she was none too serious and was probably giving him the chance to do the interceding.

In the interval of comparative quiet that followed, she thought of something.

"The builder called about that shed, daddy. He says you'd better have it in brick and make a job of it for life. If not, he says, you'll always be getting little bills for repairs—and it won't be nothing either. I told him to come and see you."

Norris nodded. "That's all right. Tell him I'll think it over and get him to send an estimate." Then, all at once, he thumped his knee with his fist. "It must be right! You can't get away from it!"

"Get away from what?"

He laughed it off. "Nothing much. Just something I happened to think about. I'll tell you later on."

He drew up to the fire with his pipe. Norris had no use for the wide net and the gradual elimination that characterized the school in which he served his professional apprenticeship. True, he recognized that such things were necessary; that they were, in fact, unavoidable evils; but what had struck him more and more in the course of his long experience, was that always, however far-reaching or theatrical the efforts, the results were rarely unexpected. "Give me motive and you can have the rest," might be summarized as his principal article of faith. Motive alone produces crime, and—except in the case of homicidal lunacy—there is no crime without motive.

That was what had been hammering away at his brain ever since he had listened to Mason's story that afternoon. Standing up stark as the line of the Himalayas was the one man—Allard; the man with the perfect motive; more than that, the man with the desperate need to commit murder. It had been just like that builder and the shed. If Allard had left Crewe alive, then all his life he'd have been paying bills, forking out a hundred here and a couple of hundred there, and having the perpetual and unsavoury threat of Crewe's company. Crewe, with those ambitions that had brought him hot-foot from America, might easily have dissipated a fortune on theatrical ventures, with Allard as the dummy behind him. No—and Norris shook his head at the fire—Allard built in brick. No makeshift job for him.

As Norris sat there he was oblivious to the quiet chatter of the children and the fact that his wife had drawn a chair up on the other side of the fireplace and was knitting steadily. It was thinking about Mason that made him realize that for best part of an hour he had been sucking a cold pipe, and Norris smiled to himself as that thought brought final conviction. Even Mason had been sure that Allard had killed Crewe. The very servants in that house had had the same idea, and there was he, with all the facts at his disposal, casting about for some other murderer. No—and Norris sat up in the chair and surveyed his pipe—there was only one solution of that part of the mystery. Allard had killed Crewe—alone or with a confederate—and the theory had become a fact beyond denial.

As Norris sat up he realized that he was very hot and the room was stuffy. When he announced that he'd go for a short stroll round the back of the woods, there was a sudden commotion.

"Oh, daddy!" said Beryl reproachfully, "and we wanted you to do something for us."

"We can do it now," burst out George.

"Sh!" She gave him a warning look, then gave a questioning one at her mother.

Mrs. Norris, who was in the secret, smiled. "Daddy won't be very long. Perhaps he'll let you sit up till he comes back."

There was jubilation over that. Norris kissed them both, promised to be back in half an hour, and went out to the hall. With hat and coat on he put his head inside the door.

"If anybody rings up for me, mummy, say I'll be in almost at once. If it's nothing important, take a message."

By the time he reached the end of the path he had laid that spring, it was raining hard, but he pulled the collar of his coat well over his ears and trudged on. It was now dark, and almost before he had recognized the lights twinkling across the valley, his mind was on the case again. Inch by inch he began to go over those two rooms where Allard and Crewe had slept. By the time he had reached the street that edged the woods, he was going over all the conjuring tricks he had ever seen, in the hope of finding something in the nature of a disappearing body or a way to kill a man without being in the same room. It was a dribble of water down his neck that pulled him up, just outside The Woodman.

He knew The Woodman for a quiet, well-conducted house, and entered the private bar where he ordered a double Irish hot, with lemon and a lump of sugar. It was early yet and the night had kept some of the regulars away. Only two men were in the room, standing at the bar and both drinking bitter. One, in bowler hat and blue overcoat, looked like an old pug, and the other, rather more plump and prosperous, looked uncommonly like a bookmaker. As Norris took off his hat and flicked the water deftly into the fire, the plump man spoke to him.

"Dirty night, sir."

"You're right there," said Norris heartily.

That was all the conversation as far as Norris was concerned. The other two resumed evidently where they had left off at his entry, and Norris, sipping away at his hot drink, couldn't help but listen. He found it interesting.

"That's how he beat him," said the pug. "Old Harry was in his corner, as I was telling you, and it was him what put him up to it. You see, the Froggy covering up and Tom couldn't get near him, so—the fourth round it was—Harry, he says to him, let on you've lorst your nerve, he says, see?"

"Made him open out," said the other, reaching for his glass.

"Just what old Tom wanted," said the pug, following suit with the glass. "This Frenchman thinks he's got old Tom groggy. Starts following him round the ring, see? Old Tom let him put him on the floor for a six and a seven. Blimey! you ought to have heard the crowd yell! Old Tom, he sort of grinned like and kept backing away. Next round he did the same and the Froggy thought he had him beat. Then Tom let him have it, see?" The pug shaped up to his companion and did some illustration. "Wallop! Wallop! like that, see? When Froggy woke up Tom was having his supper."

They both laughed, and the plump man ordered two more bitters. He seemed to be a man of some education; much better-spoken than the other.

"It's a damn funny thing," he said, "but it's always easier to let on you've lost your nerve than to kid yourself you're all right.

You can't make yourself out better than you are, can you? On the other hand, you can always let on you're beat."

They nodded at each other over the new drinks.

"Ever play poker?" asked the plump man.

"Can't say as I did. Seen it, though."

The plump man nodded. "That was an old trick of mine, letting on I held nothing. Damn sight better than trying to make a four-flusher into a straight."

"That's what they call 'bluff,' ain't it?"

"That's right. Guessing what's in the other man's mind."

He began another reminiscence and Norris caught sight of the clock. If he was to be home under the half-hour he'd have to get a move on, so he finished the drink, said a quiet good night, and stepped out into the rain. It was curious, in a way, that on that homeward walk his thoughts never reverted to the case. What he was thinking about was his garden and the new shed. The conversation he had listened to in the inn retired to the subconscious, and it was twelve hours later before he thought of it again.

As he remarked to his wife afterwards, it was strange that he noticed nothing unusual when he entered the room. The children hushed almost dramatically, for instance, and the white tablecloth was on. Even then it never occurred to him that it had been removed long before he left, and it was far too early for it to be put on for supper.

"Nobody rung up?" he asked.

"Nobody at all, dear."

"That's all right then," said Norris, and began undoing his shoes in preparation for his slippers. "Looks as if we're going to have a little peace and quiet for once."

"Daddy!" piped George, "will you come and draw something in my book?"

"Draw something?" He got up at once. "I'm not much of a hand at drawing. What would you like?"

"Daddy, you draw lovely!" said Beryl hypocritically. "Draw a pig, daddy, with a curly tail."

"Oh, yes! Draw a pig, daddy," chimed in George.

"We shall have to mind the ink on your mother's clean cloth," remarked their father, squinting at the line he was drawing.

And no sooner was the drawing finished and suitably admired, than Mrs. Norris asked to see it. The moment Norris's back was turned there was a moment or two of tremendous activity at the table. The ink-bottle was whisked away and another was overturned in its place.

Then Beryl positively screeched. "Oh, daddy! Look what you did!"

Norris turned, then his eyes popped open. On the spotlessly white cloth was the overturned ink-bottle and an oval of black ink.

"Quick!" said mummy. "Beryl, get a cloth and some salt."

"No, no!" He slipped across to the desk. "Blotting-paper's the thing to get that off with."

Again, if he had had eyes he must have seen that something was in the wind. The two children watched him as if afraid something might after all at the very last minute ruin the carefully planned scheme. Mrs. Norris looked on quietly confident, an amused twinkle in her eye, as her husband approached the spilled ink with a sheet of blotting-paper, its corner held downwards like the point of a spear.

He touched the blot of ink. Nothing happened, and he touched it again. Something was evidently wrong with the blotting-paper that it defied the laws of capillary attraction, and he tore off the corner to give a jagged edge and then applied it again. George giggled and his father gave him a quick look. Something dawned. He touched the ink blot—this time with his finger—and it was solid!

For a moment his face was blank, then he burst out laughing. Everybody roared.

"We had you that time, daddy!" said his wife.

"I'm afraid you did," said Norris. Still smiling, he picked up the ink blot and examined it. "What is it? Celluloid?"

"That's right, daddy," Beryl told him. "Celluloid, that's what the man said, didn't he, mummy? We got it at Harridge's when we went with mummy, didn't we, George?"

George nodded. "We made you an April fool, didn't we, daddy?"

"Yes," said Norris, "I rather think you did."

"Daddy's not an April fool really," put in Beryl in his defence.

Norris looked over at his wife. "I think I know who was the grand organizer of this little effort. Funny, isn't it?" He shook his head. "I knew somewhere in my mind that something was wrong. The cloth oughtn't to have been there." He laughed. "Still, I'm not an April fool really, as Beryl says. You can't be an April fool after April the First."

"We'll save it up and catch you out next year, daddy," George announced hopefully.

"You can't do that, silly," his sister told him, and, "Oh, daddy! you could get all sorts; couldn't you, mummy? Pieces of soup and red ink and gravy—"

Their mother interrupted what looked like being a long, drawn-out inquest. "Come along now. Time for bed. You're over half an hour late as it is. Put away all those things, both of you, and then say good night to daddy."

George picked up the ink blot. "You going to be here for breakfast, aren't you, daddy?"

"Oh, yes!" his father told him, and nodded confidently. "I shall be here for breakfast all right."

Norris's prediction seemed to be correct. Except for a fairly simple matter about which Lewis rang up later in the evening, he was untroubled by the case, though he went over some of its problems with his wife; rather as any man talks to any wife than with the hope of any startling suggestions.

Then, as he lay in bed, he began to wonder. Nothing had seemed to happen. That immense optimism that had flooded him until then now began to dissipate itself, and already he saw the next day dawning to the same old round of recapitulation and the same re-hash of inquiry, and with that faint pessimism as a vaguely disturbing background, he fell asleep.

It was half-past six when he stirred in the morning, and the sun was shining treacherously through the bedroom window. In a couple of seconds his brain was working at full speed. His wife felt him stir and woke too, though she lay still and made no movement. She heard him chuckle—doubtless as he remembered that ink blot of the few hours before—then he gave a quick in-drawing breath and followed it up by a grunt.

With infinite care not to wake her, he slid gently to the outside of the bed, then to the floor. He replaced the clothes, then made for the door—and in his bare feet and without troubling to put on a dressing-gown! She heard him move quietly downstairs; heard him in the hall; then heard him asking Exchange for a telephone number. Then she heard this.

"Oh, it's you, Palmer, is it? Sorry to disturb you at this godless hour. Mr. Travers there all right? . . . I see. Well, don't wake him up for another half-hour, but tell him to do this. Take it down, will you? . . . Get hold of Samuels and Drew at their hotel and say he must see them privately at eight o'clock. Tell Mr. Travers that's in case Drew has to go out. We must have them together, tell him. . . . Got that? . . . Good! Now listen to this. At about a quarter to eight I'll be along with you to see Mr. Travers and give him an outline of what he's wanted to do. Got all that? . . . Right. Good-by."

He nodded at the receiver as he replaced it, then strolled to the kitchen and put the kettle on the gas-fire. Then he made his way upstairs to wake his wife and break the news.

CHAPTER XX
EXIT FLUMMERY

THE HOTEL, comfortable though it was, didn't have an elevator, and Travers walked up to the third story. There was a vigorous holler of something unintelligible at his tap, and he opened the door of what turned out to be Samuels' bedroom—a large room with an easy chair, in which Samuels himself was sitting, and a couch on which Drew lay propped at full length. It was he who scrambled shyly to his feet as Travers entered.

"Glad to see you, Mr. Travers. Come and sit down," and he indicated the couch.

Samuels made as if to rise too, but Travers pushed him down and then shook hands.

"Far too early for violent exercise. And how's your cold? Better?"

"Sure!" said Samuels, but with a wariness that was too polite to do more than hint at an anxiety at so early a visit. "The cold and I've parted company. . . . You're out bright and early this morning."

"Yes," said Travers, seating himself alongside Drew on the couch, "like you I'm not averse to a little constitutional before breakfast."

The wry smile came to Drew's face. Samuels coloured somewhat.

"Not that we want to rake up old scores," smiled Travers. "No. The fact of the matter is I'm a bearer of bad news. Still, perhaps you won't think it so bad. I mean, you'd both rather get back to your own lovely climate than risk pneumonia here any longer."

Samuels' eyes goggled and his eyes opened wide.

Drew spoke first, with his slow, unexcited, level drawl. "You mean they're givin' us the air, Mr. Travers?"

"I'll explain," said Travers. "I only got to hear of this a short time ago—at seven o'clock this morning, to be precise, and I at once had to think about seeing you two people in a friendly fashion and seeing what we could do about it. You see, Scotland Yard is not very pleased with you at the moment. Inspector Norris believes you're still holding something back."

Samuels shook his head solemnly. "There's no satisfying that man. We gave him the lowdown."

Travers gave a shake of the head. "Well, it's no use blaming me for what Scotland Yard think. Not only that, if it's got into the hands of the Special Branch, then I'm afraid it's too late to do anything. You came over here, Mr. Samuels, on what amounted to false pretences, and you can't deny it. Once it was known who you were, the Special Branch—who deal with all sorts of people who enter the country—might have acted if they'd had information. What we want to stop, if it isn't too late, is the order for you two people to leave the country within so many hours."

"Leave the country!" Samuels appeared stupefied.

"I'm sorry," said Travers, "but that's what it amounts to."

Drew looked desperately upset. "Gosh! that's a tough break. And the Chief thinks we're holdin' back on him."

"He doesn't think it," said Travers. "He's certain of it. He's found out quite a lot of things, you know." He smiled at them both. "Won't you let me advise you? I know it'll be for your good and it can't do any harm. You're keeping something back about Crewe—and what happened that morning. I believe Inspector Norris knows what you're keeping back—I tell you that in confidence—and if he has to put you two into the . . . what I might call the witness-box at a coroner's inquest, and you're made to tell what you know, there'll be such a hullabaloo in the Press that the Special Branch'll have to take action and out you'll both go, and with a report on you to your own police into the bargain." He regarded the two mask-like faces. "Let me tell you one thing the inspector knows. He knows that Crewe mentioned the Mercer Case to you before he came over."

That blow struck home. Samuels' face showed it. "Yes, Crewe mentioned it. 'Ever hear about the Mercer Case?' he says to Zona and me, ''cause that's the bank where the dollars are kept,' and that's all he spilled."

Travers swivelled round to face the pair of them. "Let me say something very serious. If you want to keep out of trouble, forget there was ever such a thing as the Mercer Case. Cut it clean out of your minds. It's killed two men and it might jail two more. If you ever want a little excitement take a couple of rattlesnakes to bed with you; it'll be safer than remembering what Crewe said about the Mercer Case."

Samuels shook his head vigorously. "You can search me, Mr. Travers. I don't know a thing."

"That goes for me, too," added Drew.

"And now another home truth or two," went on Travers, "since we're talking frankly. Crewe was a blackmailer, and I rather gather you're beginning to know it. He got a strangle-hold on Allard and was bleeding him white. Crewe—whatever he was to you two people—was the dirtiest form of skunk, and I give you my word here and now that that's no exaggeration. If proofs are required I can give them—but I'd rather not. Now will you tell Scotland Yard what you know?"

Samuels pulled himself up with dignity. "Mr. Travers, I don't know what you folks have found out about Crewe, but when we were down to bean money he never did us dirt. If I'd had a ten-year stretch for that little affair of mine, he'd have been waitin' outside when the big gates opened." Once more he shook his head ponderously. "Guess Zona and I haven't got anything to say. We're funny that way, Mr. Travers."

Travers got to his feet and held out his hand. "Well, I'll say good-by to you both. I don't know what boat sails to-morrow, but you can take it from me you'll be on it."

At the door Drew's voice came clear and steady. "Wait a minute, Mr. Travers! Guess you won't mind if Sam and I have a little conference in the next room?"

Travers came back. "Of course not. Only I might remind you that time's getting short."

The bluff had worked, as Norris said it would, and now things must happen. The two were absent not more than five minutes, and when they came back Samuels announced that Zona would do the talking.

"You see it's this way, Mr. Travers," Zona said. "We knew there was somethin' phoney about what Crewe was doin' only, you see, it was sorta hard to wise up Crewe when he didn't spill anything. He could go places and hand out a swell line and make folks believe he was someone. That made it hard, over here, to ask questions, and Sam and I couldn't walk out on him 'cause we were in this thing together. What he was doin' was good enough for us, and we didn't want to crab nothin'."

"You were really asleep that morning?"

"Sure he was asleep," cut in Samuels. "Zona's a sleep racketeer."

Travers smiled. "Well, go on, Zona. What is it you two know?"

Zona shifted restlessly. "We guessed Crewe had my rope and knife—though we couldn't make him say so. Then the evenin' before the deaths happened he told us he was totin' a gun as

Allard was actin' kinda queer. You see, he had no shells for his gun, so I handed him my box. Sam and I didn't say nothin' about that 'cause we knew we weren't supposed to tote guns over here, and we didn't want to get in bad with the police. I hurled mine, and what Crewe had left of the shells, into the lake."

Travers nodded. "And that's all you know?"

Drew returned his nod with all the gravity in the world.

"Sure, Mr. Travers. I guess that's all."

"I see." He made a wry face, then smiled. "I'm sorry, but I still don't think the inspector will be altogether satisfied." He felt in his pocket and produced what was apparently an empty cardboard box tied, and from an inner pocket he took a letter. "I wonder if you two people would like to have another conference to discuss this?"

Samuels took the letter, and when he'd read it he passed it to Drew without a word. In its passage between the two, Travers saw that it was a series of numbered questions. The two looked at each other, and Drew spoke.

"This is confidential, Mr. Travers?"

"If Inspector Norris tells you it is, then you can depend on it," Travers told him.

He was silent for a moment or two, then, "Looks like Sam and I'll have another conference."

Travers settled resignedly to his couch. This time the wait was longer. When they finally returned, Travers was given the same small, brown-paper parcel.

"What the chief wants is inside," said Zona, and from the expression on his face that might have been anything on earth that the box would hold.

"The letter's inside too?" Travers asked.

"Sure!" said Samuels. "This time we've come clean."

Travers held out his hand to Samuels first. "I must be pushing along. Everything all right now?"

The fat man smiled. Travers went downstairs to call the Yard.

After parting with Travers that morning Norris had gone straight to the Yard. With his usual ultra-caution he refused to admit even to himself that the case was over. There would be time enough for that when Travers had induced Samuels to speak; and if even Travers failed to elicit the required evidence, then the C.C.'s conference would have to have the facts laid before them and judge for themselves.

His breakfast was sent in and during the meal he made no further reference to the case, though Lewis saw him more than once glance over at the telephone. Then all at once, with what seemed unusual stridency, the bell rang. Norris was over in a flash.

"Hallo! . . . Yes, speaking. . . . They say they've come across perfectly clear? . . . Anybody there now? . . . Good! And they put a contribution in the box? . . . Splendid! You there? . . . Not had breakfast yet? . . . Right! Come round here and we'll find you some. And, you listening? . . . We'll tell you who did the murders!"

He hung up quickly and nodded over at Lewis. "That'll fetch him at the double."

It was Lewis's turn to nod. "A fine gentleman, Mr. Travers! Never puts on any side." He laughed. "And to think that Allard and Crewe put him down as a mutt!"

Norris gave his tea a stir and reached for the marmalade. "As you say. And I wish I had his brains. And the funny thing is, he was a much bigger mutt than they took him for."

Lewis stared. "How do you make that out, sir?"

"Wait and see," said Norris not unkindly. "In a few minutes he'll be telling you so himself."

CHAPTER XXI
NORRIS EXPLAINS

TRAVERS CAME IN jauntily and handed over his small parcel.

"Here you are, then! Everything present and correct."

"You know what's inside?" asked Norris, weighing it tentatively in his hand.

"Afraid I don't," said Travers. "With that admirable restraint which has persistently characterized me during this case, I left you to undo the string. Not that I wasn't tempted, mind you." He smiled across at Lewis.

"Well, you'll know in a minute," said Norris, but he took the parcel to the desk and unfastened it behind the row of books, trying all the while to appear unconcerned, and not making too bad a job of it. Then he read the note, which Travers could now see was merely a list of questions with spaces left for answers and comments. All that took no more than a couple of minutes and then Norris got up.

"Some right and some not so right," he said, and rubbed his hands all the same. "Now, Mr. Travers, what about breakfast? You've certainly earned it."

Travers took off hat and coat and sat down again. "Never mind about breakfast. You tell me about those murders. I breakfast every morning, but it isn't often I get the chance of hearing the answer to a perfectly good riddle."

"Right," said Norris. "Draw your chair in, and you, too, Lewis. I've got some rough notes here for the Assistant Commissioner and, if you'll excuse me, we'll have a dress rehearsal."

"Good!" said Travers, and settled himself comfortably.

"First," began Norris, "all we can keep our eyes on now is the one central fact—that there was a man who hated another. Everything else is eyewash. Those two men are all we've got to deal with, and if anybody else comes in it's merely as a supernumerary."

"In other words," said Travers, "the text for this morning's discourse is that Allard must have killed Crewe."

"You've got it exactly," Norris told him. "And therefore, with your permission, I'd like to review the case from the beginning and from the point of view of those two people only. We make a start with Crewe.

"Most of our evidence is admittedly circumstantial, and we must build on hypotheses. Still, that can't be helped and I don't think, for instance, anybody could deny that Crewe's father, just before he died, told him the history of the Mercer family and the Allard children. Samuels' evidence as to the marked newspaper, and his undoubted knowledge of the Mercer Case being behind everything, gives a certain amount of solidity to that.

"Very well then; Crewe came over to England and tackled Allard. How he went to work we shall never know, but undoubtedly his receipts from the blackmailing capital consisted of directing Allard into the particular theatrical ventures for which he had a mind himself. Allard saw no way out at that moment. He knuckled under and prepared to pay through the nose. It was only when Crewe arranged for all that publicity that Allard saw a loophole.

"I should say that from then on his attitude changed towards Crewe. He no longer showed him what he really thought of him. He began to dissimulate and to adopt more of a hail-fellow-well-met attitude to allay Crewe's suspicions. He agreed to all the publicity because he regarded it all as a profitable investment."

"You mean he thought the show that Crewe was staging would really be a tremendous success?"

"Oh, no!" Norris smiled ironically. "By comparison, what Allard spent on publicity and all that for the proposed show was a very small sum indeed. A builder tells you that if you pay twenty pounds for a wooden shed, it'll always be costing you something for repairs, but if you have it in brick and tile, it'll be a job for life. Allard made up his mind to build in brick. He *invested* in murder. He determined to kill Crewe, and he was prepared to pay through the nose so long as he ultimately arrived at Crewe's death.

"But let's come to the eve of the murders. Everything's ready. The car is hidden in the woods, the hoe is in the wardrobe, the hook is in the wood below the sill, a pot of blood is ready to scatter, and the mud is on the wardrobe floor. You were ready, Mr. Travers, to act as the mutt, and Spence was ready to send out the news which should create the publicity. We mentioned the other day that this case ought to be called the Case of the April Fools because it was built round All Fools' Day and largely depended on it. It might also be called that because the principal actors in it were made April fools, and the third April fool, Mr. Travers—and I say it most respectfully—was yourself."

Travers laughed. "'Respectfully' is good—damn good. Not that I don't believe what you say. I know you too well for that."

"Mind you," Norris went on perfectly seriously, "I'm not going to mention that at the conference. That's for home consumption. But as I was saying, everything was ready, and now we'll have a look at just what was intended should happen in the morning. There we were all wrong. This was the scheme. Crewe was to pretend to be stabbed. You were to see him and think he was dead. While you were 'phoning for the police, he was to make his getaway by the private door to which Allard would take him and the hoe with him. Then Crewe would go off in the car and later reappear at The Covers as a Chinese gentleman named Wen Ti—excellent publicity, if a bit too melodramatic for my taste. That's what ought to have happened, and now we'll see what threw everything out of gear.

"To do that we've to look into the mentality of both Crewe and Allard in the particular environments in which they happened to be at the time. Allard didn't mind being thought a fool since he knew perfectly well he wasn't one—and you've made the same remark about him, Mr. Travers. He kept up that pretence of desperate secrecy during dinner so that Crewe should have no suspicions. But he reckoned without Crewe.

"Crewe, you see, was out of his depth. No matter what the relationships between him and Allard, he couldn't treat Allard as an equal or hope to understand him. All that window business was a blind, as we know. When Crewe made his getaway, everybody was to think it was by the window that his body had been carried out. Allard himself would say that nothing had come through the door, and you, Mr. Travers, would be downstairs 'phoning. Allard really was to let Crewe out by the downstair door and then get back before you did.

"Now I suggest that Crewe said to Allard, 'You'd better let me have the key. Something might turn up to stop you coming in, or something like that. After all, I know the way, and as soon as I'm ready I can slip down.'

"But Allard slipped up there. He didn't let Crewe have the key, and for a very good reason. *He didn't want him to leave that room before he himself was ready.* That must have made Crewe suspicious, and it may have been after that that he got the shells from Drew. And after he'd handed Allard his suitcase of stuff that was to be transferred ultimately to Wen Ti's room, he shut his door—and I bet he slept with his window barred. And now we come to what really happened in the morning."

It was a dramatic pause that Norris made as he looked at his notes, though he was far too honestly minded to resort to rhetorical tricks of that kind. But Travers began fumbling at his glasses, and Lewis cleared his throat with a little cough and fidgeted in his seat.

"Yes," said Norris slowly, "what happened that morning is what concerns us most. I suggest that Crewe was awake early, and the first thing he did was to get out of bed and look at himself in the glass. His eyes were dark enough, he knew that, because he had been up late and had slept badly; if he had not thought so he'd have rubbed them with charcoal or something similar and we'd have found it either on his face or on the towel. The minute the footman had left the room, he rubbed powder on his face to give the effect of deathly white. But that came later. What he did was to break the creeper with the hoe and throw out some of the blood. He also shaved himself and saw that everything else was ready. All he had to do to give the appearance of death was to stick on his bare chest—the jacket of his sleeping-suit being well open—this imitation blob of blood."

He took it from the box and handed it to Travers, who fingered it as if it were going to bite. Lewis had a look at it too.

"What is it?" asked Travers. "Celluloid?"

"That's right," Norris told him. "It's really meant to represent spilled wine. A sort of catch toy to make April fools out of people; to put on a white tablecloth, for instance, and wait till someone goes to mop it up."

Travers flushed slightly. "And what's this mark in the middle of it?"

Norris smiled. "Not in the middle. That'd have been too inartistic. Nearer one side it is. That's where they put the wooden head of the dagger thing which they copied from the handle of one of Drew's knives—the one that Crewe took and Allard conveniently forgot to return. When Crewe was supposed to be lying dead, that's the knife and the blood that you saw."

"Hm!" said Travers, and flushed again. "As you say, I was chief of all the April fools."

"Oh, no you weren't," said Norris quickly. "There's plenty more to explain yet. If I'd been in your place—even forewarned as you were—I'd have thought what you did, and I'll tell you why."

Travers laughed. "Funny, isn't it. That was what I was brought down there to see—and I stared at it like a fool and saw it."

"Wait a minute," said Norris calmly. "I did the very same thing last night. I happened to be thinking of all manner of things, and I saw something deliberately spread out to catch me, as it happened, and I didn't see it with the right kind of eyes. No, the fact of the matter is, Allard had the laugh on you. You had thought him a fool in some ways, and he wished you to think so. He thought you a fool in some ways, and he made full use of those ways. He double-bluffed you, like a man I heard about—a boxer—the other night. He led you deliberately into a trap by pretending to lose his nerve. He knew you might be suspicious when you went to that room, and he forestalled you. Before you had time to think whether or not the murder was genuine, he told you it was genuine, *and he told you in such a way that you couldn't help believe him*. He clutched your arm and he gasped out, 'But it shouldn't have been real. It was all intended as a joke!' That was what you fell for—as I should have done. You told him what I should have told him, 'And a damn nice joke it is!' or words to that effect. Then you saw he'd lost his nerve too badly to be of any use, so you did just what had been arranged—you went downstairs to 'phone and left the coast nicely clear."

He paused again to survey the notes. Travers gave another little grunt that acknowledged the justice of the summary.

"But even that's not the vital point, though a lot depended on it," went on Norris. "What we've got to do now is to see into Allard's mind as far as it was concerned with Crewe. The great moment has arrived, and Crewe—like you, Mr. Travers—doesn't know it. His overnight's suspicions are all allayed since everything has gone like clockwork. As soon as you leave, what happens? First of all Crewe hops up and wipes the powder off his face with the towel, and just as he is about to throw the blood on the floor and the jacket of the suit, in comes Allard as arranged. And here I want the help of Lewis."

Norris got up and moved back the chair that stood near the wall. He turned to Travers.

"Watch what I do, and you, Lewis, leave yourself limp and do just what I tell you to do. Ready? . . . Then try to imagine that we two represent Crewe and Allard that very morning at eight-fifteen."

Travers, in his excitement, stood up to watch. Norris went back to the door of the room, then came quickly across. He seized Crewe's arm.

"Quick! Get down again! There's somebody coming!"

Lewis got down to the position in which Crewe had been lying. Norris whispered to him.

"Who's coming?" he asked.

"Hurry up and don't ask questions. Spence is coming and we'll fool him as we did Travers."

Norris drew back. "That's all, gentlemen. Crewe lay back and Allard produced immediately from his pocket the knife he'd forgotten to return. As Crewe put the blob of blood in place and the handle of the sham knife with it, he shut his eyes. Allard whipped off the blob, but Crewe opened his eyes. There was a struggle. Can't you imagine it? 'What are you doing, Allard?' 'I've got you this time, Crewe!' and the grunts as they fought, and Allard thinking what a fool he'd been not to strike more quickly. His trouble was that the knife had to go in where you saw it, Mr. Travers, or else you'd have suspicioned something. Then Crewe reached for his gun and got it. All you see now is a tangle of arms. As Allard strikes, Crewe fires from the ground. Allard falls backward. Crewe goes forward and the knife is driven home as it strikes the floor and his body presses it." He paused and nodded. "And that's how those two were killed."

There was silence for a good minute. What Norris had said was too much to take in all at once.

"The perfect alibi," said Travers at last. "As you said, Allard must have killed Crewe and yet he didn't kill him. And to think I often thought that chap was a fool."

"The laugh's on your side," said Norris. "You've had as much to do with solving this case as anybody. You laugh last. Here's the little handle that was made to stick on the blob, if you'd like to look at it. It got broken off. It was originally all one thing. And what I'm wondering is just what would have happened if Crewe hadn't opened his eyes at that one moment; if he hadn't seen Allard about to strike; in other words, if Allard had got away with it. We'd never have fastened anything on him. What do you think, Lewis?"

Lewis grinned and scratched his head. "I don't know, sir. If he'd had time to clear up the room and so on before Mr. Travers got back, we'd have had a job, as you say. But about this blob of what was supposed to be blood, sir—"

"I know what you're going to say," said Norris, seating himself again. "There's a whole lot that wants explaining before all the loose ends are tied up. What Samuels told us this morning clears up a good many. I'll tell you just how he comes into things, though there's not much that needs explaining in his mentality. All he was out for, as he said, was peace and quietness, law and order. He wanted nothing to happen that would focus attention on himself, and there was also his loyalty to Crewe and Drew who'd stood by him when he was down and out.

"Samuels was very worried about Crewe after he'd borrowed that ammunition, and coming on top of the missing knife and rope, he had none too good a night. As soon as the footman left him—and he got his tea before you got yours, Mr. Travers—he got into his clothes, and he didn't shave, if you remember. He had a hunch that something was going to happen, and he wanted to be ready for it.

"For one thing he wanted to be certain that Crewe was all right that morning. He had got as far as the door when the shot was fired, and immediately he rushed in. You were downstairs, Mr. Travers, and he had the place to himself. His heart nearly stopped beating, and he thought at first it was some kind of joke.

Then he turned Crewe's body over and saw the knife—Zona Drew's knife—sticking in his ribs. He let the body fall again and stood there for a minute petrified with fear. Then he saw three other things, though not all at once. One was the gun lying by Crewe's hand, and he thought he knew that gun. He looked at it and saw the six shells, and he slipped it into his pocket. Then he saw protruding from under the bed the very rope that Drew had stolen. You see, if Crewe was to give the world the impression that his body had been taken through the window and down to the ground, then he'd have to leave a rope dangling from the hook, and a specially strong rope at that. Samuels grabbed the rope too and stuck it under his coat, and just as he left the room he saw that curious thing which we know to be a blob of imitation wine, with a piece of wood like a handle of a knife on it. It was the handle thing that struck him, and on the sudden impulse he picked that up too. Just as he dodged into Drew's room, Spence came round the corner on his way to hear what all the noise had been, and you were coming upstairs too, Mr. Travers.

"Drew was sound asleep, but Samuels woke him. The two saw they were in a nasty position if anything got out and, moreover, they hadn't quite time to figure out just what happened in that room. But they threw the gun and shells and rope into the lake—"

"Pardon me," said Travers, "but I think Samuels took the rope to the lake. At least he gave me that impression."

Norris consulted the letter. "You're right. Samuels took the rope and tied a rock to it and threw it in the lake. Drew had thrown his own gun in too. The one thing Samuels hung on to was the blob and the wooden handle, because he thought that would cause no suspicion if it were found in his possession, and because he had also some idea that it was a kind of mascot that might explain things and get them out of a tight corner if they were driven into one."

"Did he know what had happened?" asked Lewis.

"I don't think he did," said Norris. "He had glimmerings naturally, but I don't think he got any further or he'd have destroyed that blob too, which made Crewe out to be the killer of

Allard." He rose and stretched his legs. "Still, there you have it for what it's worth. In my opinion it accounts satisfactorily for the Case of the April Fools."

Travers had his glasses off and was blinking away. "Wonderful! And all so absurdly simple. As you said, clear away the flummery and it's all plain as a pikestaff."

"Beginners' luck," was Norris's comment. "Wait till me and Lewis and yourself get into stride."

Travers rose too. "I know. Jack the Ripper wouldn't have had an earthly." He laughed. "I've just remembered something else. Allard made an April fool of me in one other way too. He never had the least intention of purchasing that Mermaid lease. That was all for Crewe's benefit." He sighed. "Well, we've all got it coming to us one time or another and the sooner the better. I hate, by the way, to worry you about odds and ends of the case, but there's just a couple of snags I'd like to see cleared." He laughed. "Of course, they're not snags to you. The blood, for instance, probably brought from a slaughterhouse they passed that day in the Rolls; what happened to the cup or whatever Crewe kept it in?"

"Oh, that," said Norris. "I'd say it was in the spare glass above the lavatory basin, kept hidden in a corner of the wardrobe. There were bloodspots on the floor, some of them he put there before the footman came in. He couldn't see them in that light and on that maroon carpet. There were also spots, of course, from the wound that Allard gave him after. I'd say Crewe washed out the glass, then put his tooth-brushes in it as it was when we found it." He shrugged his shoulders. "That's only a makeshift solution. Anything else?"

"Yes," said Travers. "I still don't see how Crewe could count on sufficient time to dress himself during my absence. Dash it all! I might have come sprinting back almost at once. And he'd have looked devilish comical slithering down a rope with his clothes in his teeth."

Norris laughed. "I suppose he would. But I can explain all that in several ways, and the best is this. The clothes were ready laid in the drawer. All Crewe had to do was to grab the whole lot in his arms, follow Allard down to the library by the back way, Allard acting as scout, though there couldn't have been any risk of servants. Remember that Chinese screen that made a triangle before the door? Crewe thought he was going to dress there at his leisure. Then he'd have walked out of the door with only the pyjamas to carry."

"Splendid!" said Travers. "You're a great fellow, Bill! It's worked out to the last tin-tack. And what was that you were saying about breakfast?"

Norris looked startled for a moment at the unexpected question, then he laughed. "Ah, yes—breakfast. Lewis will fix you up in two shakes."

Travers suddenly felt for him some of that quiet, undemonstrative affection he had felt for George Wharton, and he smiled to himself as he watched him fingering the papers on the desk; no show, no fireworks—just sound horse-sense.

"Something I want to ask you, Bill," he said. "When are you and Lewis coming to have dinner with me to celebrate all this?"

"Dinner," repeated Norris, and thought.

"What's wrong with to-night?" went on Travers. "Sorry! I forgot there's that clearing-up conference."

"Yes," said Norris slowly. "We've got to clear up before we leave off. Not that I don't appreciate your kindness, Mr. Travers, and so will Lewis."

"Rubbish!" Travers told him. "What are you doing to-morrow, by the way?"

"To-morrow?" His eyes went to the window and the tips of the trees that were just flecked with their first yellowish-green. His thoughts went on beyond them, into the country across that valley that fell below Highgate. "To-morrow." He grunted. "To-morrow I was rather thinking of seeing the builder about that new shed of mine." He smiled, then saw Travers smiling too, and guessed his thoughts. "Yes," he said, "we're having it built in brick and tile. This case has taught me a lesson."

THE END

24954543R00120

Printed in Great Britain
by Amazon